Border Girl

Katy McKay

This book is a work of fiction. The characters, incidents, and dialogue are drawn from the author's imagination and are not to be construed as real. Any resemblance to actual events or persons, living or dead, is entirely coincidental.

Cover artist: Alexander Chau

Interior design by WriteIntoPrint.com

Acknowledgments

First and foremost, I must thank author, mentor and dear friend Kathryn Lance for her expertise, unflagging encouragement, and persistence in asking "So how's the novel coming along?"

I offer many thanks to readers Katie Hubert and Kimberly Morris for their enthusiasm and suggestions, and I am forever grateful to my teachers, who believed in me.

Dedication

For my sons, whom I love more than breath or measure or reason.

Spanish-English Glossary

acequias irrigation ditch
Adiós goodbye
Agua Prieta dark water
alamosa cottonwood tree
albondigas meatballs
Arroyo Codorniz Quail Creek
Ars Poetica poem by Roman writer Horace

bandidos bandits
Bendita tú eres entre todas las mujeres, y bendito es el fruto de tu vientre, Jesús.
   Blessed art thou among women, and blessed is the fruit of thy
   womb, Jesus.
bien, mi queridos well, my dears
buenos dias, queridos good morning, dears

caballo horse
canales water channels
Casa sin madre, rio sin cauce A house without a mother is a river
   without a channel
cenizo purple sage
champurrado a rich hot chocolate drink thickened with corn flour
chatelaine (French) a housekeeper's belt of keys and necessities
Chico little boy
Chinche bedbug
Chiricahuas an Apache tribe
chorizo spicy sausage

De AmiciTía   essay by Roman author Cicero
deshilado   open-work embroidery
Dios en cielo   God in heaven
Dios te salve, María. Llena eres de gracia, El Señor es contigo.   Hail Mary,
      full of grace, the Lord is with thee.
Dos Ríos Two Rivers

ejido   small community
El Cocinero Chino   the Chinese cook
el Día de San Juan   June 24, when prayers are offered to St. John the
      Baptist for an abundant rainy season
El Ojito de San Ramón   Saint Ramón's Spring
el venadita   little deer
estancia: Spanish land grant

gracias   thank you

hermancito   little brother
hermano   brother
¡Hola! ¿Cómo estás?   Hello! How are you?

las aguas   the rains
las apariencias enganan   Appearances are deceiving.
la señora periódico   the news lady; a gossip
la vieja chismosa   the old gossip
llueve a cántaros   it's pouring from pitchers
llueve a mares   it's raining oceans
Lo que esta escrito, escrito esta   That which is written, is written.
Lo que no se puede remediar, se tiene que aguantar   That which cannot be
      remedied must be tolerated.
Lo siento, llego tarde   I'm sorry, I'm late

Más tira el amor que una yunta de bueyes Love pulls stronger than a yoke of oxen.

mija my daughter

mijo my son

milagros religious charms offered to a saint

mi pobrecita my poor little one

miro look

pórtate bien behave yourself

Poquito venemo no mata A little poison won't kill you.

querida dear

¿Quién es? Who is it?

Rancho de los Cien Aguas Ranch of a Hundred Waters

Rancho sin Agua Ranch Without Water

rapido quickly

Santa María, Madre de Dios, ruega por nosotros pecadores, ahora y en la hora de nuestra muerte... Holy Mary, Mother of God, pray for us sinners, now and at the hour of our death.

Siempre que llovió, paró. Whenever it rained, it stopped. Bad times pass.

tía aunt

vaya con Dios go with God

¿Y que? And what?

zaguán entryway

Chapter 1

Nattie shivered as cold rain trickled down the back of her neck. A windswept branch snagged on the saddle horn; she tugged it loose and watched it spin away. This was the wildest storm she had ever seen, and by great good luck she was out in the midst of it. Unlike other occasions when Nattie had given Adventure an encouraging nudge, this time she was the blameless victim of circumstance. *Mostly* blameless, Nattie amended. Her assessment of wrongdoing was scrupulously fair, if cheerfully unrepentant.

Her family would worry when she didn't return, but no one could reproach her for being stranded on the far side of the rain-swollen river. The storm had roared north out of Mexico without warning or regard to season. The winter rains were past and it would be months before *el Dia de San Juan* brought *las aguas*, so this was "unusual weather," observed Nattie, as she surveyed the roiling sky. "But as Papí says, if we didn't have unusual weather around here we'd have no weather at all. Which would be unusual."

The wind whipped under her wide hat brim and lifted it from her head. She snatched it just in time and fastened the strap under her chin. She disdained chin straps, but it would be unfortunate to lose her hat, especially since it really belonged to her brother Tomás. She had snatched it from the rack by the door and fled before Tía thought of yet another recipe or pattern or bit of gossip to bring to

Mrs. Stockton. Ordinarily Tomás wouldn't notice that his hat was missing. As the ranch business manager, he spent most of his time at a desk. But this storm would send everyone out to move the cattle to high ground, so he'd lecture her when she got home. Nattie was well accustomed to lectures. She shrugged off the prospect and reveled in the wild exhilaration of the storm, standing in the stirrups and shouting into the gale.

"Blow, winds, and crack your cheeks. Rage, blow, you cataracts and hurricanoes, spout till you have drenched our steeples—" The wind swept her words away. Chico tossed his head and stomped impatiently.

"All right, we're going," Nattie told him as she gathered the reins. She considered the options for shelter as they followed the sodden trail south along the river.

The San Rafael was higher than she had ever seen it, surging against its banks with a force that shook the ground. Streaks of foam sketched the currents as the wind whipped spray from peaks of muddy water. An uprooted tree swept into view, its bare branches slowly rising and sinking as it rolled. Like fingers, thought Nattie. She patted her horse's neck, reassured by his familiar warmth.

She rode on, fascinated by the torrent raging where, only hours ago, a peaceful stream had meandered, clear and sparkling in the morning light. A great slab of earth disappeared with a splash, warning that the river was devouring its banks.

The storm eased briefly, but the greenish hue of the low clouds warned of more to come. Nattie was grateful she had ridden Chico. A sturdy dapple-grey, he was her most reliable horse, calm and intelligent. Nothing ever spooked him, but nothing ever induced him to hurry, either. He picked his way through the mud with slow deliberation, "at a full mosey," her brother Robby would say.

"There's no use in rushing anyway," Nattie said. "We don't have anyplace much to go." She shifted in the saddle and looked behind her at the trail, a wet ribbon gleaming in the false twilight.

She could, should, turn tail and go back to the Stockton place. Worried by the dark clouds building over the mountains, they had urged her to stay the night. She really should return to the hospitality they would be delighted to offer. That would be the sensible thing to do.

"But what if we can't cross Kettle Creek? It's probably over its banks by now," said Nattie. "And by the time we make sure of it it'll be nearly dark, and this trail will be under water, and we'll be worse off than we are now."

These were all reasonable arguments. But there were others, less reasonable but more compelling, that kept her from turning back.

Mr. Stockton had told her she would be caught out in the storm. He had told her that the river would rise before she could cross it and she'd do better to stay where she was and avoid a cold, wet ride that would end at the river. Mr. Stockton had been right, and Nattie hated to admit she was wrong.

Furthermore, Mrs. Stockton would fuss over her as though she had narrowly escaped certain death, insisting that Nattie drink this and wrap up in that, and Nattie hated fussing. To go back, soaked and bedraggled, mewing for shelter like a helpless kitten, was not how she wanted to end a day that had begun so well.

She had ridden over in the cool of early morning, leading the chestnut mare Mr. Stockton had purchased for his eldest daughter's sixteenth birthday. Alethia and her three younger sisters were waiting on the porch with their mother, who rocked the baby's cradle with her foot while her hands, never idle, mended a small pinafore. The girls all spoke at once while they patted the mare. Nattie found it best to focus on one conversation at a time and let the others flow around her. No one seemed to take offense, and it prevented headache.

She admired Alethia's new forest-green riding dress as her friend pointed out all the fashionable features she had chosen and described others that would not have done at all. Nattie hoped she looked knowledgeable as Alethia chattered happily about basques and passementerie, shoulder caps and sleeve puffs, embossed buttons and serpentine braid.

"It *is* a lovely dress," said Nattie, when the fashion lecture came to an end.

"And quite grown-up, don't you think, now that I'm sixteen?" asked Alethia. "I've caught up with you."

"Only for a little while, until my birthday," replied Nattie. "But I promise I'll let you catch up again next year."

"Do you think I look older with my hair up like this?" Alethia asked. She patted her hair, carefully arranged in shining red coils.

"Turn 'round," said Nattie. She tilted her head thoughtfully as Alethia pirouetted, skirt swirling.

"It's very elegant. I like the way it twists round and then tucks inside itself."

"It's easy to do; I can show you," offered Alethia. Her hands smoothed the sleek coils and she sighed. "I think my hair looks older, but with these freckles, my face still looks like I'm twelve."

"I have freckles, too," offered Nattie helpfully.

"You don't either! Where?" Alethia peered under the brim of Nattie's hat.

"On my nose. See? All across here." Nattie took off her hat and pointed to a few spots slightly darker than her brown skin.

"Those don't count!" said Alethia. "You need a strong light and a magnifying glass to see them. I'm speckled all over like a bird's egg."

"And well worth it, to have such beautiful red hair," said Mrs. Stockton, bustling up to welcome Nattie. "You have beautiful hair, too, my dear," she went on. "Black as a raven's wing and just as glossy. And it wouldn't hurt you to be more careful about wearing a hat when you're out of doors."

Nattie obediently put her hat back on, then realized the admonition was directed at Alethia. Conversation with Mrs. Stockton required careful attention.

Nattie presented her friend with a green saddle blanket that complemented the mare's chestnut coat, Alethia's red hair, and, by a stroke of luck, the new riding dress.

"Pretty as a picture," said Mrs. Stockton. She watched as Alethia put the mare through her paces, then hurried off to the kitchen. The younger girls begged to ride Chico, who adjusted his gait to suit each girl's ability. He padded serenely around the corral as Deborah bounced in the saddle, her chubby legs sticking straight out. He allowed Pauline to urge him into a sedate trot, and startled Molly with a dancing sidestep.

"That's a compliment," Nattie told the girl. "He wouldn't try that unless he thought you could handle it."

Molly beamed with pride.

Alethia was delighted with her mare. Mr. Stockton appeared and voiced his approval, proclaiming the horse a "pretty little thing and a fit mount for any lady. And with an excellent temperament, to stand all this commotion."

The younger girls surrounded their father, clamoring for ponies of their own. "And Miss Nattie must train them all. Please, Papa?"

"We'll see, we'll see," he repeated calmly, pacing slowly to the house while his daughters skipped and chattered around him.

The morning passed quickly while Nattie simultaneously cuddled baby Mary Jane, perused fashion periodicals with Alethia, discussed novels with Molly, admired Pauline's drawings, played dolls with Deborah, and traded news with Mrs. Stockton.

"How is your dear sister? She is a wonderfully faithful correspondent, but we miss her company," Mrs. Stockton said. "I remember her sitting in that very chair, always holding one of my babies on her lap. We were so sorry to hear of her disappointment. Such a shame... I know how Floralinda yearns to be a mother."

"There is nothing Flo wants more," Nattie replied. "The doctor says she needs to rest and regain her strength before she tries again."

"Do you think she might visit?" asked Alethia.

"I hope so. We're trying to convince her to come home for the summer."

Alethia smoothed her skirt. "Flo says the hot weather's a bore. She joined the Ladies' Society for Civic Improvement, but in summer the women do nothing but play cards, fan themselves and complain about the heat."

The mantel clock chimed.

Mrs. Stockton said, "She and James will make that cowtown into a proper little city, just you wait." She stood. "Well, out here in the country we have plenty enough to save us from *ennui*. Big girls, come help in the kitchen. Little girls, mind the baby."

At dinner, Mr. Stockton smiled down his long table of daughters.

"We're doing our part to settle the territory, aren't we, dear?" he asked his wife. "Think of all the young men condemned to bachelorhood without our contribution."

Instead of offering her usual laughing protest, Alethia blushed, folding and refolding the napkin on her lap. Did she have a suitor? And if so, why hadn't the news bubbled out of her already? Alethia had never been good at keeping secrets. She and Flo had chattered endlessly to each other about their suitors, although Flo's were mostly unwelcome and Alethia's were mostly wishful thinking. Nattie had always rolled her eyes and left them to it. But now she was intrigued. Could it be one of her brothers? A ranch hand? Could she have met someone on a visit to Flo? No. Flo would have let it slip. She couldn't keep secrets, either.

After the meal was finished and the kitchen was tidied, Nattie rescued Chico from the attentions of the girls. By the time Mrs. Stockton finished pressing gifts on her "for your dear family, with our best regards," and good-byes were repeated, and future visits were promised, banks of clouds blocked the sun and wisps of dust spun across the yard.

Nattie had brushed off the Stocktons' concerns, expecting nothing worse than a wet ride home, but here she was on the wrong side of the river and likely to remain so. At least she wouldn't go hungry. She twisted in the saddle to rummage through the bulging bags of food tied on behind. Mrs. Stockton had sent jam, pecans, honey—

"Apples!" said Nattie.

She took her knife from her belt, cut an apple in half, and leaned forward to give Chico his share. Girl and horse munched companionably while Nattie considered where to wait out the storm.

Her half of the apple held the stem. She twisted it. "South, north, south, north, south—" The stem snapped, and she tossed it into the wind. "South it is."

As Nattie picked up the reins she froze, squinting against the rain. The hair rose on the back of her neck as she peered at a dark shape in the water, caught on a downed cottonwood. "Just some debris, maybe," she said, but there was no mistaking the outline of shoulders and head.

Nattie stood in the stirrups, her apple forgotten in her hand, and appraised the situation. The man—or body—was facing downstream, pressed against a thick branch that barely broke the surface. The fallen tree that held him angled inshore, out of the swiftest current, but clods of earth splashed into the water, exposing more and more of the anchoring roots.

"That won't hold long," said Nattie, dropping to the ground.

Chico gently lipped her apple from her hand as she stood by his head, gauging the water's depth.

"Well, we can't leave him out there," Nattie said. "So I guess we'll go fetch him." She hoped she sounded more confident than she felt.

She pulled off her leather gloves, stuffed them into a pocket and threw her long riding coat over a branch. She considered stripping down further but decided against it. She couldn't spare the time and "if this goes badly, it won't much matter. I'll drown regardless," she said.

Nattie tied a loop in her rope and dumped everything else in an untidy pile. She had a sudden vision of her father and brothers searching for her and finding only her gear, but she thrust it out of her mind and swung up into the saddle. A glance upstream to check for approaching debris, a deep breath, then she urged Chico to the water's edge where the bank had crumbled into an uneven slope. He took step after careful step until suddenly the water was midway up his side. It was much colder than Nattie expected and she gasped as it washed over her legs and filled her boots. "We'd better do this quick," she said, and headed her horse toward the dark shape nearly submerged in the brown water.

Chico side-stepped out to the fallen tree. As they neared the man Nattie shouted to him, but her voice was lost in the rushing water. She was relieved to see that his arms gripped the branch.

"All right, Chico, he's alive. Let's try to keep him that way."

She edged Chico closer and leaned forward with the rope ready in her hand. It was precarious work, leaning low in the water to inch the rope under the man's arms without losing him, or herself, to the current. A broken branch tore her sleeve, and her flesh too, but she didn't feel it. The cold water numbed her fingers and the water's roar filled her head, driving out everything else. She focused intently on each accomplishment; one arm through, both arms, tighten the rope, bring him in close, then, "¡Let's go, Chico! *Rapido, rapido!*"

As the horse turned toward shore the man was on the downstream side, with the current tugging at him. Nattie grasped his belt and hauled him up until he lay face down in front of her. A sudden surge caught them and Chico lost his footing as the current swept them back toward the tree. For a heart-stopping second Nattie feared they'd be tangled in the branches, but Chico pushed on until his hooves found the bottom. He scrambled up the bank and Nattie slid to the ground, gasping and shivering. The man retched and coughed, a gush of water streaming from his mouth down Chico's side.

"Well, we're none of us drowned," said Nattie, giddy with relief. "If we don't freeze to death this could be a good day yet."

She checked Chico for injuries, then tugged the man's limp form to a more secure position across the saddle's seat and draped her coat over him. She glanced at the sky. They were safe from the river but the storm was strengthening. Thunder followed fast upon each lightning bolt and a hard rain fell as she searched her coat pockets for her gloves. One was missing; "Naturally," said Nattie.

It was nearly dark, but they weren't far from shelter. A mile or so downstream was the trail to East Camp. With luck, someone would be there to help her. There was a cookhouse and bunkhouse and barn, a fireplace and blankets and stove and maybe food—but she had food.

"Bless you, Mrs. Stockton," said Nattie as she retrieved the heavy bags.

Loading them back on Chico was a challenge. The saddle was occupied by the rescued man. Nattie would ride behind, so all the food and gear had to go forward. Her cold fingers could barely form a knot, but she tied everything in a tangled mess and looped it over the saddle horn. Chico seemed mildly puzzled by the odd arrangement bumping against his shoulders, but didn't object.

"We're a sorry sight, but it's only for a little while and you are the greatest horse that ever lived," said Nattie, teeth chattering. Buttons flew as she tore off the unnecessary front placket of her riding skirt and pulled it around her shoulders.

The trip was an endless misery of cold and rain, interrupted only when Nattie saw the pile of rocks that marked the ford, impassable now under the torrent. She used her knife to slash a ragged strip of cloth from her makeshift shawl and tied it to a branch. Her family would come looking for her as soon as the storm allowed; they'd see the fabric sign across the river and know that she was all right.

Past the ford Nattie paused, searching for the gap in the trees that marked the trail head. The storm's false twilight had deepened into night. She let Chico have his head, trusting him to follow the trail she couldn't see.

Each dazzling flash of lightning illuminated a frozen black-and white world. Raindrops paused in midair, trees held unnatural angles for a brief instant, then all was lost to darkness again. Nattie closed her eyes against the blinding white flashes, but the jagged images still streaked across her eyelids. The pounding thunder and howling wind assailed her like physical blows. Leaves whipped her as they whirled by. She wondered if she'd have the strength to climb back up if the wind pushed her to the ground. Best not to find out, she thought grimly, and willed her weary muscles to hold. She rode on, huddled over the man lying across the saddle in front of her. His flesh felt cold even to her numb fingers, but she thought she could feel a faint pulse in his throat. There was nothing to do but wait until they reached shelter. Wait and endure.

She fell into an uneasy half-sleep until she was roused by painful jabs on the back of her gloveless hand. It took her weary mind a moment to puzzle out the cause; rain had turned to hail. Chico snorted and tossed his head, but trudged on through the howling darkness. Nattie checked that her coat covered the man's head, then stretched forward to pat her horse's neck.

"This won't last long, my sweet boy. I'm so sorry to have you out in this, but it can't be much farther now. Just a little more and we'll be all right. Just a little more."

Chapter 2

Chico stopped and whickered softly. Dazed by cold and fatigue, Nattie pulled herself upright and strained to see through the darkness. The next lightning flash showed the East Camp barn in front of them. Chico whickered again.

"Soon, I promise," Nattie told him. Her lips were so cold she could barely shape the words.

She looked around the clearing, hoping to see a light, but all the windows were dark. "Looks like we'll have to manage on our own," she said. She shook off her disappointment and slid stiffly off Chico's rump.

She led Chico to the cookhouse. A few steps rose to a small porch. Nattie positioned Chico next to the porch and pulled the man from the saddle. He was heavier than she expected and they tumbled in a heap. The back of her head hit the door with a loud crack. Chico snorted.

"Don't laugh, *caballo*, if you want grain tonight," Nattie said, rubbing her head.

She grasped the man under his arms and dragged him inside, depositing him near the fireplace. Groping blindly, she searched until her fingers brushed the glass base of the lamp she knew she'd find on the long table. Her cold fingers fumbled with the match holder, but soon a match flickered and the lamp illuminated the room. The accomplishment energized her. She triumphantly slammed the door against the wind.

There was plenty of wood by the fireplace and Nattie knew there would be more in the shed. Impatient for heat, she used an extravagant amount of kindling. The fire crackled softly at first then suddenly blazed up, sending waves of warmth to her outstretched palms. She shivered violently as the heat penetrated her wet clothes.

She turned to contemplate the man sprawled on the floor. She was tempted to linger by the fire but, "What do I do about you?" she asked. "There's no sense saving you from drowning to let you die of cold. You need to get out of your wet clothes and into warm blankets. How about I fetch the blankets and you wake up and do the rest for yourself?"

She shifted him closer to the fire and rolled him onto his side, "So you can rid yourself of any more river water you might contain. Better out than in." He lay on his left side, his holster on his right. Nattie unfastened it and removed the revolver, "in case you wake up in an unfriendly mood." She stuck the revolver in her belt and thought that she would look quite fierce if she weren't dripping wet and shivering.

Nattie held her coat in front of the fire a moment, hoping to trap enough heat to sustain her until she returned. She picked up the lamp and went out the back door, past the pump and into the bunkhouse, where a wooden chest held blankets. She gathered as much as she could carry and hurried back to the fire. The man hadn't moved.

"You're not going to help at all, are you?" she asked as she put the lamp and his revolver on the table.

Nattie rolled him onto his back. The current had taken his coat and his shirt was torn. A muddy stream trickled onto the floor when she pulled off his boots. The boots were intricately stitched; "custom made for you, I'm guessing. Maybe that's why the river didn't pull them off."

She unbuckled his gun belt and put it on the table, then arranged blankets over him the way Tía had taught her; one for the upper body, one for the legs, and one for the nether regions.

"I'll still see more of you than is customary on such short acquaintance," she told him, "but this will maintain the proprieties."

She unbuttoned his dark shirt, revealing a silk-trimmed undershirt with mother-of-pearl buttons at the neck. "Quality right down to the skin," said Nattie. She considered leaving it on him as a nod to modesty, but "in for a penny, in for a pound," she said.

She peeled off the wet fabric to reveal an assortment of fresh scrapes and old scars. "Looks like this wasn't your first adventure," she said. She pulled the top blanket up to his chin and tucked it in.

"Now for the other end." She folded the lower blanket up to reveal his feet and ankles and, with some difficulty, tugged off his trousers. His drawers came with them. "Just as well, I suppose. The sooner you're dry the sooner you'll be warm."

She tucked the blankets around him and put another on top. "There. Swaddled like a baby."

She stood and pulled herself away from the fire for one last trip to the bunkhouse. The euphoria of being out of the storm was giving way to weariness, but she couldn't rest yet.

Nattie returned with the last of the blankets. The wind banged the door closed behind her but the man didn't stir. He breathed evenly and his pulse was regular, but his hands were icy and his fingernails had a blue tinge.

She piled blankets to warm by the fire and fetched a flour-sack towel from the kitchen. She folded the blanket up to reveal his feet and legs and nodded in approval. "Pinking up nicely." She found no injuries as she dried his lower limbs, but bruises were beginning to mottle his skin.

"No broken bones, but you're going to be sore for a while," she told him. She tucked his legs in again and folded the upper blanket down to his waist. As she dried his arms and chest, she spotted a cord around his neck that led to a leather pouch under his back. She pulled it around to the front in case he awoke and felt for it.

Nattie arranged a generous layer of blankets near the fire and shifted her patient onto it, then covered him with more. She sat back on her heels and studied him. She had seen the scar of a bullet wound below his collarbone, and a long straight line on his upper arm; souvenir of a knife fight, Nattie judged. *If I weren't so tired I'd be wildly curious*, she thought.

She picked up the lamp and stepped out the front door. The wind had eased but the rain fell unabated. Chico stepped toward her, then turned his head away, ears pricked. She edged toward him and lifted her rifle from its sheath on the saddle. Slowly raising the lamp, she peered past Chico and glimpsed the shadowy outline of a horse.

"Who's there? *¿Quién es?*" she called.

The only sound was the hiss of raindrops on the hot lamp chimney.

Nattie moved closer. The horse's saddle was empty and the blanket hung low on one side. She relaxed and put the lamp on the ground.

"Did you follow us here?" she asked. "You're missing a rider, and I know someone who's missing a horse. I don't suppose that's a coincidence."

The horse was a mare with clean lines and an intelligent head. Nattie led her in a circle around the lamp; the horse moved easily, but her head stayed low.

"*Pobrecita*, you're just worn out. Food and rest will put you right."

Nattie picked up the lamp and led the mare to shelter, with Chico close beside. Both horses perked up as they entered the hay-scented barn. She led them into adjoining stalls, "so you can get acquainted," she told them. As she slung the stranger's saddle onto a rack, a glint of metal on the underside of the cantle caught her eye. A small rectangle of silver was engraved in flowing script. She held the lamp close to read it: *A C M Butterfield Overland Mail Co.*

"Perhaps ACM is the half-drowned soul I left by the fire. And I need to get back to him, so food and a quick rub-down is all you get tonight. I'll lavish you with attention tomorrow." She left the horses contentedly munching and trudged back to the house.

Nattie put the lamp on the floor as she knelt to examine her patient. The stranger's eyes were still closed but his pulse was stronger, and color was returning to his lips and fingernails.

She stood by the fire a moment, wishing again that she could stay there. Soon, she promised herself. She picked up the lamp once more.

After a trip to the privy, the pump and the woodshed, Nattie was in for the night. She made a fire in the cookstove and filled the reservoir; there would be the luxury of hot water tomorrow. She peeled off her coat and rotated by the fireplace, like a chicken on a spit, she thought. But even when the outside of her clothes were hot to the touch, the inside remained cold and wet. If she were alone she would just wrap up in a blanket while her clothes dried, but under the circumstances—"Maintain the proprieties," Nattie said, yawning, and picked up her coat. It was tolerably dry and tolerably modest, except for the slit back.

"Good enough, considering that the only other person here is unconscious."

As Nattie held the coat by the fire, a small red volume fell on the floor. She had slipped it into her pocket that morning, hoping for a chance to read in the cool green of the riverbank. It seemed a very long time ago. She checked the book for damp, riffling its delicate pages and examining the leather binding, then placed it on the mantel.

She undressed in the corner of the kitchen, where she wouldn't be seen if her patient chose an inopportune moment to open his eyes. There was a ragged gash on her forearm. That's going to hurt once it thaws out, she thought. The cut was seeping blood so she tied a dish towel around it.

Nattie buttoned her coat with fingers clumsy with cold and returned to the fire. She gathered the stranger's wet clothes and spread them out on a bench with hers to dry.

She knelt by the sleeping man. His breathing was deep and even, his pulse strong, but "I'd be relieved if you'd open your eyes," Nattie told him. She sat back and studied the pattern of shadows the firelight cast on his face. Even softened by sleep and a few days growth of beard, his face was all planes and angles. His nose wasn't quite straight; "You've got in the way of bullets, knives, *and* fists, apparently," said Nattie. She judged him to be in his mid-twenties, although people look younger when they're sleeping, she thought. Younger, and more vulnerable.

But, "*Las apariencias enganan,*" she reminded herself briskly. She wondered where he was from, and where he was headed, and what he carried in the pouch hanging from his neck.

A smear of red appeared on the towel as she dried his dark hair. She scrambled up to fetch the lamp and placed it near his head as she searched for the wound. There was a lump a hand's-breadth above his right ear. Her fingers delicately pressed around the swelling and she sighed with relief.

"I think you'll live," she told him, "and I'm about dead on my feet."

Nattie blew out the lamp and, with her rifle near at hand, curled up in a nest of blankets as close to the fire as she could get without smoldering. She was asleep in an instant.

Chapter 3

Drifting to the edge of consciousness, his first awareness was of quiet. The roar of water that had surrounded him, pummeling his body and dazing his mind, was blessedly still. Now and then he heard—or dreamed?—the soft murmur of a woman's voice. He tried to respond, but the effort overwhelmed him. He could do that later, he thought. It was enough for now to know that he could rest. He slipped again into dreamless depths.

Nattie woke with a sharp intake of breath and listened intently for— what? She sat tensed, heart thudding, knowing only that some sound had awakened her. Whatever it was, it wasn't repeated.

She added wood to the fire and wondered how long she had slept. More than a few hours, she judged. The wind had calmed, but a hard rain still beat on the roof. The river wouldn't go down today.

She lit the lamp and knelt by the stranger. She was encouraged to see that he had moved; his hands were out from under the blankets. Nattie placed the back of her hand on his forehead and he muttered a little. "Maybe you're what woke me," she said. "I expect you might be ready for some food soon. Clothes, too, which promises to be awkward."

She checked the garments on the bench. They were still damp, so she could postpone deciding whether she should try to dress him. She turned the clothes over, brushed off the worst of the mud, and shook her head as she examined her shirt. It was blotched with dirt and the torn sleeve was blood-stained. Nattie shrugged and laid it down with the rest.

"Now that I've finished the laundry," she said, "I shall apply my domestic skills in the kitchen."

She had a sudden craving for coffee. A coffeepot waited on the stove, its blue-and-white enamel blackened with long use. She hunted for coffee beans in the tin-lined larder and planned meals as she took inventory. A bin was nearly full of pinto beans; those would dominate the menu. Flour, baking powder, salt, lard—she could make tortillas and biscuits. But coffee first.

A glimpse of yellow at the back of a shelf rewarded her search. She shoved containers aside to reveal two Arbuckle's packages with the coffee mill next to them. Both were open but nearly full; probably opened just for the peppermint sticks, thought Nattie. Armando, the camp cook, had a sweet tooth. She found cans of condensed milk and opened one with her knife.

At last she held a heavy crockery mug of coffee and the world seemed brighter. Halfway through her second cup she realized that the world really was brighter; the sun was rising. She blew out the lamp and opened the front door to the day.

A steady rain fell and there was no break in the clouds. Water poured from the roof *canales* and flowed across the muddy yard. Nattie shivered in the cool air. Violent storms were common here but she had never seen rain like this. At home her father would be everywhere at once, a general marshaling his troops against the invasion of water; ally turned enemy. Tía and Mrs. Dresen would be flying around the big kitchen, maintaining a steady supply of coffee and food for the hands. Her brothers would be working like demons; Tomás grim, thinking of the damage, and Robby bright-eyed with excitement. He and their cousin Ignacio would be trying to outdo each other describing the storm:

"*Llueve a cántaros.*"

"*Llueve a mares.*"

"Raining cats and dogs."

"Snakes and pitchforks."

"Gully washer."

"Fence lifter."

"Toad strangler."

"Frog floater."

"Duck drowner."

They'd invent their own increasingly ridiculous terms until the game ended in laughter.

"Sister strander," Nattie said, and turned to go back in.

The air in the cabin was heavy with the smell of smoke and wet wool. The window frames had swelled shut with damp so she used a stick of kindling to prop the door open a few inches. She'd need to fetch more wood soon.

Her coat was drafty with nothing under it. She checked her clothes again and judged them to be dry enough. She dressed quickly by the kitchen stove and revolved slowly in front of the fireplace to take the chill off the damp fabric.

"I appreciate your concern for my modesty, but I'm decent now," she told the man at her feet. "You can wake up any time."

She knelt beside him. He groaned as she gently examined the bump on his head. "You really do need to start taking care of yourself," Nattie told him. "Your clothes are almost dry and I don't want to put them back on you. Getting them off was hard enough."

She thought she saw his eyelids flicker, but that was all. She pulled on her hat, coat, and still-wet boots.

"I'm going out to the barn now, but I'll be back soon to start breakfast," she said, picking up her rifle and the stranger's gunbelt. "I'll take these with me in case you're not a cheerful riser."

She plodded through the mud, boots squelching inside and out. The horses turned their heads as she opened the barn door. Chico whickered a greeting.

"*Buenos dias, queridos*," Nattie replied. "Feeling better? Let's have a look at you."

She found halters and walked the horses. They moved easily and were cheerfully interested in the prospect of breakfast. Nattie ran her hands down their legs and found no heat or swelling. Chico leaned against her companionably and snuffled her hair.

"Get over, you great lump," said Nattie fondly, trying to push him away with her shoulder. "You'd sit in my lap if I'd let you."

She replenished their hay, grain, and water, and began to look forward to her own breakfast. The thought of food reminded her of Mrs. Stockton's generosity. She untied the bags from the tangle of rope and squelched back to the cookhouse.

She carefully lowered the bags onto the long dining table, mindful of the jars of jam and honey she'd seen yesterday. She found the apples and took an enormous bite, chewing happily as she explored the bounty spilling out onto the table. The jars had survived the trip and her mouth watered at the prospect of biscuits and jam. There were pecans, and onions to season the pinto beans, and—her next discovery, a slab of bacon, sent her flying to the kitchen. She tossed thick slices into a skillet and hurriedly made biscuits, shaping them with her hands. She had seen an empty beer bottle that probably served as a rolling pin, but she was too hungry to take time to roll out the dough.

She munched crisp strips of bacon while she waited impatiently for the biscuits to brown. When they were ready, she piled a plate high and ate more than she thought possible. Full at last, she refilled her coffee mug, put the remaining bacon and biscuits in the warming oven, and scooped a generous measure of beans into a pot to soak.

"Now to remove some mud," she said. She knelt by the stove, a towel close at hand and a basin of steaming water in front of her. She added miserly amounts of cold water until it was "perfect—not *quite* scalding." She sluiced water over her head with a tin cup, closing her eyes and shuddering pleasurably as fingers of warmth flowed through her hair—and down the back of her neck. Changing her technique, she submerged her head in the water and vigorously scrubbed her hair with a bar of brown soap. Water streamed into the basin as she raised her head.

Nattie twisted her long hair into a thick dark rope and squeezed out as much water as she could, then groped blindly for the towel. She dried her hair, sending droplets flying to hiss on the hot stove, then rocked back on her heels and quickly lifted her head, sending her hair up and over to hit her back with a heavy smack. She wiped her face with the towel and opened her eyes.

The stranger was sitting up, watching her.

Chapter 4

Alan McTurk jolted back to consciousness between one heartbeat and the next. One instant he was aware of nothing; in the next his mind was racing, trying to recall where he was and how he came to be there. The last thing he remembered was fighting for air in a confusion of cold water. Now he was warm and dry—good signs, but he remained cautious. He kept his eyes closed while he tensed and relaxed his limbs; they were sore, but functional. His pulse pounded in his head. He dismissed the pain and sat up slowly.

An almost imperceptible sound caught his attention. He froze, listening intently, trying to identify the rhythmic soft noise. Peering through the dim light, he saw what appeared to be a headless creature hunched on the floor by the stove. The sound, he realized, was coming from hands moving on a white blur where a head should be. When the apparition sat up, the puzzling shape resolved itself into a girl with a towel over her hair. For a long moment he stared at her while she knelt, wide-eyed, still holding the towel on her head. Then he sneezed.

Nattie relaxed and tossed the towel onto the bench. "There's a sign of life," she said, moving closer. "You've been half-drowned and three-quarters frozen, and you have a knot on your head the size of my fist. How do you feel?"

"I was in the river," Alan said slowly. His eyes slid past her to his gun belt on the table. He thought a moment, then asked, "What day is this? Where is this place?"

"It's Tuesday, and this is a cattle camp south of Swede's Crossing."

"Am I still east of the San Rafael?"

"You are. The river's still in flood. The ford won't be passable until tomorrow, even if the rain stops today. I doubt it will."

"Is there a bridge?" he asked.

"Upriver, at Alamosa Station."

"It's gone," Alan said.

"Gone?" repeated Nattie.

"The flood took it out…yesterday, it must have been."

"You were there?"

Alan nodded. "I was on it when it collapsed."

Nattie was silent, imagining his journey down the river to where she had found him.

"So I expect I'm very fortunate to be here, or anywhere on dry land," he continued, "although I had hoped to be in Dos Rios by now." He looked up at the beamed ceiling and listened to the steady drumming of rain on the roof. "Ah, well. What can't be cured must be endured."

"One of my Aunt Constancia's favorite sayings. *Lo que no se puede remediar, se tiene que aguantar.*"

The man said, "It's a true thing, in any language." His gaze searched the cabin, then returned to Nattie.

Sizing me up, she thought.

"My name is Alan McTurk."

ACM, thought Nattie. She was sizing him up, too.

He said, "I had a letter of introduction which might assure you of my respectability, but it was in my saddlebag, which is now somewhere downstream, I suppose."

"You were traveling on horseback?"

"Before I took to traveling by water? Yes. And my horse was very reluctant to step onto that bridge. I should have taken heed of it."

"Your horse—a dark sorrel mare with three white stockings?"

"You found her?" asked Alan.

"She found you. Your mare, and saddlebags, are in the barn."

She stood. Her evaluation was complete. This man was no threat to her.

"It's a pleasure to make your acquaintance, Mr. McTurk. My name is Nattie Johnston. I expect you're ready for some breakfast."

Alan looked at his clothes on the bench and raised an eyebrow.

"Not quite ready, perhaps."

Nattie wished she had managed to dress him before he woke.

"I think your clothes are dry now," she informed him briskly, and busied herself with gathering them up from the bench.

"I do hope word of this doesn't get out. It might damage my reputation," said Alan, his grin contradicting his pious tone.

Nattie wished she had left him in his wet clothes. She stood over him, her arms full.

"Since I don't know what sort of reputation you have, I'm sure I couldn't say."

She dropped the clothes in a heap next to him and said, "I'll fetch your bags while you restore your respectability."

She lingered in the barn to give him time to dress. Her arm had stopped bleeding so she discarded the bandage. She brushed the horses and her clothes, and wove her hair into a loose braid, tied with a bit of twine instead of her mud-stained ribbon.

When she went back in Alan was slumped at the table, holding his head in his hands. He straightened at once and smiled at her.

"What is it like out there? I'll need to be on my way as soon as I can."

Nattie fixed him a plate and poured coffee.

"What you need is rest and a doctor's care," she said. "Even if the river were passable, you're not fit to ride and won't be for a while. And you must be half-starved." She put the heaping plate in front of him.

"I'm afraid there's no butter," she said, but Alan didn't seem to miss it. He happily slathered jam on biscuits and finished off the bacon.

Nattie tidied the kitchen while Alan finished eating. At last he sighed, stretched, and brought his dishes to the wash basin.

"Thank you, that was splendid," he said. "Is there more coffee?"

He leaned against the wall, cup in hand, and looked steadily at Nattie. She met his gaze, then turned away to the stove. She had expected his eyes to be brown, like her own, but they were a deep blue-grey.

"Your mare seems fine," Nattie said as she reached for his cup.

"I'm happy to hear it; she's a good horse. I wonder how she got out of the river. In fact, I wonder how I got out of the river."

"You were caught in some branches. I helped you out of the water," said Nattie casually.

"Ah."

Nattie decided she'd be more comfortable with a new topic.

"The river took your rifle and any other gear you had. Your saddle and bridle are all right except for being covered in mud. I'm going to clean them now." She moved toward the door.

"We can do that in here while you expound on how you saved me from a cold, wet doom."

Nattie sighed. "All right. You bring in the bridles. I'll get the saddles."

They went out the back door together, Nattie to the woodshed and Alan to the barn. He walked slowly but seemed steady on his feet.

Back inside, Nattie stoked the fire and the stove and put the beans on to cook. She surveyed the cabin seating; one rickety chair and two long benches by the table. She dragged a bench to the fireplace and tipped it on its side. With blankets piled on the floor in front, it made a tolerably comfortable legless sofa.

She gathered up the food bags from the table and was surprised to find that one wasn't empty. She had stopped excavating upon discovering the bacon. Now she uncovered more treasure; a packet of brown paper containing six cleaned and plucked quail.

"Mrs. Stockton, you are a wonder, a marvel, and a gem," said Nattie.

Alan carried his saddle in, doing his best to look comfortable under the burden.

"I said hello to Bella. She seems no worse for wear."

"I can't say the same for you," Nattie replied. "You're in no condition to be lugging saddles around." She turned toward the door. "You're doing much better than you have any right to, so don't press your luck," she said sternly, and slipped out while she had the last word.

The rain was easing. Nattie opened the doors to the corral in case the horses wanted exercise, but they were content to stay inside.

"Had enough of rain? I don't blame you," she told them.

She looped the bridles over her shoulder, shoved saddle soap and rags into her pockets, and picked up her saddle. When she returned to the cookhouse Alan was cleaning his revolver. He had neatly arranged the contents on his saddlebags on the table. Nattie saw the pouch he had worn around his neck, an oilskin-wrapped packet next to it.

Alan followed her gaze and said, "No treasury notes or deeds to gold mines, I'm afraid. Just papers. Letters. I was worried they may have gotten wet but they seem all right." He changed the subject. "Does anyone live here?"

"Armando Padilla is the camp cook and general caretaker. He's usually here, but he broke his foot—dropped a case of canned peaches on it—and went to stay with his daughter in Agua Prieta until it mends. I hoped his sons would be here, but no such luck."

"And where do you live?" asked Alan. "Near here?"

"Not far. On the other side of the river."

"Speaking of the river," Alan said, "I've told you how I came to be in it; now it's your turn to tell me how I got out."

Chapter 5

They settled comfortably by the fire. The air was rich with the scent of saddle soap and leather when Nattie finished speaking and looked up from the bridle on her lap.

"So here we are," she said.

"So here we are," Alan echoed thoughtfully. "You took some chances."

"It wasn't as though I had a choice."

"You could have swooned on the river bank."

Nattie shook her head. "I've never been much for swooning. Although it must be useful."

Alan raised an eyebrow. "How so?"

"To avoid unpleasantness." She assumed an upright posture and stern voice. "Nattie, finish your needlework. Nattie, conjugate these verbs. Nattie, Mrs. Beamish is here, come and visit. Nattie—" She held her hand to her forehead, closed her eyes, and let her head fall back. Holding the pose, she looked at Alan through her dark lashes. "You see?"

"Brava!" said Alan. "Although I suspect you have other ways of avoiding things you don't wish to do."

"True enough," agreed Nattie cheerfully. "I am a willful, disobedient daughter, a trial and tribulation to my family who don't know what is to become of me despite their best efforts and what they've done to deserve me I'm sure I don't know." This was rattled off with an ease that spoke of frequent hearing.

"My father told me much the same thing." Alan stood and stretched.

Nattie winced as she picked up her saddle. Blood appeared on her torn sleeve. Alan fetched a dish towel from the kitchen and held it on the ragged tear.

"You're really in no condition to be lugging saddles around," he said mildly.

He lifted the cloth to inspect the wound. The bleeding had slowed to a persistent ooze of red.

"See, it's not bad," Nattie said. "No need to fuss. It'll stop in a minute."

"Only to tear open and bleed again. I'm afraid I'll have to fuss a bit." Alan tore the towel into strips. "I promise to cause as much pain as possible, to distract from the fussing."

He was really very gentle, frowning with concentration as he bandaged her arm.

"Nattie; from Natalie? Natalia?" he asked.

"Natividad. It was my grandmother's name."

"Pretty. Were you born at Christmas?"

"No, but she was. My birthday's next month."

"And you'll be…?"

"Seventeen."

Alan stole glances at her as he worked. High cheekbones, determined chin, tip-tilted eyes that hinted at mischief—he saw that she was watching him and quickly looked down to finish tying the bandage in place. When he looked up again her dark eyes were still on him, serious and thoughtful. He met her gaze and they studied each other with unblinking intensity, scarcely breathing.

A log popped with a spray of sparks and they quickly moved apart.

Alan looked out the window. "I think the rain has stopped."

They stepped out onto the small porch. Weak sunlight filtered through the breaking clouds.

"If this holds, the river might be passable by mid-day tomorrow; the morning after that for a surety," said Nattie.

"Your family must be worried about you."

"I hope not. They probably think I stayed with the Stocktons, which I would have done if I had any sense."

"Well, I'm very grateful you didn't choose the sensible course."

Nattie nodded, imagining him clinging to the tree until his strength failed him, and then… She shook off the thought.

"I'm going to chase the horses out to stretch their legs," she said.

Alan watched her walk away, her braid swaying. She had a small waist, the kind women tried to achieve with corsets and laces. He found himself wondering if his hands would encircle it, then shook his head.

"Idiot," he said, and went back inside. He poured two cups of coffee, picked up the bridles, and joined Nattie. They leaned on the corral fence and watched the horses.

Alan asked, "Who owns this place? I should compensate them for—"

Nattie interrupted. "It's all right. I know them. They'll be glad to have helped. They would say, *Cuándo uno es mas pobre, se le debe socorro mas.* To one who needs the most, give the most."

" 'The wicked borrow and do not repay, but the righteous give generously,' " countered Alan.

"So let the people who own the camp attain righteousness by giving generously. If you sacrifice their righteousness to save yourself from wickedness, then you're still wicked."

Alan said, "I'd challenge you to a theological debate, but I fear I might swoon."

They drank their coffee in companionable silence until Alan spoke again.

"You don't ask many questions, do you? Don't think I'm complaining; it's remarkably restful."

"If there's something you want me to know, you'll tell me. As for the rest—pieces come together."

"Oh yes? What have you pieced together about me?"

Nattie looked down, as though reading the answers in her coffee cup. Finally she said, "You have information in that pouch that you need to deliver, soon, west of here. You expect that someone may try to stop you. The information is about an issue that doesn't affect you personally so I'd guess…the new rail line."

She saw a fleeting change in Alan's expression at the mention of the railroad.

That's a hit, she thought, and went on. "Money isn't a concern for you. You're well educated, but you haven't led a sheltered life. You've done your share of fighting, maybe for or against the law. You're disciplined, so I'd guess it was for."

"Impressive," Alan said. He turned to face her. "Expound, young seeress."

"Does that mean I was right?"

"Too right for comfort."

"Well then. You tried to cross a flooded river on a questionable bridge, so the papers must be important, and needed soon. If you were personally concerned you'd chafe at this delay, but you accept it with good grace. Your horse is remarkable, your clothes and gear are the best quality, and you weren't much troubled by losing some of it."

Chico ambled over to the fence. Nattie scratched his head.

"Go on," said Alan.

"You carry some scars." Nattie felt her cheeks grow warm, and hurried on. "You cleaned your revolver first thing; maybe you expect you might need it. And maybe you were given these papers to deliver because you can fight your way through if you need to."

She hesitated, trying to judge his reaction, but his face was expressionless.

"And the purpose of my journey?"

Nattie said, "My sister's husband is on the territorial committee about rail routes. I know that meetings will be held next week; Flo's letters are about little else. She's going with her husband to Prescott and she's all a-flutter about what to wear. The railroad is all anyone talks about lately. It seemed likely that your papers might relate to it somehow."

She glanced at Alan; still no response.

"Of course, people around here want the southern route. We thought we had a good chance, especially when a survey crew came. But then they disappeared. People who want the northern route say that shows the borderlands are lawless and violent and not suitable for a rail line. But there's no sign that the crew was attacked; they just…vanished. Everyone is talking about how it will affect the decision, and wondering if maybe that's why it happened, and who might be behind it—every day there's another rumor."

"Hmm," said Alan absently. "Your sister Flo—would her surname happen to be Peller?"

"Yes."

"So her husband would be James Peller."

"Yes."

"Owner of Peller Mercantile."

"Yes. Do you know him?"

"I know of him. He's one of the men waiting for these papers."

"I'm not surprised. He has a finger in every pie in the territory."

Alan thoughtfully rubbed his thumb across his chin.

"So then your surname would be Johnston, with a 't'."

"Yes."

"Not Johnson, without a 't'."

"No."

"Ah. I missed that during our introductions."

"Understandable."

"And your father would be Martin Johnston."

"Yes."

"Owner of the largest spread in the territory."

"People exaggerate."

"Would you have mentioned that you are Martin Johnston's daughter if I hadn't asked?"

Nattie mulled it over. "Probably not."

"I see. You don't ask questions, and you're extremely selective about the information you share. This could hinder free and open communication between us."

Nattie laughed. "I don't believe you have cause to complain. I've told you more than you've told me."

"True. But you have the advantage of superior local knowledge. I'm just a courier, hired to deliver papers."

Nattie suspected he was more than that.

Alan watched the horses a moment. "Right," he said decisively. "I'd like you to tell me everything you've heard about the railroad and the vanished surveyors. I'll tell you all I know, as well."

He put his hand on his chest where he carried the pouch. "These papers contain information that'll shake the rail committee up, down, and sideways. I'm inclined to trust the man who's sending these letters; we were Rangers together, in Texas." He flashed Nattie a quick grin and said, "You were right about that, young seeress. But I don't know the people who gave him this information, or the people I'm delivering it to. Before I hand these papers over, I'd like to know all I can about the game and the players."

Nattie nodded and threw the dregs of her coffee out on the ground. "We can talk in a little while," she said. "I need to start supper, and then I'm going to ride down to the ford. I left a signal for my family; they may have left one for me."

"What sort of signal?" asked Alan.

"A piece of my skirt. This outing has been hard on my clothes."

Alan handed Nattie his cup and said, "I'll saddle your horse."

"Thanks, but it's a short ride. No need for a saddle. You can give me a hand with supper, though."

Alan stared when Nattie uncovered the quail. "A seeress *and* a magician! How'd you conjure this up?"

"I can't take credit. We have Mrs. Stockton to thank."

"Thank you, Mrs. Stockton," said Alan fervently.

Nattie regarded the quail. "Should we cut these up and fry them?"

"With some of those onions." Alan's head disappeared into a cupboard. He emerged with a cast-iron frying pan in each hand, then found two knives and handed one to Nattie. "Birds or onions?" he asked.

"Birds, I think. Onions make me teary."

"And you'll shed no tears over these poor little corpses? Heartless creature." Alan picked up an onion.

"Hungry creature," Nattie corrected him. "We're also having beans, if that would better suit your superior nature. I'll enjoy your share of the poor little corpses." She brandished the knife with a dramatic flourish and began cutting.

"No need for that." Alan picked up a second onion. "My superior nature has starved to death; a tragic loss. It will be sadly missed by all who knew it."

Nattie wiped her hands on a towel. "If you would put the bacon and onions in with the beans, the rest can wait until I get back."

Alan picked up a third onion and began to juggle. "This is an amazing spread of food, you know. I haven't eaten this well since I set out on this jaunt."

"Mrs. Stockton would be thrilled to hear it. She's never happier than when she's feeding people."

"How long will it take for you to ride to the river? I don't seem to remember the trip here."

"I'm not surprised," said Nattie, remembering the limp figure draped across her saddle. "I'll be back in well under an hour."

"I'll accompany you. I don't think I've brought any trouble with me, but I'd feel better if I rode along."

Nattie pulled her hat on with a sharp tug. "You'd feel better if you'd lie down for a while," she said sternly. "Admit it; you're tired and sore and you need to rest."

"Nonsense. I've never felt better."

"You don't have the sense God gave a gopher. And I sound exactly like my aunt, which is deeply upsetting." Nattie turned to go.

"You should wear your coat," said Alan.

"Now *you* sound exactly like my aunt," Nattie called back as she went out the door.

Chapter 6

Chico danced as they started down the trail. Birds flitted about on self-important errands, loudly voicing their opinions. The air was fragrant with the scent of plants and wet earth. Water still dripped from the trees and rivulets ran across the trail. Nattie's shoulder brushed a low-hanging branch, bringing a cold shower down upon her. Alan was right. She should have worn her coat.

She could hear the San Rafael before she saw it. Air and ground thrummed with raw energy. The river had retreated from its high-water mark, leaving debris clumped in branches like untidy bird's nests, but the torrent still filled the channel from bank to bank. She shook her head. It seemed impossible that she had ventured out into that angry flood.

"Ay, Chico, what were we thinking?" Her voice was lost in the water's roar. They turned upstream toward the ford.

Nattie's signal was matched by a bandanna hanging from a branch across the river. Her message had been received. At some point she would have to give an account of how she came to be stranded with a stranger in East Camp, but "I'll cross that ridge when I come to it, as Tía would say."

She watched the river for a few moments, marveling that only one day had passed since the storm had blown her off-course. Somehow her life had changed and there was no way to reverse it, anymore than this racing water could turn and flow back to its source.

Something had been put in motion and she'd be pulled along with it, to whatever destination awaited her.

Nattie was solemn a moment, then shrugged.

"*Lo que esta escrito, escrito esta.* In the meanwhile, I have supper to cook."

She took a last look at the river. Barring more rain, she judged it would be passable in twenty-four hours. And then Alan would continue on his journey, and she would go home, and then—what?

"*Lo que esta escrito,*" she said.

She sang as she rode. Chico's ears swiveled like weather vanes.

"I hope that means you like it," she told him. "Lord knows no one else does."

She watched the ground and slid down several times to gather plants and narrow strips of bark. She tied her finds into neat bunches and tucked them into her belt.

"Hold up, Chico, I want to clean my teeth," Nattie said as they passed under a low branch. She cut a slender twig and rotated one end against the branch until it flattened into a fibrous disk. Riding on, she lay flat on Chico's broad back while she scrubbed her teeth and idly watched leaves and sky take turns passing above.

She sat up and threw away the twig as they entered the camp clearing. She thought she glimpsed a flicker of movement by the barn, so she dismounted and crouched low to look around the corner of the cookhouse. Alan emerged from the barn and quickly crossed the yard. She heard the back door of the cookhouse, and then boots on the wood floor.

"Interesting," said Nattie, her eyes narrowed.

She led Chico to the barn. Bella was in her stall, wisps of hay hanging from her mouth. There were splashes of fresh mud on her legs.

"You've been busy," said Nattie. She settled Chico in his stall and headed for the cookhouse. Alan was standing by the fire with Nattie's book open in his hand.

"Remarkably well-read drovers you have in these parts. I wouldn't have expected to find Shakespeare's sonnets in a cattle camp."

"Poetry calms the herd," Nattie replied, hanging up her hat. "Did you have a pleasant ride?"

Alan closed the book and placed it on the table.

"I wanted to be sure you didn't encounter any problems," he said.

"So you skulked along behind me."

"I was not skulking. I just rode a short way down the trail and back. There was not the slightest element of skulk."

Nattie stirred the pot of beans and pointed the ladle at Alan. "I saw you lurking in the barn when I came back."

"You don't miss much, do you? But again I must object to your choice of words. I was not lurking. I was watching in case you were followed."

Nattie raised her eyebrows.

"All right," Alan said. "I admit, it sounds ridiculous. And I'm probably being overly cautious. But the men who lost these papers have a lot more to lose if they're delivered."

He looked at Nattie. "I just didn't want you to think I was…fussing."

"Although you were. Well, it's my turn to fuss now."

She stripped leaves from the plants she had gathered and put them in a small pot of water to brew, then dropped in a bundle of bark strips. Alan picked up a leafy sprig and sniffed it, wrinkling his nose at the smell.

"Don't make faces. This will ease the pain in your head," Nattie admonished.

"Did I say my head hurt?"

"Of course not. But it does. So you'll drink this remarkably bitter tisane and it will make you feel better."

"Yes, ma'am." Alan examined the plants. "I assume you know what you're doing."

"I learned from my aunt. Tía doctors everyone around here. I've had to drink this myself more than once."

Nattie stirred the pale green liquid. "It's truly dreadful," she added cheerfully. "Enough to gag a maggot, Papa says."

Alan studied the brew with deep suspicion.

"You can try putting sugar in it, but it won't help," Nattie told him. "The best thing to do is let it cool and then gulp it down before you retch."

"You could at least pretend to be sympathetic." Alan watched as she cut up another green bundle. "What's that for?"

"It's a poultice for your head, to bring down the swelling." She wet a strip of cloth in the steaming tisane and wrapped the chopped leaves in it. "Here; hold it on that goose-egg."

Alan sniffed the damp bundle before placing it gingerly on his head. "This smells better than the other. Are you sure you don't have them mixed up?"

Nattie ignored him and strained the tisane into a mug. "It just needs to cool."

"No hurry."

Nattie turned her attention to supper preparations. Soon biscuits were in the oven and meat sizzled on the stove. She picked up the mug and offered it to Alan. He didn't take it.

"That cut on your arm must be painful," he told her. "I think you need this more than I do. I'll wait for the next batch."

"Oh, for heaven's sake. Don't be such an infant. *Poquito venemo no mata.*"

Alan took a deep breath and gulped the liquid down.

"That—is—terrible," he said, grimacing.

"Yep. But it will do you good, I promise. And supper will taste like nectar and ambrosia after that."

"Dirt and potato peel would be delicious after that," said Alan, wiping his mouth with the back of his hand.

Soon dishes clattered as they hastily set the table and filled their plates. In a remarkably short time the quail were reduced to piles of bones and the level in the bean pot was considerably lower.

"I'd like another biscuit," said Alan, eyeing the golden survivors arrayed on a platter.

"Me, too," said Nattie.

"But I can't eat another bite," said Alan.

"Me, neither," said Nattie.

"I'll clear the table," said Alan.

"I'll make coffee," said Nattie. Both sighed with satisfaction; neither moved.

Alan wiped his hands and picked up Nattie's book. The red cover was soft as glove leather, the pages like tissue. He opened the slender volume to the page marked by a red satin ribbon and read:

" 'Why didst thou promise such a beauteous day

And make me travel forth without my cloak,

To let base clouds o'ertake me in my way—' "

He closed the book and handed it to Nattie. "An appropriate verse." He stood and began gathering plates. "A writer I once met said you can divine a person's true self by their favorite Shakespearean comedy, tragedy, and character."

"An interesting concept. So if one person adores Romeo, and another prefers Benedick…"

"You and your sister?" asked Alan.

"Not necessarily. It was just an example."

"And you prefer Benedick. I applaud your discernment."

"What is your complaint against Romeo?"

Alan snorted dismissively. "Romeo. Quick to love, quick to anger, influenced by others, impulsive, impetuous—"

"In a word, young," protested Nattie. "The only difference between Romeo and Benedick is age."

"Not so. Romeo is in love with love. He craves love and pursues it like a terrier chases a rat. Benedick mistrusts love. He ducks and dodges until there's no avoiding it."

Nattie nodded. "So we agree; their only difference is age. Or, more specifically, the wisdom that comes with age."

Alan shook his head. "You are much too young to have such a jaded outlook," he said severely.

Nattie laughed as she put the coffee on. "Without such a jaded outlook I would doubtless prefer Romeo. You can't have it both ways, you know."

"I must remember not to engage you in debate," said Alan.

Nattie ladled hot water into the basin of dirty dishes, then looked up in surprise as Alan took the cloth from her hand and gently steered her out of the kitchen.

"You go sit by the fire. I'll tend to the kitchen and the horses. And I would like to clean up a bit, so I'll take a bowl of hot water out to the bunkhouse and leave these lavish accommodations to you in case you wish to do the same." He gestured grandly, his hands dripping water.

The thought of soap and water was irresistible. Nattie's skin felt tight with dried mud.

Alan picked up his saddlebag and handed her a bundle. "Here; I have an extra shirt. Yours looks like it's been through the wars."

"Thank you. I won't say no to a clean shirt. How did it stay dry?"

"Packed in oilskin."

"Like your mysterious papers."

"Right. I'll show those to you later. But for now I will leave you in peace. Let me know when you're ready for company." Alan called back as he went out the door, "I may nap for a bit, now that my head has stopped hurting."

"There, you see!"

If Alan heard Nattie's cry of triumph he didn't acknowledge it.

Nattie gathered cloths and towels, then carefully carried the wash basin to the fireplace. Drops flew as she scrubbed herself with the bar of brown soap. Clean and dry, she put on Alan's shirt and rolled up the cuffs, then threw out the murky water and refilled the basin to wash her underthings, stockings, and tattered shirt. She would need to wear it home; there would be enough questions without arriving in a stranger's clothing. Her skirt would take too long to dry so she settled for sponging it with a wet cloth. She remembered her hair ribbon and scrubbed it too.

Warm and content, she poured a cup of coffee and wrapped up in a blanket by the fire to wait for her clothes to dry. She undid her braid and combed her hair with her fingers as she considered her strange situation. Most of the time, it didn't seem strange at all. Most of the time, she felt as comfortable with Alan as she did with her brothers. But when she looked into Alan's blue-grey eyes, it was very strange indeed.

Nattie stared into the fire. She knew nearly nothing about Alan, but there was a shock of recognition that passed between them whenever their eyes met, like seeing someone in a shop window and then realizing it's your own reflection. Except—breathless, like having the wind knocked out of you.

The coffee cup felt heavy so she put it down. So many questions remained about Alan McTurk, but none of them really mattered. She knew all she needed to know. Her head nodded and she fell asleep.

Chapter 7

It took Nattie a moment to realize that she had dozed off, and another moment to determine that she hadn't slept long. Night had fallen, her undergarments were fairly dry, her coffee was cold but the fire still burned. She dressed quickly, lit the lamp, and put it on the back porch to let Alan know he could come in. As she threw out her wash water he appeared, yawning and clean-shaven.

"I found candles in the bunkhouse," he said. "We're low on kerosene."

They moved awkwardly around each other. Nattie had left her hair down; it made her look more womanly and exotic, thought Alan. He had shaved; it made him look younger and not so fierce, thought Nattie.

By the time they finished fetching firewood and water they were hungry again. They finished off the biscuits with generous dollops of honey and declared it an excellent dessert. Nattie remembered Mrs. Stockton's pecans, so they lit candles and went in search of something to crack them. The night was surprisingly warm despite a restless breeze that threatened the candle flames and lifted soft tendrils of Nattie's hair to brush across Alan's face. He closed his eyes—then stumbled and spilled hot wax on his hand.

A sudden gust blew Nattie's hair across her face. With a few quick movements she twisted it into a dark cloud at the nape of her neck. Alan wondered what it would be like to hold that heavy softness; he could still feel its touch on his face. And the burn on his hand, he reminded himself sternly.

The moon had not yet risen and the sky was thick with stars. The candle flames danced wildly and went out. Excited by the night, the horses ran and snorted in the corral. Alan and Nattie leaned on the fence, intensely aware of each other.

Nattie looked up at the sky and counted slowly.

"What are you doing?" asked Alan.

"Testing my eyes. I'm counting the stars I can see in Pleiades."

"I think that would depend more on weather than vision. I'd wager that last night you couldn't have seen any."

"That's true. I just like to see that all of the sisters are at home. Of course, one never knows with Electra."

"I didn't know that people out here learned the constellations."

"My family has walls of books and endless curiosity. And a telescope." Nattie paused. "Just where is it that people *are* expected to know the stars?"

"Forgive me; I didn't mean to condescend. It's just that I associate stars with navigation at sea. We're far from the ocean here."

"I've never seen the ocean." Nattie's voice was wistful.

"I grew up on the water." In the sheltering darkness, Alan told her something of his life.

Chapter 8

Alan Charles McTurk hadn't grown up on the ocean, but very near it. He was born and raised in New Haven, where his father was the founder of a prosperous shipping line. As Willoughby McTurk's only son, Alan was expected to take over his father's business, take a wife, and take his place as a pillar of New Haven. Alan viewed this sensible plan as a life sentence in a pleasant prison.

His father was exasperated by Alan's resistance. "The single solitary reason he won't do it is because I want him to. If I were a landowner that boy would run away to sea as a deckhand, but I offer him a fleet of ships and he turns me down."

Alan had to admit there was some truth to that, but didn't change his mind.

"What *do* you want to do?" asked his sisters when Alan emerged from their father's study after a particularly intense discussion of his future. Alan's face showed no expression, but his jaw was clenched.

"I don't know," Alan said. "Maybe have my own ships, someplace far away."

"Like Boston?" asked Mary Grace, the youngest.

"No, someplace more exciting," said Edith, the adventurous. "Argentina, or China."

Alan would have been as surprised as anyone to know that, in less than a year, he would abandon New Haven for the western frontier, swept away by prairies as vast and alluring as the sea.

"Well, well, well," said Nattie. "You ran away from home. Pray continue with your shocking confessions."

At seventeen, with his father's reluctant permission, Alan joined an excursion of schoolmates eager to see The West.

"Get it out of your system and be done with it," his father told him.

"Be careful, dearest," his mother whispered as she kissed his cheek. "Come back safely."

But Alan never came back. He slipped away in Kansas, in a dusty, chaotic, piecemeal town that funneled cattle from the Chisholm Trail onto the Atchison, Topeka and Santa Fe railroad. He left a note asking his parents not to blame the unfortunate teacher who led the expedition, and promised to come back for the next school term if he had no prospects, although he was confident he could carve out a place for himself in this energetic land where fortunes were just waiting to be made.

Alan found work in a livery stable mucking out stables, grooming horses, and harnessing teams. He slept in the stable, made enough money to get by, and thought it all a grand adventure. He met men who had been everywhere, done everything, and could sometimes be persuaded to tell their stories to a wide-eyed young Easterner.

Alan earned a reputation as a tireless worker, skilled with horses. This led to a job on a ranch, which led to replacing an injured drover on the final leg of a cattle drive. He learned later that the crew had wagered he wouldn't last a day. He was an experienced horseman, but herding cattle was nothing like the riding he had done at home. He was given the least desirable jobs, horses, and gear, but he was supremely happy. The crew called him Turkey, which was only to be expected. He cheerfully tolerated all the hazing and was accepted as a good sport.

"You're called *Turkey?*" Nattie asked. "Turkey McTurk? It sounds like a character in a children's story."

Alan gave her a look.

"A very imposing character, of course," she added hastily. "Do go on."

Alan watched and listened and learned. He swallowed some tall tales, which amused the crew, and disbelieved some true ones, which amused them even more. He used his sailor's skill with needle and thread to mend gear, cursed with a depth and creativity that was greatly admired, and taught the drovers sailors' knots and bawdy sea chanteys. His increased prestige earned him the name of Admiral.

Another new nickname was offered and rejected. At the end of a long day riding drag through clouds of alkali dust, Alan rode into camp covered with fine white powder that stung his throat and eyes. The crew humorist said, "Look at our little Turkish Delight, powdered all over with sugar. He should be in a candy shop sitting on a lace doily."

Alan took a swing at him by way of objection, and the discussion continued until the trail boss stepped in to end it. There was no clear winner, but the name was put to rest.

His story was interrupted while Nattie laughed a great deal more than was "necessary or courteous," he told her sternly.

Alan became browner, tougher, and more confident each day. He was immensely proud to earn acceptance on his own merit, not as his father's son. He returned to Texas with the outfit and drove a herd north once more. With his earnings he bought himself a good horse and gear, and left the cattle outfit to lead a group of settlers heading to Oregon. They invited him to stay but farming held no appeal, so he moved on. He tried logging and mining and found them tedious except for the occasional episode of heart-pounding danger. But he made enough money to keep traveling, and to attract the attention of three men who thought he'd be easy prey. A night attack ended with his pack mule and one bandit dead. Alan loaded his supplies onto the remaining two men and led them into Albuquerque. Their unconventional arrival attracted attention, which increased when his captives were identified as the bandits who had annoyed the Butterfield Overland Mail Company by robbing stage passengers, then amusing themselves by setting the empty coaches on fire and rolling them off cliffs.

Alan received a reward from Butterfield and, more important, the offer of work. He became a stagecoach messenger on payroll runs, guarding the green strongbox under the driver's seat. Alan learned to shoot from a moving stage and while being fired upon, "which adds a whole new level of interest," he told Nattie.

The job suited him and he planned to stay with it, but his driver and a clerk had plans of their own. The driver stunned Alan with a gun butt to his head and took the strongbox. He regained consciousness in time to open fire—"You *do* have a hard head," said Nattie—but the thieves escaped unharmed. He was left with a bullet hole under his collarbone and a grudge against the driver. Alan had considered him a friend.

It was believed that the thieves had fled to Texas. Alan followed as soon as he was able to ride, carrying a letter of introduction from the Butterfield manager to the Texas Rangers in San Antonio.

The thieves were eventually located in Cuidad Acuña. Alan helped apprehend them and recover most of the money. Reputation restored, Alan returned to Albuquerque just long enough to make his report and settle his accounts, then returned to Texas to sign on with the Rangers.

He enjoyed the work until he broke his leg diving from the saddle to bring down a miscreant who was preparing to fire on a fellow ranger. Alan's old nickname was reborn, thanks to a callow young journalist who breathlessly described Ranger 'Turkey' McTurk's courageous flight to save a colleague, and the unfortunate landing that clipped his wings. As soon as he could hobble, Alan paid the writer a visit and gently explained the inaccuracies of his account, but the damage was done and Turkey he remained.

"Oh dear," said Nattie, stifling laughter. "That's really very unfortunate."

Alan found enforced inactivity worse than the injury. As soon as he could walk with a cane, he took the train to New Haven to see his family. But he felt out of place, and relations with his father remained strained. He was relieved to head west again.

Back in San Antonio, Alan sought to relieve his restlessness by drinking and gambling. After an altercation with a prominent citizen, his superiors sent him to a sleepy little town on the Gulf Coast. He suspected he had been exiled to keep him out of trouble.

He was eventually reassigned to San Antonio, but the saloons and faro tables had lost their appeal, the outlaws seemed to have lost their ambition, and Alan had lost interest in his old life. When he received a stiffly-worded letter from his father informing him that his Great-Aunt Alice had died and left him a tidy sum, he bought some land near the Davis Mountains and settled in to build a little ranch.

"It's coming along nicely," said Alan. "My sister Edith and her husband Gus live with me—or I with them, more like, since I'm away a good bit of the time."

"Like now."

"Like now. Lately I've split my time between Texas and a place on the Gila River. I've been working with two Englishmen to start up a cattle outfit. They began as silent partners, but now they want to settle there. I'll probably buy out my share now that the place is up and running."

The wind had quieted. The horses stood side by side with their heads over the fence. Nattie patted them absentmindedly until Chico shouldered Bella aside.

"*Pórtate bien*," Nattie chided him. She turned to look at Alan.

"So now you know all about me," he said.

"Not all," she replied quietly.

Alan waited for her to say more, but she was silent.

Finally, he nodded. "No, not all."

Nattie said, "You needn't look so concerned. You didn't babble any secrets while you were unconscious, if that's what you're thinking. It's just—people never tell all about themselves. Especially out here. A lot of them have left so much of their lives behind, they're like puzzles with pieces missing. You only see the bits they want you to see." She leaned back against the fence and stretched her arms above her head. "So I don't know all about you. But I think I know enough."

Chico dropped his head over Nattie's shoulder so horse and girl were cheek to cheek. Nattie murmured to him in Spanish. Chico lifted his head and rested it atop hers.

"Ah, you're heavy," she said as she ducked out from under his chin. "I'm going in; you cuddle up to Bella."

The night was brighter now. The moon had risen above the trees, flooding the clearing with a pale light.

"New moon in the old moon's arms," said Alan.

"My aunt says that means good fortune in new endeavors. She says that about a lot of things, though."

"Well, it's good to take an optimistic view."

After settling the horses for the night, Alan and Nattie remembered why they had gone out. They lit the candles and resumed the search, finally unearthing a mallet in the woodshed. They sat in front of the fire, cracking pecans and throwing the shells into the flames.

Nattie saw that Alan winced as he wielded the mallet. She jumped up and headed to the kitchen.

"Time for your medicine."

He watched as she quickly prepared the brew. A hip closed a cupboard door, a foot nudged a stray piece of firewood back into the pile, and all the while her hands were busy with leaves and cloth and cup.

"While this cools, let me see that knot on your head," Nattie said, putting the cup down on the table.

"I can't even feel it; it's fine."

"Of course it is. Tilt your head over here into the light."

Alan obeyed, grumbling, then yelped as her fingers gently pressed the swelling.

"You can't have it both ways," Nattie admonished him. "First you complain because I don't believe that you're fine, then you complain because your head does, in fact, hurt."

"But, my dear angel of mercy, if you weren't pounding on my skull it wouldn't, in fact, hurt."

"Delirious ravings. Drink this, and then take a spoonful of honey to kill the taste."

Alan gulped down the bitter liquid and followed it quickly with honey.

"There, that wasn't so bad, was it?" Nattie asked sweetly.

Alan's reply was muffled. Nattie reached for the empty cup and his blue-grey eyes met hers. She jumped up and took the cup to the kitchen.

Alan said, "You could have told me before about chasing that poison with honey."

"You could have stayed here and rested instead of following me."

"Fair enough. Truce?"

"Truce," she agreed.

"How is your arm?" asked Alan. "Should we re-bandage it?"

"No, it's all right. I've kept it dry. My aunt will be happy to fuss over it when I go home."

"Will there be other fussing? I doubt that your family will be pleased to hear that you risked your life and your…your…"

"My reputation?" Nattie suppressed a smile and turned to face him. "I appreciate your concern, but we're practical out here. My family will understand. Of course, because I didn't wait out the storm at the Stockton place I'll hear the usual lecture; that I should use better judgment and I take foolish chances and I worry them past all forbearance and the saints themselves are weary of looking after me." She folded a dish towel and hung it over a cabinet door, then came back to the fire. "But no one will think I was wrong to help you. They'll say—it needed doing."

"Still, I'll see you home and talk to your father. I can explain—I mean, assure him that—well, I should talk to him."

Nattie laughed and threw a pecan at Alan. "That really isn't necessary, although I'm sure my father would be delighted to meet you. And you could replace your lost gear."

"Is your home on the way to Dos Rios?"

"No. It's south of the road you want."

"This delay hasn't left me time to spare." Alan considered a moment, then asked, "Is there a telegraph office?"

"At Dos Rios? Yes, but the storm may have brought down the lines. Probably washed out roads, too."

"So I may have to go swimming again. At least I'll see it coming, instead of being dropped in with bits of lumber."

"Do you remember anything about the bridge collapsing?"

Alan stared into the fire. "Not much. The bridge was shaking and groaning. When I felt it start to give I turned back, but it was too late. I remember hitting the water—Lord, it was cold—and grabbing a plank. Bella must have scrambled out."

"She's a lot tougher than she looks. A little rest and food and she perked right up."

Alan nodded. "She's hardy as any mustang. Fast and smart, too."

"My father's favorite obsession is horse-breeding. He'll want to buy her."

"Not at any price," said Alan.

"Well, at least promise him a foal or he'll badger you to death."

"I've heard that Martin Johnston is a man of...great determination."

"Tactfully put," said Nattie. "He's a bit of a madman. Once he gets an idea, no matter how preposterous, he sinks his teeth into it and chews it and shakes it and worries it like a dog with a bone, until all the reasons why it's impossible give up and go away. Even the ground beneath his feet parted and gave him what he wanted."

"Silver? Gold?" asked Alan.

"Something more precious," answered Nattie. "Water."

"And thereby hangs a tale, I expect."

"Mmm. How his land went from *Rancho sin Agua* to *Rancho de los Cien Aguas*. It's a long story," said Nattie.

"Well, until the river goes down I have no place to go," said Alan cheerfully.

He propped his elbow on the back of the bench and rested his chin in his hand. Nattie looked into the fire and began.

Chapter 9

"My father came here with his two brothers, down from Minnesota. They had decided farming wasn't for them and set out to seek their fortunes. They had many adventures, which I won't relate because I suspect at least half of them are fictional. They bought the land we're on and a small herd of cattle from a man who was going back East after the Chiricahuas burned him out. They built this cabin and cleared the river trail and the ford."

"Swede's Ford?" asked Alan. "Your father's Swedish?"

"No. His family came over from England. But if you saw him you'd understand where the name came from. He's shockingly fair. Papa says we children turned his hair white with aggravation, but it's always been white, really. His brothers look just like him, tall and tow-headed. Papa says while they were building here they saw a group of Indians watching from the trees. Papa burst out the front door, Uncle Harvey went out the back, and Uncle Trout came running out of the barn. The Indians looked like they'd seen a ghost and left in a hurry. Papa figures that's why this place never had any trouble."

"Lucky."

"Crazy. My father and uncles were absolutely insane to try to settle when everyone else was being driven off. But they succeeded. And that was just the beginning."

Alan added wood to the fire and arranged it to his satisfaction. He picked up the mallet and moved closer to Nattie.

"Continue," he said, "while I ply you with nutmeats."

Accompanied by the whack of the mallet and pausing to munch on pecans, Nattie went on with her story.

"After a time, Uncle Harvey decided he didn't want to leave the girl he left behind, so he went back to Minnesota. He's still farming there. Uncle Trout moved on in search of new adventures; he shows up every now and then. My father knew that big dreams require big land, so he jumped at the chance to buy an old Spanish *estancia*. It was promptly dubbed Swede's Folly and *Rancho sin Agua*; lots of land, all dry as dust. But Papa had read about a place in France where water wheels and pumps and pipes brought water from the Seine five hundred feet up to a palace—"

"The Marly Machine," said Alan, trying not to laugh.

"Right. Go ahead and laugh; everyone else did. My father was sure he could construct a system to bring water where he needed it, but he didn't have all the king's horses and all the king's men to help him. In fact, he had no money at all after buying the land. So he decided to postpone building the New World's Marly Machine and went down to Cananea to buy a prize bull."

"With no money."

"Right," said Nattie. "And yet it almost makes sense when he tells it."

"Go on. He wanted water and a bull. What happened?"

"He found something else he wanted; my mother. But I'm getting ahead of myself."

Nattie took a deep breath and collected her thoughts.

"The rancher in Cananea was polite, but adamant that he wouldn't sell the bull. He invited the madman to stay the night, and at supper Papa saw the rancher's youngest daughter, Rosario. They hardly spoke; Papa says he knew only cattleman's Spanish, and she spoke little English. But they looked at each other, and that was enough. When Papa left he said he'd make his fortune and come back in one year to ask for Rosario's hand. And the bull, too, of course. The rancher laughed and wished him well. As Papa left the house, a rose fell at his feet. He kissed it and waved to the window above, then rode away.

"While Papa was asleep on the ground one night he dreamed of thunder, but there was no storm. When he arrived home he found that there had been an earthquake and springs had opened up all over his land. He says the valley turned green as he stood there watching.

"One year later to the day, he returned to find Rosario waiting for him. He had spent the year building a home and a herd and learning lover's Spanish. Rosario had spent the time learning English and convincing her parents that she was going to marry the tall madman, with or without their consent. Her father still refused Papa's offer to buy the bull, but gave it to them as a wedding present."

She smiled. Alan found Nattie's smiles fascinating. They began with a slight upturn on the right side and often went no further, easily missed if he didn't watch carefully.

Nattie looked away, embarrassed by his attention.

"And so it began," she said.

Alan whistled. "Quite a story."

"It was our favorite," said Nattie. "We'd beg Mamá to tell it to us."

Nattie still smiled, but a little crease formed between her dark eyebrows. Alan had studied that, too. It appeared when Nattie was troubled or deep in thought.

"When my mother became too ill to leave her bed, we children would sprawl around her and she would tell us stories. Fairy tales and legends and family stories got all jumbled up in my head. I was quite a bit older before I realized that Uncle Trout was a real person and Paul Bunyan wasn't."

They continued to talk of home and family. There was a note of regret in Alan's voice when he spoke of his father.

"I refuse to go back, and he refuses to accept that. And he blames me because my sister Edith came west, too. My father always wanted to stop time and keep all of us as children, safe at home with him. Except during the war, when he wanted to pack us off to safety with his family in Scotland. But my mother refused. She's a very quiet, gentle person, but there was no persuading her. She told him her place was at his side in her own nation. And that was that."

"The war rarely reached this far," said Nattie. "But your family must have been in the thick of it."

"I was very young, so I only remember bits and pieces. I remember seeing the soldiers marching, and my mother being busy all the time. And sometimes my mother cried."

"And your father? What did he do?"

"I don't really know. My father and uncle would disappear periodically, no one ever said why. They both were injured, no one said how or where, but I'm sure it was at sea. My father took a large splinter of wood through his thigh, and my Uncle Charles lost three fingers."

Alan was silent a moment, then went on in a voice so low Nattie had to strain to hear it. "We lost family members, of course. And my cousin Daniel returned long after we had given him up. We heard that he was wounded, but after that there was no word of him. He just appeared one day when the war was over. It was rumored that he had been a spy, but he never spoke of it. He stayed with us for a time. He couldn't bear to have his door closed and always wanted a light in his room, even in the day. He couldn't sleep at night, but he'd doze off in a chair while we played at his feet. He'd wake with a start sometimes, wild-eyed and sweating, and my mother would soothe him. He says she led him back to the living."

"She sounds like an extraordinary woman."

"She is that. My father worships her; she led him back to the living, too."

"And thereby hangs a tale."

"Yes, indeed," replied Alan. "And one that I wouldn't know if not for my Great-Aunt Alice. She told me about my father, hoping that it would help me understand him. I was angry because he only let me sail the coast, and I wanted to travel the world."

"And did it help?"

"Not really. I was too young. Now, though—now I can understand why he held on so tight."

Nattie pulled blankets around her and settled in happily.

"Well, we're not going anywhere for a while, and I love stories. So tell."

"It's not as dramatic as your father's story," Alan warned. "No earthquakes or prize bulls."

"I'm sure it will not disappoint. Begin."

Alan began.

Chapter 10

Like his son, Willoughby McTurk had run west in his youth, from one side of the Atlantic to the other. He sold his share of McTurk and Sons to his brothers and, without a backward glance, left Scotland behind. He left the only home he had ever known, left the wind-blown house overlooking the bay, left the three granite headstones in the churchyard. His wife and children had died in the space of a week, taken by diphtheria. Six months later he booked passage on a Royal Mail steamship to the United States.

Willoughby stood at the railing hour after hour, staring at the empty ocean. He realized, with a detached interest, that he was completely numb. Nothing mattered to him at all. There was a freedom in not caring, he realized. It was nothing like being carefree, as he had been before he lost everything, but it would serve. He had no desires, no ambitions, no hopes. He might succeed, he might fail, but it didn't really matter either way. He would do his best, of course. It wasn't in his nature to do less.

He did succeed in America, far beyond any expectation. He worked tirelessly, was scrupulously fair, treated everyone with sober courtesy, and made no friends. Willoughby didn't notice the lack. He was trusted and respected; that was enough. He had no interests outside of work. Work filled his days, and thoughts of work filled his nights. That was enough.

His life was satisfactory and he had no desire to change it, but his business outgrew his ability to run it alone. He needed a partner. He thought of asking his younger brother Charles to come, but hesitated. When he ran out of reasons to postpone writing the letter, he had to admit the truth. He was afraid that seeing a familiar face would bring it all back to him, all the memories that ended with a row of headstones in an old churchyard.

Willoughby sat quietly at his desk, thinking of home. He was surprised that his memories remained so vivid after three years, and even more surprised that his pain had dulled to an aching sadness. It had settled in his bones, but no longer crippled him.

One last test; he retrieved a picture case from the depths of a bottom drawer and studied the lost faces that smiled at him from a far-away life. The mantel clock chimed, and chimed again, but he didn't hear it. He didn't notice the patch of sunlight moving across the floor, didn't notice that the room darkened until he could no longer see the photographs.

At last he stretched in his chair. He closed the picture case and held it in his hands a moment, then lit the lamp and reached for his paper and pen.

Charles was delighted to come to America, and Willoughby was pleased to have him. Charles was an able assistant and pleasant company, but he brought more than that to his brother's life. After three years, Willoughby knew only those people who worked for him, bought from him, or sold to him, but Charles soon knew everyone in town. He was tall, attractive, and blessed with a cheerful disposition that brought more invitations than he could accept.

His popularity spilled over to include his brother. People began to notice that Will McTurk was also tall, attractive, and a pleasant, if quiet, addition to social gatherings.

"It's good for business," he told Charlie, but he found himself looking forward to the parties and dinners and dances and picnics. Both brothers were valued as eligible bachelors, although Charlie was the only one aware of it. Will would have been dismayed to know that he was considered a marital prospect; that part of his life was over and done. Charlie planned to marry sometime, but he enjoyed his flirtations too much to settle down just yet. So the McTurk brothers formed no romantic attachments but "It's just a matter of time," people told each other, nodding wisely.

Will couldn't have pinpointed just when he fell in love with Marian Cole. It's like the turn of the tides, he thought. You don't see any difference, wave after wave, but land turns to sea or sea turns to land. You can't say just when it changed, but there's no denying it.

Later, when Will and Marian talked, as lovers do, about the when and the how and the where, Marian said she knew the exact moment she fell in love. It was when she first saw him, when he followed his smiling brother into her cousins' parlor. This wasn't quite true, but she did think he was the most handsome man she'd ever seen, and the most courteous, and intelligent, and thoughtful.

Nothing could come of it, of course. Marian had no illusions about herself. She was thin and colorless and plain-featured. She wasn't talented or witty or wealthy. There had been someone, years ago, but he had gone away to seek his fortune. Eventually word came back that he had found it, attached to a wife.

Since then Marian had carefully guarded her heart, but Will McTurk made her wish that things could be different. He was kind and attentive to her, but that meant nothing. He offered the same quiet courtesy to everyone, from the smallest children to the eldest grandparents. That was what she loved most about him.

Marian looked forward to every occasion that she might see him, although she knew she might see him with someone who wasn't thin and colorless and plain-featured, someone who would laugh prettily and place a hand on his arm. She knew it would never be her hand on Will's sleeve, never be her face that made his light up. There was no use being unhappy about it, she told herself sternly. It was just the way things were. Then she wept into her pillow.

For his part, it took Will most of a spring and summer to realize that Marian had become the reason he looked forward to social events. Nothing could come of it, of course. He would never take such a risk again. Still, he looked forward to every occasion that he might see her, and perhaps talk to her, although he was often frustrated in his attempts to claim a few moments with her. Everyone in need of comfort came to Marian, who listened as though there was no one else in the room, nodding encouragement, her gray eyes never leaving the face of the supplicant. She offered the same sweet, thoughtful attention to everyone. That was what Will loved most about her.

Even Charlie brought his secret trouble to Marian. Sitting on an ottoman at her feet, he told her that he loved her cousin Anne.

For once, Marian's attention wavered. With the self-absorption of the unrequited lover, she could only think of what this news meant to her. Charlie, equally self-absorbed, didn't notice.

The news itself wasn't the problem. She was truly happy for Charlie and Anne and saw no real obstacles before them. Anne was young and a bit silly, but her family would approve the match. Marian suspected that Charlie's torment would end as soon as Anne tired of the game. She offered Charlie reassurance and sympathy, and nodded as he praised Anne's perfection.

Marian tried to pay attention, but she longed to go to her room and collapse into misery. She was sure this news explained Will McTurk's recent attention to her. She had foolishly allowed herself to hope, but now she knew that his behavior was only that of a future cousin-in-law, nothing more.

When Marian had first noticed that Will appeared wherever she went, she had reasoned it away. After all, she looked for him everywhere; of course she would see him often. She was more aware of him, that was all. But when her cousins commented on how often Will sat by her, walked with her, joined her in conversation or cards, she began to wonder. She could dismiss her own observations as wishful thinking, but if others saw it too...

Now she knew she hadn't imagined Will's attention to her, but she had misread it. She wouldn't make that mistake again.

Will was surprised and confused by the sudden change in Marian. She was pleasant as always, but she seemed guarded somehow, and distant. It was impossible to talk to her. Her youngest cousins swarmed around her constantly, an impenetrable barrier.

Will thought of confiding in Charlie, but what would he tell him? He couldn't even explain to himself what troubled him. Besides, something was bothering Charlie, too. He was distracted and irritable, so Will left him alone.

By mid-summer, Marian and Will were deeply unhappy. Seeing each other was torment, being apart was agony. They looked forward to each unsatisfactory encounter, then ached to be alone with their suffering.

To make matters worse, Anne began to encourage Charlie's courtship. Marian was genuinely pleased for her cousin, but it was painful to hear her endless happy confidences. Will was glad to see that Charlie had regained his high spirits, but it made him feel old and tired.

As the weeks passed and Marian's spirit dwindled, her family became concerned. After a flood of tonics did no good, they called in Doctor Mackie. He found no sign of illness, but thought he recognized symptoms of a different trouble, more difficult to cure. He discussed his suspicions with Marian's Aunt Claire.

"Of course she's in love," Claire told him. "The silly little thing's been pining away the whole time I've been here, and who knows how long before that."

She poured tea and handed the doctor a cup.

"Do you know who the man is?" asked Doctor Mackie.

"She hasn't said anything, of course, but I'm quite sure it's Will McTurk. He seems to be smitten as well. I don't know what the problem is between them. I've been waiting for them to work it out but they seem determined to suffer," Claire said with stern disapproval.

"Well, she can't go on like this much longer or she'll make herself ill."

Claire's face showed her concern. Marian was her favorite niece.

"Would a change of scene help? I plan to go home to Hamden next week; perhaps Marian would like to go with me. Her Aunt Alice would be happy to have her come back early."

Marian agreed without protest. They would leave on Monday, so she would see Will only twice more; at the picnic Saturday and at church Sunday. She wouldn't return until Christmas, and by then her feelings for Will would surely subside.

The Coles traditionally hosted the last picnic of the season, a day at the shore. For weeks before the event there was endless discussion of weather and transportation, food and games. Will and Charlie supplied boards and trestles for tables and wagons for transport. Rain Friday caused concern, but Saturday the sun rose in a clear sky.

"A perfect day," people congratulated each other as they arrived. Excited children chased each other around the tables as their mothers counted chairs and debated every detail of serving the food. Somehow, out of the swirling commotion, a feast appeared. Everyone agreed they had never seen so much food. The Presbyterian minister, who had a healthy appetite and could be counted on to be brief, was asked to say grace, and after that said very little except to ask that dishes be passed.

Marian found herself sitting between Anne and Will, with Charlie on Anne's other side. She had encountered Will repeatedly as they fetched and carried, and decided that she felt much better already. It helped to know that she was leaving. She could smile and join in the conversations around her, despite the pressing awareness of Will at her side.

Across the table, Claire watched Anne and Charlie. "Will we be coming back for a wedding, Marian?" she asked quietly.

Will froze, his fork in the air, as he tried to sort out the question's meaning. Coming back? Was Marian leaving? What wedding?

He strained to hear her soft reply. "Hush, Aunt Claire. They aren't even engaged yet, or at least they haven't announced it. And if there is to be a wedding, it won't be until next year."

"Who is to marry?" Will asked.

"Anne and Charlie, of course."

Will couldn't conceal his astonishment. "Charlie plans to marry? My brother Charlie?"

Marian stared at him. "Surely you knew. They've had an understanding for weeks now."

"I knew Charlie was—I didn't know he—"

It was Marian's turn to be astonished. Had he really not known? It didn't matter now, she reminded herself. She was leaving Monday.

As if he read her mind, Will said, "You're not going away, are you?"

Marian realized that she didn't feel better at all. She wanted to tell him that she wasn't going anywhere, that she was staying here where she could at least see him and hear his voice.

She said, "Aunt Claire and I are going home to Hamden."

Will wanted to ask her not to go, to ask her to stay until he found the courage to tell her—he wasn't sure what he wanted to tell her.

"How long will you be away?" he asked.

"Until Christmas, I think."

He nodded slowly.

Aunt Claire watched the two of them and wondered again what the difficulty was. Surely Will McTurk must know how Marian felt, and there was no mistaking his dismay at the news that she was leaving. The best thing would be to strand the two of them on a deserted island until they sorted it out, she thought.

After the meal, Will watched as Charlie and Anne tried to fly a kite. What was it Marian said? They had 'an understanding.' It was so obvious now that he knew, and he realized it had been obvious for some time. He had been so wrapped up in his own misery that he hadn't seen anything else. Will wondered what else he had missed.

It was time to take part, he thought. No more standing like a great lump while life swirled around him. He remembered when he had been in a play at school, watching nervously from the dark wings until it was time to step out into the dazzle of light onstage. It was time now.

Marian's young cousins brought out their kites. They ran until they dropped, panting.

"Let's take them down by the water," Marian said. "There's a better breeze."

Will helped carry the kites, seeing the seven children as individuals for the first time. He had always thought of them as a swarm keeping him from Marian. Now they sorted out into three girls and four boys. Will tried not to think of his own lost children, but the small footprints, the laughter, the sunburned noses in need of a handkerchief were all so familiar. It was somehow comforting to know that these things stayed the same.

He found his handkerchief and wiped the small nose of a bright-eyed boy who said his name was Henry Joseph.

Henry Joseph's kite was taller than he was. Will helped him get it aloft and stood back as the boy held the spool with fierce determination. The other children ran and shouted with excitement as their kites swooped and dipped overhead.

Suddenly a different cry shrilled above the others. One of the girls was on her knees in the sand. Her forgotten kite sailed away as Will and Marian ran to her.

Marian knelt and put her arms around the crying child. Will, ready to stand against any danger, saw an emaciated puppy stretched on its side, all paws and ears.

"Is it dead? Is it?" sobbed the girl.

Will placed his hand on the dog's protruding ribs and was surprised by a feeble wag of its feathery tail. The puppy tried to stand but fell back. Marian gently stroked its head and it licked her hand.

"Poor little thing," she said. "It's alive, but it needs our help. Hush now, Sarah. Let's get it something to eat and drink, and we'll see if Dr. Mackie can help make it well."

Will took off his coat and gently wrapped the puppy in it. "I'll carry the puppy if you children can manage the kites," he said. "Sarah, perhaps you could help Henry Joseph."

"His name is Daniel. He's always making up names for himself."

"Well, he and I agreed on Henry Joseph, so that's what I'll call him until he tells me otherwise."

"The puppy's name is Henry Joseph, too," said Henry Joseph.

"Perhaps we should wait to name the puppy until we know it better," said Marian.

"If it's a girl, it could be Henrietta Josephina," said Henry Joseph.

"A big name for such a small pup," said Will.

"I wonder how the poor little mite came to be out here. Do you think it washed ashore?" asked Marian.

"Shipwrecked in a terrible storm," said the youngest girl.

"Jettisoned by pirates," Henry Joseph said solemnly.

By the time the little procession found Dr. Mackie at the pie table, the puppy's history had become an epic of fantastic dangers narrowly escaped through unfailing courage and intelligence. The children told the marvelous tale to the doctor as he examined the small patient on Will's lap.

"Well, if he survived all that, I'm sure he'll pull through. There seems to be no injury, but he's starved and dehydrated. He needs frequent small feedings and a quiet place to rest undisturbed."

Dr. Mackie considered the children pressed around the puppy. He glanced at Claire, who sat next to Will with Henry Joseph on her lap.

"That poor dog won't have a moment's rest around these children," said Claire. She paused, then asked, "Mr. McTurk, could you keep him?"

The puppy slowly lapped water from his cupped hand, then

dropped its head on his lap again.

"I suppose…I could keep him in my office. Just until he's stronger."

"What will you call him?" asked Sarah.

"Well, I think Henrietta Josephina has been ruled out," said Will.

He gently stroked the dog's soft ears.

"I wonder if he did wash in from the bay. His coat is matted with salt."

"Call him Flotsam," suggested the eldest girl.

"Or Jetsam," said one of the bigger boys.

"That doesn't make sense. Jettisoning him wouldn't lighten a ship enough to make any difference. No one would throw him overboard," said Sarah.

"Pirates would," said Henry Joseph, nodding wisely.

Marian fed the puppy tiny shreds of chicken.

"Flotsam, jetsam… How about just 'Sam'?" she suggested.

The dog sighed contentedly and closed his eyes. Will stroked the unkempt bundle of brown fur sleeping on his lap.

"Well, then. Sam it is."

Dr. Mackie chuckled as he escorted Claire back to her seat in the shade.

"You engineered that very neatly. But if you and Marian are to leave on Monday they don't have much time."

"The children will make Marian take them to visit that puppy every hour, so there will be plenty of opportunity for love to bloom. Besides, if they haven't come to their senses by Monday—well, I'm a frail old woman and I may be too ill to travel. I expect I could persuade a doctor to tell my family that I should be coddled and cosseted and have my every whim indulged until I've recovered."

The doctor snorted. "You are neither old nor frail, and I doubt you've ever had a whim that wasn't indulged. Ordinarily I would deplore your meddling, but no one is more deserving of happiness than Marian."

He looked away. "And for myself—I'd be pleased to have you stay a little longer."

Claire patted his arm. "Dear Caleb. Perhaps someone should meddle on our behalf someday."

"Perhaps. Although one of the advantages of growing older is the freedom to meddle in our own lives."

Claire stopped and turned to face him.

"And if we were younger I'd have to pretend not to understand you, or tell you I had no idea—but we've known each other too long for that, I think. Although I must admit I'm surprised. We've both been alone for a number of years, long enough to become set in our ways. Do you really think—?"

"Yes, I really do," said Caleb, taking her hands in his. "And you?"

"I think—the idea merits consideration," said Claire.

They found seats away from the others and happily considered it for the rest of the afternoon.

The children tired of watching the puppy sleep and ran off to play.

As Marian stood to follow them, Will blurted "Stay, please. I'd—I'd like you to stay. If you wish. That is, if you don't mind."

"Yes, of course." She looked puzzled, but sat down.

After a brief uncomfortable silence that seemed endless to them both, Marian said, "I was going to get some lemonade. Could I bring you something?"

Will felt like a complete fool.

"Yes, please. Lemonade would be fine. Thank you." He watched her walk away and shook his head.

"That went very well, eh, Sam? She probably won't come back at all now. I should let you speak for me; you'd make a better job of it."

Sam's tail wagged at the sound of Will's voice.

Marian returned, carrying two glasses of lemonade. Sarah was with her, holding two plates, and Henry Joseph walked behind, trailing a small blanket on the ground.

"We brought a blanket for Sam so you can have your coat back," said Sarah.

"And cookies," said Henry Joseph.

"Those aren't for Sam. This plate is for him," said Sarah.

"The cookies are for all of us," said Henry Joseph hopefully.

Marian laughed. "I'm sure Mr. McTurk is willing to share. But we forgot the bowl of water for Sam. Could one of you—?"

"I'll get it," both children shouted and raced away.

Will carefully transferred Sam to the blanket on Marian's lap, then shook out his coat and put it on. The children came back with small slow steps, careful not to spill the water they carried.

Sam devoured the morsels of food they offered and noisily lapped some water. He looked better already, they all agreed. As if he understood them, he suddenly sat up. His legs shook but his eyes were bright. He accepted their accolades, dog-smiling with his pink tongue lolling out of the side of his mouth, then lay down and went to sleep.

The children wandered off with cookies in hand, leaving Will and Marian alone. They talked about Sam and laughed about Henry Joseph. Will desperately wished he knew what Marian was thinking. He crumbled a cookie, silently cursing himself for a great daft lump.

It's time, he told himself sternly.

He sat up, looked out over the water, and said "Don't go."

Marian's grey eyes were huge and dark as she stared at him.

Will forged ahead.

"Stay here. Please. You have become—essential—in my life. Please don't go."

Marian was silent.

Will said quietly, "Perhaps I should have spoken sooner, or perhaps I shouldn't speak at all. I'm afraid I may have caused you pain. Please believe me; I would never—"

He glanced at Marian. Her face was turned away from him, her head bent low. Will saw shining drops fall onto the rough coat of the puppy sleeping on her lap. He took her hand and knelt in front of her, looking up into her face.

"Don't cry, Marian, please."

He pressed his handkerchief into her hand. She made a sound that could have been a sob, a laugh, or a hiccup. He searched her face for a clue and saw a wavering smile.

The conversation that followed was largely incoherent, but Will and Marian understood each other perfectly. Sam woke up and happily licked their clasped hands.

Finally, "But what am I to tell Aunt Claire?" asked Marian.

"Tell her she'll be coming back for a wedding," said Will.

Chapter 11

Nattie was silent so long Alan wondered if she was asleep. Her head rested on the bench behind her, her face upturned to the ceiling. The collar of her borrowed shirt was loose around her neck and revealed a small silver cross nestled in the hollow of her throat. It flashed with reflected firelight in rhythm with her pulse. He saw a scar under her chin and wondered how she got it.

At last she sighed happily. "That was a *splendid* story," she said dreamily.

Alan laughed. "You sound exactly like my sisters. Of course, Mother tells it better. I'm sure I left out a lot of the details."

"That's all right. I just filled it in with imagining."

Alan said, "My father is a very private person, so we only heard the story of 'How you and Father fell in love and got Sam' when he was away. Which added to our enjoyment of it; forbidden fruit, you know. And even so, my mother didn't tell us the whole story. We pieced it together from bits of information we gathered here and there."

"There are few mysteries in my family," said Nattie. "Everyone knows everybody's business. My brother Robby is worse than an old woman for prying and nosing about."

"Well, I'm grateful to the old women in my family," said Alan. "I learned a lot from my aunts that my mother would never tell. She respects my father's desire for privacy, even from her children."

"It must pain her, this rift between you and your father."

"It does, but she's working to mend it. She's trying to persuade my father to come out here—to Texas, I mean—to see for himself that his wayward offspring's lives aren't fraught with deadly peril."

Nattie asked, "And just where were you two days ago?"

"All right, there is that, but be fair. I don't spend much of my time in rivers."

"It seems to me that this journey could be somewhat fraught, even on dry land."

"Minimally fraught. Safe as houses, really. And, speaking of my journey, I would like to hear your impressions of the rail-related events around here. Tell me everything you can think of; fact or rumor, important or trivial."

Nattie nodded. "Well then," she said, "let us begin our lesson with a map." She held a stick in the fire until the end was aflame, then blew it out and drew a charcoal sketch on the hearth, describing and explaining as the map took shape.

When she finished, Alan studied it in silence for a few minutes.

"Right," he said at last. "Thank you. That gives me a clear picture of the stage; now how about the players? What do you know about the survey crew?"

"Very little. The chief surveyor, Sullivan, was not at all friendly," said Nattie with prim disapproval.

Alan suppressed a smile.

"The Dutchman, Langelaar, seemed a decent fellow, but Sullivan kept him on a short tether. He refused all offers of hospitality; said they couldn't spare the time. A lot of people rode out—hoping to get inside information about the railroad's plans, if the truth be told—but Sullivan discouraged visitors."

"Most unfriendly," commented Alan, echoing Nattie's tone.

She glanced to see if he was making fun of her, but his expression was blandly innocent.

"It was odd, though. Sullivan told everyone they were behind schedule, but my brother and cousin rode out twice—"

"Nosing about."

"Exactly. Anyway, Robby and Ignacio said the surveying hadn't advanced at all that they could tell. And there were instruments scattered about, but they weren't moved between one visit to the next."

"Odd, indeed," said Alan. "But not entirely unexpected."

Nattie raised her eyebrows, but Alan offered no explanation. She went on.

"And there's a fair amount of mystery swirling about Edwin Dagleish, or young Edwin's absence, to be exact. The surveyors hired him to haul supplies and clear brush, cut trees, that sort of thing. The job brought Edwin lots of attention, which suited him fine. He makes up in self-importance what he lacks in stature. He can hardly see over the back of one of his mules."

"A harsh assessment," Alan chided with mock disapproval.

"Ordinarily I'd be more kind, of course, but in the interest of accuracy—"

"Of course," said Alan. "Please go on."

"Edwin hinted that the surveyors had taken him into their confidence and that he was privy to a great many secrets which everyone would find fascinating, if only he could tell them. This was typical of Edwin so no one paid it much mind at first. Then he disappeared with the other two men—"

Alan interrupted. "Did Edwin stay in camp or in Dos Rios?"

"Both. He'd take supplies out about once a week and usually stay a day or so. Then he'd come back to town, strutting and preening like a peacock. But before his last trip out he said he'd be clearing a thicket so he'd be gone longer."

"Hmm. How long was it before they were missed?"

"Only a day. Some layabouts from Dos Rios rode out and found the camp deserted."

"Mr. Sullivan should have been more forceful in discouraging visitors," Alan said.

"Nothing short of cannon fire would have kept people away, with Edwin all puffed up and ready to burst with secrets. Every time he came back to town he drummed up more curiosity. All his cryptic hints have taken on new meaning since he disappeared. No one agrees on just what that meaning *is*, but they're having a grand time speculating."

"It would almost be a pity to solve the mystery and spoil the fun. Does our Edwin leave a grieving family?"

"No, but he has a young lady who isn't grieving nearly as much as you'd expect. I thought she'd be playing the tragic heroine to the hilt, drifting around all pale and Ophelia-like, but I hear she's been acting rather smug. *And* there was talk that she'd been seen walking by the river with a young man not even a week after poor Edwin vanished. But when the witnesses caught up to her, she was alone. That inspired the tale that Edwin is dead and his spirit was accompanying his beloved, bereaved Lucy as she paced in lonely sorrow."

"A touching interpretation, and convenient for young Edwin." Alan stared into the fire and seemed to reach a decision.

"Well," he said with a note of finality. "Your information has been most helpful. I know now where I need to go and what I need to do. The problem is time, or the lack of it." Alan studied the map again. "If we can cross the river early tomorrow, I might be able to deliver the papers—and perhaps a few other items—in time to do some good. Your suspicions were correct, and I'd like to bring in the evidence that proves it."

Nattie nodded slowly.

"The survey was a sham, then. The southern route was never even considered."

"I'm afraid not. The papers I'm delivering contain an agreement made months ago, promising support of the northern route. You might be surprised at some of the names signed to it."

Alan pulled the leather pouch out from under his shirt, removed the papers and handed them to Nattie. They were warm in her hands.

The little crease appeared between Nattie's eyebrows as she read.

"Well, well, well. This would put a hitch in some political careers if it were to come out." She tilted her head and considered Alan thoughtfully. "*Is* this going to come out?"

"That's not my decision. I'm only the courier."

"It might be better to keep it quiet," said Nattie. "If these lying swine are exposed they'll just be replaced with more of the same. Leave them in office with the threat of exposure hanging over them and they might be forced into honesty."

"What a devious mind you have. Machiavelli behind the facade of a country maiden."

"Hardly," replied Nattie. "I just object to being taken for a fool. Last Fourth of July we heard these scoundrels make impassioned speeches demanding the southern route, and all the while their pockets were stuffed with payment to support the other. It's enough to make a person cynical."

"You don't seem terribly disappointed that the railroad won't be coming your way."

"It will, sooner or later. We've managed without it this long, we can manage a while longer."

"What would the railroad mean to you, to your family?"

"Well," said Nattie, "it would open up new markets for our cattle. My father's happy enough with how things are, but my brother Tomás wants to expand. He's the family businessman. And we'd get our mail and newspapers sooner, but that might be a mixed blessing. Papa says it's much less agitating to read about events several days after the fact, knowing that they've already become history and the world has moved on. Puts things in perspective."

"That's true, you know. I've learned to check the date on a paper before I pitch a fit. It makes a man feel foolish, throwing the paper down and ranting about the sorry state of the world, only to realize that was the state of the world a week ago. All that righteous indignation wasted. What else?"

"It would be easier to get ice. We could make masses of ice cream whenever we wish."

"That's a powerful draw."

"Oh, yes. Flo says the town ice cream parlor is the real reason I visit her."

"So the train would put an end to visiting your sister. That's not much of an endorsement. How else would you benefit?"

"Faster delivery of all the nonsense Papa orders from catalogs. He loves the promise of technological advances, even though they never live up to their advertisements. We have a shed full of gadgets that claimed to revolutionize the future of one thing or another." She shrugged. "He has fun tinkering with them, though. And he uses parts of them to build his own gadgets, some of which actually work."

"Such as?"

"An adjustable telescope tripod. It earned a patent so he's very proud of that. And he made a system of buckets and pulleys and pipes and gears to irrigate the vegetable garden, but it needs constant adjustment and repair."

"A miniature Marly Machine?"

"Something like that. I expect the one in France was more reliable, but ours is a tinkerer's dream. It's been redesigned and rebuilt more times than I can recall."

She stretched and yawned, then pulled off her boots and wiggled her toes near the fire. Despite the washing, her stockings were in a sorry state.

Alan said, "I expect you'll be glad to get home to clean clothes and a proper bed."

Nattie tried to picture the coming day; going home, stepping back into her life... The thought of saying good-bye to Alan made her throat tighten. She rubbed her eyes.

"You should sleep," Alan told her.

"I'm not tired." She was relieved that her voice sounded normal. "It's just that I've been talking so much. Now it's your turn."

"All right. What do you want to hear?"

Nattie thought a moment. "Tell me about the ocean."

So Alan spoke of the ever-changing color and rhythm of sea and sky until Nattie could feel the rise and fall, the sun on her shoulders and a breeze moving her hair. She fell asleep dreaming of sleek cattle grazing on streaks of sea foam, dotted on shining green slopes rolling to the horizon.

Chapter 12

Nattie woke to the sizzle of cooking. The fire had burned to embers and she was nested under a pile of blankets with another folded under her head. A hand appeared beside her, offering a cup of coffee.

"Good morning," Alan said. "Breakfast will be ready soon. The horses are groomed and fed, the stalls and bunkhouse are clean and the privy is limed. I had a look at the ford; I wouldn't want to try it at the moment but the water's going down fast. I think we might manage it in a few hours."

Nattie stretched and unsuccessfully resisted a yawn.

"Don't you ever sleep?" she asked.

"I've learned to get by without much rest when I need to."

"That might be all right ordinarily, but you are injured, you know."

"I appreciate your concern. But I feel remarkably well, thanks to your medical skills, and I can sleep for days once I deliver my information to your brother-in-law."

"And you'll see a doctor."

"Perhaps, if I get the chance."

Nattie's eyes narrowed.

"You'll see a doctor," she repeated firmly.

"Yes. Of course. I will see a doctor, even though it's completely unnecessary."

"Promise?"

"I promise. Would you like me to put it in writing?"

"No-o," said Nattie. "But if we can find some paper, I'll send a note for you to give my sister. She'll have the doctor in to see you."

"I feel you don't trust me."

Nattie ignored him. "I've been thinking. You have a lot of ground to cover and not much time. If you take some of the old trails instead of the road, it'll shorten your trip."

"Would that give me time enough to escort you home?"

"No, but that doesn't matter."

"It matters to me," said Alan.

"Hear me out," Nattie insisted. "My father wouldn't want you to risk the old trails at night, especially after this rain, and he'd certainly want you to deliver those papers in time to confound that pack of pompous scoundrels." She paused. "He's probably not at the house anyway. Everyone will be out cleaning up after the storm."

"You may be right, but—"

"Mando's accounts book should be here somewhere," Nattie interrupted. "You can write my father a note."

Alan grunted noncommittally.

Nattie pulled on her boots and jumped up. She smoothed her hair back with one hand and searched her pockets with the other.

"What did you lose?"

"My hair ribbon." Nattie's tone brightened. "Although it's really no great loss since it matched my shirt which is ruined anyway."

"Ah. Well. That's good, then."

"I'll go get some twine from the barn."

Alan opened the door for her. She paused in the doorway, half her face burnished by the sun, the other half in shadow, and looked up at him, keenly aware of his arm behind her. Alan wished he could reach out and feel the warmth of her cheek. He dropped his arm and stepped back, his boots loud on the wood floor.

Nattie stopped at the pump for a quick wash. She lifted her face to the sun, squinting into the brilliant blue sky. Chico whickered from the corral.

"*¿Y que*? Do you wish me to believe that you haven't already been fed?"

Bella peeked out from the barn as Nattie approached.

"*Bien, mi queridos*, are you ready to try the river again? It shouldn't be quite so exciting this time. Chico, you'll have to set a good example for Bella. She might be a little nervous, and who could blame her?"

Nattie cut a length of twine with her knife, then rapidly braided her hair and tied the end.

"There. That's as presentable as I'm going to get."

Alan called from the cookhouse. "Breakfast's about ready. C'mon and eat."

Nattie clattered up the steps and paused to let her eyes adjust to the darker interior. A shaft of sunlight slanted from the open front door.

"Smells good," she said refilling her coffee cup. "What did you find to cook?"

"The last of the beans, baked apples, and cornmeal splat cakes."

"What are splat cakes?"

"Observe." Alan scooped up a ladle of yellow batter and dropped it into a skillet of hot grease where it spread and sizzled. "They'd be better if we had eggs, but I think these will be tolerable with honey." He turned the cake over and watched it with a judicious eye, then lifted it onto a plate.

Nattie broke off a piece and popped it in her mouth. "It's really good," she exclaimed.

"Thank you, but you needn't sound so surprised. I'm a competent cook, which saves me from food in tins."

Alan placed a second cake on the plate.

"I can't take full credit for these, though," he said. "An old woman in Shreveport taught me how to make them."

"Mmm," said Nattie, her mouth full.

She set the table as Alan brought the plate of cakes to the table and sat down.

"That's a remarkable stove to find in a camp cookhouse," he said. "It must have been a job to get it here."

"It took all of a very long, hard day. It used to be in the kitchen at home."

Nattie poured honey over the stack of cakes on her plate.

"I told you my father can't resist technological advances. Every year he'd see the Stove of the Future in a catalog and just have to order it, so our old stove would go elsewhere. I think every place around here has one of our old stoves."

Alan said, "I wouldn't have thought there's that much difference from year to year."

"There really isn't. Anyway, Papa had to give up on having the Kitchen of the Future. The cook finally said if the latest stove went, she'd go with it. She'd just get comfortable with a stove and it would be whisked away."

"Whisked?"

"Ye-es; a very slow, laborious sort of whisk, involving a team of oxen and a crew of men."

"Y'know, this isn't how I pictured life out here in the wilderness. Marly Machines, stove whisking—"

"Maybe out here in the territories people have more room to be–" Nattie searched for the word.

"Eccentric?" offered Alan.

Nattie nodded. "Eccentric is one word for it."

"Forward-thinkers are always considered eccentric until everyone else catches up."

Alan started a new batch of cakes, singing softly as he worked. Nattie could make out a word here and there.

"I don't know that song. Is it French?"

"A dialect. And it's a most improper song."

"Who taught it to you? The same one who taught you to make these cakes?"

"Yes. Marie-Elise. A most improper woman. And most kind. She'd feed anyone who came to her door. Whenever I cook these I always remember her singing in the kitchen."

The oven door creaked as he opened it and peered inside.

"Apples are done. Bring your plate over."

Nattie hoped he would say more about the most improper Marie-Elise, but the subject seemed closed. She brought both plates to the kitchen and Alan placed an apple on each, spooning syrup from the pan into the cored-out centers.

"Like apple pie without the crust," said Nattie, inhaling the aromatic steam.

"Do you speak French?" Alan asked.

Nattie nodded, blowing on a spoonful of apple.

"Papa wanted us all to have the education he lacked, so he brought in an endless series of tutors and teachers. At first he hired women, but every man in the Territory came courting so they didn't last long. Papa said he was tired of playing matchmaker and started hiring men to teach us. By that time Flo was old enough for them all to fall in love with *her*, which rendered them pretty much useless. Then the priests came back to the mission so we continued our education with them."

"Including Latin, I suppose." asked Alan.

Nattie made a face. "Cicero and Horace, *De Amicitia* and the *Ars Poetica*; I think any language that's been dead that long should be left to rest in peace."

"Do you still have lessons?"

"I'm supposed to. The problem with not officially going to school is that there's no point when you're done with it. Flo went away to a girls' academy in California so she had an end to her education. Mine's still dragging on."

"Your father didn't send you to the academy, like your sister?"

"Not exactly."

"What does that mean?"

"He sent me. I just didn't go."

"An interesting distinction. Would you care to explain?"

"Not particularly," replied Nattie cheerfully.

"But you will," prompted Alan.

Nattie sighed. "All right. It's really very simple. Sister Euphrasia was taking a group of nuns from the mission to California, so they were to escort me. I explained very clearly that I wasn't going, but Papa put me on the stage anyway. I got off at the first stop and just didn't get back on."

She shrugged dismissively.

"This is really very good," she said, gesturing with her fork at the plate in front of her.

"Thank you, and don't change the subject. You refused to get back on the stage?"

"I didn't refuse. I just—left."

"How? Where did you go?"

"It was dark. I walked away. The next day I found an *ejido* and traded some frills and folderols for a mule. Then I rode home."

"What happened?"

"Papa was furious, of course. It was months before I was allowed out of sight of the house."

"I recall that you had something to say about my running away from home, and yet you did the same thing."

"I did not!"

"All right; you ran away from school," amended Alan.

"I didn't do that, either. How could I run away from a place I never went?"

"Can we agree that you defied your father's wishes and took unauthorized leave of a stagecoach?"

Nattie thought it over and nodded. "Yes. That sounds about right," she said.

"I'm beginning to feel sorry for your father."

"Tomás and Flo have always been sensible, even when we were children, but Papa says Robby and I were demons and if Tía hadn't come to help he would have run away to a more peaceful life in equatorial Africa."

"She's your mother's sister?"

"Yes; the eldest. She helped convince my mother's family to let her marry the crazy giant. Although Mama would have married him anyway."

"Walked away in the dark and traded for a mule to get here?"

Nattie laughed. "Something like that. Papa says I'm very like her. So he really shouldn't complain too much about me. If Mama had been an obedient daughter he never would have won her."

When Nattie's plate was empty she jumped up and began searching the kitchen.

"I know I saw a pencil somewhere…"

Alan joined her, puzzled but willing to help. Nattie turned and tripped over his boot. He caught her and they stood close to each other, his hands warm on her shoulders.

"Mando's accounts book," said Nattie. "Paper. To write notes."

Alan tilted his head, questioning.

"It might be with the pencil."

"Oh, right," said Alan. "That makes sense. I'll help you look for it."

They didn't move. Nattie looked into Alan's eyes and again forgot how to breathe. He dropped his hands from her shoulders and abruptly turned away.

Nattie opened a drawer and stared into it, not seeing its contents. Alan examined the same cabinet several times before he noticed that it contained a pencil. He looked deeper and uncovered the accounts book. The first few pages contained writing; "Hieroglyphics," said Alan.

They could pick out only a few words from the cryptic scribbles.

"I suppose it makes sense to Armando," said Nattie. "You write while I tidy up breakfast."

Alan's pencil was still scratching across paper when she turned the wash basin upside down and draped the dish towel across it. She retrieved the remains of her shirt and went out to the barn to change. When she returned, Alan was folding the letter to her father. He handed it to her, along with the pencil and book.

"Your turn," he said.

Nattie sketched a map of his route for him, then tapped the pencil on the table as she wondered how to explain him to her sister. Finally she wrote a brief message that she knew Flo would find maddeningly incomplete. She described Alan's injuries and need for medical attention, but gave only the sketchiest account of the part she played in his journey.

"My sister will badger you for the whole story," she warned him.

"So Mrs. Peller will interrogate me and drag me to a doctor. Perhaps I should just give my information to Mr. Peller, and run."

"No, there's no need to fear Flo. She's the sweetest person you'll ever meet. You'll adore her; everyone does. She and James will insist that you stay with them. Don't even try to argue."

Nattie re-read her note to Flo. Dry and matter-of-fact. Perfect. Nothing of her feelings had slipped in. She would have been dismayed to know that her sister would parse the meaning behind the sentences as clearly as if she had poured out her heart.

Alan had returned the blankets to the bunkhouse. Nattie retrieved some to replace his lost bedroll. She insisted that he take her rifle as well.

"There's no need," Alan protested. "I'll replace my gear in Dos Rios."

"When you do, you can leave mine with Li Jun. He used to be our cook until he started a restaurant. Anyone can tell you where to find *El Cocinero Chino*. He'll put you up for the night and tell you tales of how he was tormented by the dreadful Johnston children."

"Intriguing. I will certainly look him up."

"We weren't that bad, really. He just wanted a quiet, undisturbed kitchen with no children underfoot. The funny thing is he has five of his own now."

Nattie made packages of food for Alan while he put the cookhouse in order. Again he protested that he'd buy supplies in Dos Rios.

"Just in case," she replied. "And I found a canteen which I am going to fill with the vile potion, and which you will be very glad of when your head starts to pound."

"All right, I surrender. If it makes you happy we'll load up Bella till her knees buckle."

"I'm glad you're ready to be sensible. There's one more thing; you'll need to take my hat. I know, I know—you'll buy one in Dos Rios. But the sun will give you a splitting headache by then."

"Certainly not. How can I complete my daring mission wearing a girl's hat?"

"It's not a girl's hat. It's my brother's."

"All the same, I won't send you home bareheaded."

Nattie twirled in front of him. "Do you really think that Tomás' hat could redeem this ensemble? And he'll lecture me about taking it whether I bring it back or not."

They continued to pack and clean until the cookhouse showed no trace of their stay. Soon there was nothing left to do except saddle the horses. Alan and Nattie were quiet as they prepared to go. Nattie could think of nothing except the moment she would watch Alan ride away.

Alan tried to skip past thoughts of saying good-bye. He filled his mind with distances, trails, and times but he didn't feel his usual enthusiasm for moving on.

"Let's go see what the ford looks like," he said.

Chapter 13

The tree-shaded trail was a dim green tunnel flecked with golden dapples of sunlight. The woods were cool and quiet except for bird song and the soft thud of hooves on damp earth. Alan sat relaxed in the saddle but his eyes were alert, searching the woods for movement and scanning the trail for tracks.

They heard the sound of rushing water as they approached the river trail, but it was no longer a flood's menacing roar. Sections of the trail had been taken by the river and other stretches were obscured by debris. The horses picked their way through the clutter of brush and branches.

Alan asked, "What do you think?"

Nattie shrugged. "Hard to say until we reach the ford. I wouldn't want to cross here, that's for sure."

Nattie dismounted once to gather a bundle of leaves. She wrapped them in a cloth and reached up to tuck them into Alan's saddlebag. "Crush these a bit, wet the cloth and put it on your head tonight," she told him.

"As long as I don't have to taste it."

Nattie touched the silver rectangle on Alan's saddle. "A reward from Butterfield?"

"Yep. For bringing in the hooligans who had been burning their coaches. There was a ceremony and photographs and an endless series of stout gentlemen giving speeches. Very impressive."

Nattie swung up into her saddle. "ACM. What does the C stand for?"

"Charles."

"After your uncle Charlie?"

Alan nodded. "What's your middle name?"

"Which one? It takes five minutes to recite them all."

"Your favorite, then."

Nattie swung up into the saddle. "That would be...Irazema. From my great-aunt."

"Natividad Irazema," said Alan. "Natividad Irazema Johnston. I am very pleased to know you, Miss Johnston."

"The pleasure is mine, Mr. McTurk."

"You're missing a glove," Alan observed.

"The marvel is that I didn't lose both. Papa says it takes half his herd just to keep me in glove leather."

They reached the ford, a great slab of rock wide enough for a wagon to cross. It was usually clearly visible under a few inches of water. Now it would have been hard to find without the markers on the riverbanks. Nattie retrieved her signal cloth and looked across the river. The first cloth had been joined by a second.

"Good. They've been watching the river so they knew not to expect me."

"And will everyone fuss over the prodigal daughter?"

Nattie said, "A little fussing doesn't sound so bad right now. Tía knows how to fuss without being tiresome."

They watched the water pour over the ford in a smooth sheet that crumpled into whirls of foam on the downstream side.

"Still a bit dicey," Alan said. He studied Nattie's profile, shaded under her wide hat brim. "I'd wait a while if I didn't have someplace to be. You could stay on this side till the water goes down a bit more."

"Not likely," said Nattie. "Chico knows the ford; we'll go first."

"Not likely," replied Alan, grinning.

He urged Bella into the brown water. She stepped carefully across. Chico followed, calm as always. The gentle slope west of the ford had been washed out by the flood. The horses scrambled up the bank to the road.

"This will need some work before wagons can go through again," said Nattie. "The roads may be in bad shape, too."

"I can make my own path if need be."

They rode side by side, knees nearly touching. They talked of routes and landmarks and where to find good grazing and fresh water. Trees thinned as the road left the river. Alan and Nattie blinked in the bright sunlight as they emerged from the cool green shade into wide grasslands. The clarity of the rain-washed air showed every detail of the surrounding mountains in sharp relief, bringing them deceptively close. Soon Alan would disappear over a ridge and Nattie would continue on into the valley.

They rode on in silence, stealing glances at each other, until Nattie reined Chico in.

"This is where I leave you," she said. "You can't quite see the house from here; it's past that rise."

Alan looked down the road that would take Nattie home.

"I know what you're thinking," she told him. "But you really can't spare the time. You need to finish what you came to do. And you needn't feel unchivalrous. Out here, this is considered delivering me to my doorstep."

"An extremely long doorstep. Well, then, make my sincere apologies to your father and tell him he'll have the chance to horsewhip me as soon as I can manage it."

"I most certainly will not."

"My letter will have to do, then."

Alan smiled at Nattie, but his eyes were serious.

"I hope that your father will understand what I wish I could tell him face-to-face; what I want to tell you."

He looked out over the valley.

"There aren't words enough to thank you, or to tell you what a remarkable young woman you are. I just wanted you to know—to know that."

Nattie's throat was tight; she couldn't speak. She tried to smile but her face felt frozen.

Alan thought, if I don't leave now I never will. He turned Bella and galloped away.

Nattie watched as horse and rider became small with distance. She knew the point where they would vanish behind the ridge and Alan would be gone. She blinked away a blur of tears, then blinked again, confused. They were returning. Nattie dismounted and stood waiting.

Alan leapt off Bella as she came to a halt in a flourish of dust. He took Nattie's hands in his own.

"Look," he said. "I'll come back as soon as I can."

Nattie nodded. Her eyes were wide and dark.

Alan released her hands. He snatched the hat off her head and clapped it onto his own, then grinned and swung up into the saddle.

"*Adiós*," he said. At the top of the ridge Alan paused and turned in the saddle. He waved his hat and Nattie raised her hand in farewell.

Then he was gone.

Nattie stood, hand raised, long after Alan was out of sight. She felt numb, incapable of thought or movement. Her legs seemed unwilling to support her so she sank onto the ground. She sat cross-legged, listening to the buzz of insects and the rhythm of Chico grazing. Two bites, then teeth grinding. Tear tear grind. Tear tear grind.

Chico lifted his head, grass hanging out of his mouth, and looked down the road that led home. Nattie stood and saw her brother Robby, riding fast as always.

"Nat! Hey, Nat!" he called.

She waved and waited.

"I was on my way to check on the river," Robby said. "Are you hurt? Can you ride?"

"No. Yes. I'm fine. Just awfully tired." She forced a smile and said, "I'm glad to be home."

"You may change your mind on that," Robby told her.

Chapter 14

He brought her up to date as they rode.

"I might as well tell you the worst first," he said. "Mrs. Beamish is staying with us."

"Oh, *no*! Why? For how long?"

This was serious. Mrs. Beamish prided herself on being the first to broadcast any news. She was relentless in her pursuit of gossip, and Nattie didn't feel up to being quizzed by *la señora periodico*.

"The storm damaged her roof, so she's with us until it's repaired. It shouldn't be much longer, though. Mrs. Dresen's ready to poison her tea, and she's driving Papa mad so he sent more men than we can really spare to work on her house. The damage was to her parlor, mostly."

"The Mausoleum? No great loss."

Mrs. Beamish's parlor was a memorial to her deceased husband and many other dearly departeds.

"Not to hear her tell it. You know those awful hair wreaths and things? Some of them got wet. She's afraid they're ruined."

"We should lock our doors at night. She'll likely scalp us to replace those horrors," Nattie said.

"You're arriving at a good moment, anyway. Tía took La Beamish to see how work is progressing. With luck you can claim illness and take to your bed until she goes home."

"Bed sounds wonderful, but I need to talk to Papí first."

"You'll have to wait a while. He's out with Tomás figuring out where the new *Arroyo Codorniz* fence line will be. When the creek flooded it changed course and washed out the fence."

"What other damage did we take?"

"Some windmills and trees blew down. The *acequias* are silted up so we have water running where we don't want it and not running where we do. The old chicken coop was flattened, but the little-littles got the chickens out before it blew down. They're very proud of themselves."

"And rightly so," said Nattie. The smallest ranch children were in charge of tending the poultry and collecting eggs.

"Mostly we've been pulling cows out of bogs," Robby continued.

"Did we lose many?"

"No, we got them to high ground in time. Now the problem is keeping them there. They insist on wandering down to play in the muck."

Nattie was grateful for the distraction of her brother's conversation. She was trying very hard not to think about Alan, or what he said, or how he looked at her... She would save those thoughts for when she was alone.

A final turn in the road brought the house into view. It had begun as an L-shaped adobe, but over the years it grew to be a two-story rectangle enclosing a central courtyard. A covered breezeway ran from the house to the ranch hands' dining hall and then out to the summer kitchen. Vines climbed the walls and a rose-covered portal led to the rarely-used front door.

They rode around to the back of the house. Nattie slid to the ground, grateful to be home. Chico trotted eagerly to the barn, Robby following.

Nattie entered the shade of the *zaguan* that led into the courtyard. This was her favorite place in the house. A tiled fountain trickled in the corner, and plants tangled everywhere in a profusion of green leaves and bright blossoms. A fat black-and-white cat dozed on the clay tiles. Nattie scooped him up and held him close, feeling the lazy vibration of his purr against her cheek.

"Ah, Chinche. Did you miss me?"

She put him down and, suddenly hungry, hurried to the kitchen. Mrs. Dresen wasn't there; probably taking her afternoon nap. The coffee pot was on the stove, along with a smaller pot of hot chocolate. Nattie's favorite cup, patterned with violets and pansies, sat ready on the sideboard. She poured herself a cup of chocolate, then lifted the lid of an enormous pot and sniffed the rich aroma of *albondigas* soup. It smelled wonderful, but she craved sweets. She surveyed the kitchen and pounced on a plate of spice cookies. "Bliss," she murmured with her mouth full.

She was drinking her second cup of chocolate when she heard her father's footsteps. He limped when he was tired; he limped heavily now. He dropped a heavy hand on her shoulder as he crossed behind her to the coffee pot. Cup in hand, he lowered himself onto the opposite chair.

"So you found your way home, *mija*," he said. "I was beginning to wonder if I still had a wild black-haired daughter. Tía was worried sick."

"I'm sorry, Papí. I know I should have stayed with the Stocktons but I didn't and then I found a man in the river so I took him to East Camp. He gave me this letter for you and asked that you send a telegraph for him if you can."

She handed him the paper and watched as he read it, then read it again.

"He writes a pretty letter, this fish you hauled in. McTurk...that name's familiar. And he was on his way to James? Well, well. Small world, as they say. I swear, this whole territory is just a little village with the houses scattered farther apart."

Nattie said, "There's a lot more I need to tell you—"

"It'll keep till tomorrow. Get some rest."

"I want to tell you now, while I remember everything."

Nattie told him about the railroad and the storm and Alan McTurk's papers. Mrs. Dresen came in, gave her a hug, and put steaming bowls of soup in front of them. Papí reluctantly rose from the table when they heard the carriage.

"Guess I'd better give poor Constancia a break from Mrs. Beamish's company. The news of your return should give her something to chew over for a while." He winked at Nattie as he left.

Nattie's eyelids were heavy as her aunt bundled her away to bed. Tía shook her head over the ruins of her clothes, but approved Alan's bandage as neat work. Nattie tried to tell her aunt about him but her words trailed off into sleepy silence. Tía shooed Chinche off the bed as she tucked Nattie into sheets scented with lavender. Nattie fell asleep wondering where Alan was now.

Chapter 15

Nattie slept, half-woke, and slept again. Once or twice she was dimly aware of Tía's hand on her forehead, soft and cool as a fallen leaf. When she awoke, bright sunlight pierced gaps in the shutters. She thought about getting up, then thought about going back to sleep, but did neither.

It felt unreal to be home. She wondered if the storm and the cabin and Alan would soon seem unreal, half-dreamed and half-forgotten. A warm weight on her knees told her Chinche was in his usual place. She stretched out a hand and he moved closer, purring, to sit on her stomach while she rubbed his head.

"Oof. You're squashing me," Nattie told him.

She rolled onto her side, dislodging him. He floundered to his feet, grumbling, and burrowed under the blankets in search of toes to nibble.

"Oh no, you don't."

Nattie pulled her feet to safety and swung them out onto the floor. She glanced at her little china clock; it was mid-afternoon.

"No wonder I feel discombobulated," she said.

The cat emerged from the bedclothes and stalked to the door.

"Go scout it out and tell me if it's safe to go down," Nattie told him.

She felt a bit head-achy and her throat was scratchy. She wanted food, but had no desire to face Mrs. Beamish. She opened the door a crack and listened for the strident tones of *la vieja chismosa* baying on the scent of fresh gossip, but the house was quiet.

Nattie pulled on her wrapper and slipped out, her bare feet silent. If she could make it to the kitchen she'd be safe. Even Mrs. Beamish would hesitate to face Mrs. Dresen on her own ground.

She hesitated at the bottom of the stairs. There was a murmur from the sitting room; she strained to make out the words, then jumped as Mrs. Beamish blared "...sleeping the day away. It isn't healthy to lie abed so long."

Poor Tía, thought Nattie. She moved quickly down the passageway to the kitchen. Soon she was installed at the big wooden table with a great mug steaming in front of her. Mrs. Dresen prescribed tea with honey and lemon to soothe her throat and a late breakfast to soothe everything else. She beamed as Nattie devoured eggs, chorizo and tortillas. Finally Nattie sighed in satisfaction and got up to carry her dishes to the sink. Mrs. Dresen took them from her.

"Oh, no. You sit and tell me about your adventure before the girls come in to help me get supper."

Nattie glanced at the door.

"Oh, don't worry about her," said Mrs. Dresen. "She won't set foot in the kitchen. Thinks it's common. I tell you, I had a duke stand in this very spot, paying me the prettiest compliments you ever heard. But I'm glad to be left in peace, I'll tell you that. I feel sorry for the lady, her house damaged and all, but she hasn't been pleased with anything the whole time she's been here. Maybe it was a blessing to have her, though. Gave your aunt something to think about besides you."

"Was she very worried?"

"Well, she did have a few chats with her saints. I'm not sure it's proper to tell the saints their duties." Mrs. Dresen's tone was disapproving.

"It's not *telling*. More like reminding."

"Whatever you call it, I'm glad it worked and here you are, safe and sound."

Mrs. Dresen looked closely at Nattie's face.

"Maybe not so sound, though. Your cheeks are flushed." She felt Nattie's forehead. "You feel a bit warm. And here I let you sit all this time with nothing on your feet. Back to bed, now. I'll send up more tea and let your aunt know you're awake and fed."

Nattie judged the outdoor staircase in the courtyard to be the safest route. She paused at the corner of the landing that ran all around the inner square of the house and leaned over the railing to survey the garden below.

Her mother had planted her favorites in the beds that circled the courtyard, but after her death they had run wild. The children had run wild, too, until Tía came. Her calm restoration of order was welcomed by Tomás and Floralinda, and tolerated by Robby. Nattie, however, seemed oblivious. She serenely came and went, hair tangled, feet bare, busy with her unfathomable activities.

"Does the child ever wear shoes?" asked Tía.

"She doesn't need them," explained Robby, who usually spoke for his little sister. "Her feet are so tough that she can have a devil's-head thorn in her foot and never feel it. She doesn't even know it's there until she comes in and hears it clicking on the floor."

Tía was horrified. She waited for Martin Johnston to make one of his brief visits to the house. Since the death of his wife, he had let his land and herds consume him.

"I have no concerns about Tomás and Floralinda," Tía told their father. "Roberto is a challenge, but there's no malice in him. It's just a game, trying to outwit me. But Natividad…"

"I know," Martin said heavily. "She wasn't strong during her first years so we indulged her, and we were so relieved when she improved that we indulged her still. She was little more than a baby when Rosario became ill. And since she died… *Casa sin madre, rio sin cauce.*"

99

He looked down at his large hands, awkward at rest.

"I'm grateful you're here, Constancia. They need you."

"They need their father, too," Tía said gently. "They're all grieving for their mother; Nattie especially."

Martin looked up in surprise.

"Do you think so? I thought it would be hardest for the older ones."

"They're old enough to understand their loss. Nattie just feels it. But I can't begin to guess what's going on inside that head of hers. She appears and disappears like a wild thing. I don't know where she goes or what she does. If the other children know, they aren't saying."

"I might be able to help you with that. When the children became old enough to wander I asked William Begay to keep an eye on them. You might get him to tell you what she's been up to." He paused. "The children think he just raises hounds and does odd jobs. If they knew he's watchdogging them—"

"I'll be discreet," said Tía.

She found William Begay feeding his dogs. They exchanged greetings and Tía waited in silence until he finished. He led her to a rickety bench where they watched fat puppies tumbling over each other in a nearby pen.

Finally William said, "You want to know about *El Venadita*."

An apt description, Tía thought. Nattie did seem like a little deer, graceful and wary.

"Yes, please. I am very worried about her."

"Yes. A young one should be happy, like them." William gestured toward pups. "But *El Venadita*, she misses her mama. She visits her, up on the hill."

"She goes to her mother's grave?"

"Yes. She goes and makes pictures on the ground, with rocks and sticks and flowers. She talks and sings, and makes pictures."

Tía's eyes filled with tears.

"Not at night, though," he continued. "At night she just sits and talks. Sometimes she sleeps."

"She goes at night? *Dios en cielo!*"

"It's all right. I watch her. Her papa's dog goes with her. Her mama's cat, too."

Tía sat in silence, imagining the little procession of child, dog and cat slipping silently through the night to the small graveyard on the hill.

"*Pobrecita,*" she said softly.

"I watch, to keep her safe. But—" He shook his head.

"I know. Thank you. I'll try to help her not miss her mamá so much."

That afternoon, Tía put on her wide-brimmed hat and work gloves and went out into the courtyard. She lined up buckets and pots and arranged all the gardening tools in a pleasing display.

Like playing shop, she thought. Then she rolled up her sleeves and set to work.

Soon two children were drawn to help, then a third, and finally Nattie. She watched for a time, then gathered up a set of tools that fit her small hand.

"Mamá gave these to me," she said.

"Your Mamá's garden needs care," Tía told her.

Nattie nodded. She watched and copied everything that Tía did, working on after the older children became bored and left, stopping only when it became too dark to tell weed from flower.

Morning found Nattie at work in the garden.

"Shall I bring her in for breakfast?" asked Flo.

"Leave her be," said Tía. "I'll take a plate out to her."

As Nattie ate—Tía ignored the dirt caked on her hands—Tía told her the English and Spanish names of the flowers and plants, and pointed out the ones that Rosario had brought from her home in Cananea.

"This one," she said, pointing to a climbing vine, "is the rose that your mother threw to your father."

Nattie gently touched a leaf and looked up, as though imagining a dark-haired girl smiling from a high window.

As they worked, Tía told the child stories of her mother. Nattie gave no response, but when Tía's voice faded she quickly looked up and stared wide-eyed at the tears rolling down her aunt's face.

Nattie lifted the hem of her dirty pinafore to gently wipe the tears away. Tía sobbed and opened her arms. Nattie carefully stepped close and stood stiffly for a long moment, studying Tía's face—it's the first time she's really looked at me, thought Tía—then relaxed against her side.

Tía gently pulled the child onto her lap, rocking her and singing as she had sung to Rosario when they were children.

"Mamá sang that to me," Nattie said. "Sing it again."

Tía sang, smiling through tears.

Now Nattie surveyed the greenery with a critical eye. She wished she could work in the garden. It had always been her refuge and solace, but it wouldn't shield her from the prying eyes of Mrs. Beamish. Best to go back into hiding.

Nattie returned to her room just as she heard Tía's light steps approaching. She threw off her wrapper and jumped into bed as the door opened.

Tía appeared, wearing a brown dress with black at the collar and cuffs. Her key-laden *chatelaine* jingled as she put down a tray. She was slight and spare, with slate-grey hair in a braided coil. She tilted her head, dark eyes narrowed, as she gave Nattie a long appraising look. Nattie thought she looked like an inquisitive bird.

"Mrs. Dresen told me you're not feeling well," said Tía.

"Just a touch of cold, maybe. I think I'll have a bath and stay in bed today."

Nattie tried to look ill enough to stay in her room, but not so ill that Tía would feel she needed doses and poultices.

"Hmm. Well, a little rest will do you no harm."

Her eyes strayed to the window. Nattie knew what she was thinking. The vines outside the window were a favorite escape route.

"Tía, really, I'm not going anywhere. I'd just like to stay quiet in my room."

Tía smiled, remembering when young Nattie was confined to bed with a bad cough during a rare snowfall. Tía had hauled her back through the window by the tail of her nightgown.

"What a naughty little thing you were," said Tía. "Trying to go out barefoot in your nightgown."

"I still think I was right. I couldn't *get* sick if I was already *was*."

"Well, there's no snow on the ground now so perhaps you'll stay put. You can make use of the time to improve your needlework. I'll bring you your *deshilado*," Tía said sweetly. "And I'll check in on you. Frequently."

"Yes, Tía. Make my apologies to Mrs. Beamish, please. How much longer will she be staying?"

"I'm sure you'll see her before she leaves. Enjoy your peace while you have it."

Tía straightened the bedclothes and plumped Nattie's pillow, then left her to rest.

Chapter 16

Nattie woke to Tía's light touch on her forehead.

"I believe you really do have a cold," Tía told her. "You won't be able to come down to supper tonight. Mrs. Beamish will be so disappointed."

She pulled a small bottle and a large spoon from one of her apron's many pockets and poured a syrupy dose. Nattie swallowed it and made a face, then sneezed. Tía reached into her apron again to produce a handkerchief and said, "Her house will be ready soon. You may not have the chance to see her before she leaves us. Try to rest now."

Nattie felt achy and restless. Now that she was legitimately ill she felt trapped in her room and longed to go out, even if it meant enduring Mrs. Beamish. She tried to read but couldn't concentrate, tried to sleep but her thoughts raced. Tía brought her a tray of food but she didn't feel like eating.

Tomás stuck his head in to say hello. He said she owed him a hat, but spared her the lecture she expected. Robby came in later. He flopped his lanky frame down on the edge of the bed and grabbed Nattie's long braid, dangling the end to tickle Chinche's nose. The cat moved away in annoyance as Nattie reclaimed her hair.

"You look awful," said Robby. "Your nose is red, your face is blotchy, your eyes are bleary; all very convincing. I applaud your dedication to verisimilitude."

Nattie counted on her fingers. "Six. What's Ignacio's score for today?"

"He topped out with inundation."

"Only four? Tell him I said he needs to apply himself more assiduously."

"That's only five. I still win."

"Five is pretty good, considering I feel as awful as I look."

"That *is* bad." He dodged the pillow Nattie threw at him and settled by Chinche, who stretched and rolled onto his back.

"Bedbug," said Robby, tickling the expanse of white fur on the cat's stomach. "What an awful name."

"You're the one who started calling him that," protested Nattie. "I wanted to name him something imposing, like Charlemagne or William the Conqueror."

"The only thing that cat ever conquered is his food dish. Speaking of food, what do you have to eat?"

"Why? Are you hiding from La Beamish?"

"I won't deny it. I'll trade information for edibles."

"What information?" asked Nattie, pointing to the tray.

"As your Mr. McTurk requested, Papí sent the message for James over to the telegraph office but the lines are down until tomorrow, probably."

"That's not much information, and he's not my Mr. McTurk."

Robby swallowed a huge bite of rice pudding.

"If you saved his life he belongs to you. I'm sure I read that somewhere."

"I refuse to respond to your indefatigable idiocy," Nattie said with dignity.

Robby headed for the door, carrying the bowl of pudding. "Six. We're tied. Also, I heard that your Mr. McTurk said very nice things about you in his letter to Papí."

He waggled the spoon at his sister. "Does the mere mention of your Texas Ranger make you blush, or is it your girlish modesty at being complimented? Or maybe you're just getting blotchier."

"How do you know he was a Texas Ranger?"

"Well, I suppose there could be more than one Alan McTurk in Texas. Is yours exceptionally fierce and cunning, swathed in firearms and righteous bravado? The famous Turkey McTurk?"

Nattie sat up. "What are you talking about?"

"Don't you remember? We read dime novels about him."

"Maybe you and Ignacio did. I certainly don't waste my time on that nonsense. Misspellings and errors on every page—"

"Right. And you pointed out each one until we took them away to read in peace."

"Oh. Do we still have them?"

"Doubt it. I'll ask Ignacio. Are you sure you can lower your standards enough to read them?"

"I'm just curious, that's all."

"Ah. Well, far be it from me to stand in the way of curiosity. Or true love. Whichever."

Nattie reached for a pillow to throw at him. He vanished, then his head reappeared.

"By the way, the Stocktons came through the storm pretty well. They send their best wishes and Alethia says she'll ride over in a few days. I hope you look better by then."

When Nattie was sure Robby had really gone, she checked her face in the mirror. Had she blushed? If Robby thought he could needle her about Alan she'd have no peace. Nattie felt a twinge of regret, remembering how she and Robby had tormented Flo about her many suitors. She wished she could talk to Flo now. She couldn't bare her heart to Alethia as she could to her sister. Nattie wondered again if her friend had a beau. One of her brothers, perhaps? She couldn't imagine ever-serious Tomás in love, and Robby was too much of a flirt to settle down.

Nattie stuck her tongue out at her reflection and climbed back into bed. She wondered what Alan had said about her in his letter and tried to think of a casual, offhand way to ask. She settled back on her pillow and closed her eyes, trying to remember every detail of her time with him. Sleep brought dreams of rain falling hard on a sheltering roof.

Chapter 17

Alan was thinking of Nattie, too, much more than he expected or intended. He was accustomed to enjoying feminine companionship while he had it, and promptly forgetting as soon as he left it behind. But each landmark reminded him of Nattie in the firelight, sketching his route on the hearth. He wished she was with him to see the hawk drifting on invisible currents, the lizard sunning on a rock, the little owl bobbing by its burrow, looking so much like a portly gentleman bowing a welcome that Alan found himself nodding in response.

When he crossed a slender stream that curved around a red rock beside the trail, he dismounted and led Bella up the hill. Nattie had told him it led to *El Ojito de San Ramón*. "It's a restful place," she had said, "and the best water you'll find."

The well-worn path followed the stream, then disappeared around a house-sized boulder. On the other side there was a small reed-encircled pond nestled between rocky cliffs and a tree-shaded green crescent. Alan unsaddled Bella and waited while she rolled on the grass. He staked her to graze and, taking the candles and matches Nattie had packed for him, set out to explore the canyon above the pond. Nattie had said he wouldn't see the entry to the upper canyon until he was in it. He studied the wall of rock, trying to detect a gap in the featureless cliff.

He scrambled up a rocky slope and turned to face the cliff again. A cool current of air on his face led him to a narrow cleft, barely wide enough to enter. Alan slipped in and followed the path that twisted and turned between rock walls that nearly met above him. As he walked on the breeze became stronger, bearing a faint, familiar scent that prompted him to remove his hat.

The canyon path ended in rough steps that led to a dark opening in the wall above. Alan stooped to enter and found himself in a small cave. It was barely high enough for him to stand upright, and he could almost touch the walls with arms outstretched. The ceiling was velvet black; he touched it and his fingers came away dark with soot.

A shaft of light shot through an opening in the ceiling, illuminating a statue of a bearded saint. As Alan's eyes adjusted to the dim light, he saw that every surface was covered with candles, prayer cards, and notes. Flowers stood in an assortment of cans and vases. Small metal *milagros* gleamed in the light of a dozen candles of varying heights. One guttered and went out, reminding him of Nattie's instructions.

First he tidied the shrine, putting dead flowers and puddled wax in a small wooden box by the entrance. "Who empties the box?" he had asked. Nattie shrugged and replied, "Someone will."

He lit the fresh candles and distributed them throughout the cave, carefully dripping melted wax on the rough rock to anchor each one.

"Then what do I do?" he had asked.

"Whatever you like," Nattie told him.

Alan looked into the saint's serene dark eyes and breathed in the familiar scent of flowers and candles. If he closed his eyes he could be back in the spired church of his childhood, surrounded by stained glass and polished wood. He wondered how many candles had burned, how many prayers had been offered in this natural chapel. A shrine, Nattie had called it. A shrine to San Ramón, in gratitude for protecting a family from Apache warriors.

"There are many stories of how the shrine came to be, but this is the most accepted," she had told him. "A family from New Mexico joined up with a wagon train traveling to California. This family was plagued with bad luck from the start. Axles broke, their wagon got stuck where all others crossed; one thing after another. The other travelers grew tired of being slowed, especially when they entered Apache territory. So when an ox went lame, the others said they had to move on but they'd send help. So there was the family, with small children and an infant, all alone.

"They had just settled in to wait in the hills above the road when they spotted a small band of Apache warriors. They scrambled through the rocks, looking for a place to hide. Someone felt cool air rising out of the rock; that led them to the opening into the cave. They could hear the Apaches camped by the spring. If the baby cried, or the children made a sound, they would be lost. The family prayed to San Ramón Nonato to protect them. They made *una manda,* a promise that if they were spared they'd make the cave a shrine. And the children slept silently all night."

"Maybe the air was bad and the children were the most affected. That would make them sleep."

"Maybe," Nattie had said. "You can decide when you see the cave for yourself. Anyway, the Apaches moved on and soldiers came to escort them to safety. And the shrine has been there ever since. People say that as long as one candle is burning, prayers will be granted. Everyone takes care of the shrine."

Alan felt above the entrance for the small ledge where Nattie said matches were kept and left some of his for future visitors. He stooped to leave, then turned back and bowed his head to offer inarticulate thanks for his life and for the girl who saved it.

He ducked out of the shrine and put on his hat. The light was dim now. He imagined the terrified family huddled in the cave through the long night, with the children sleeping peacefully.

Alan slept peacefully as well. The next morning he made good time to Dos Rios, where he found Li Jun to be a generous and helpful host. Provided with supplies and information, Alan regretfully refused Li Jun's offer of a bed for the night. He now knew several places where his quarry might have gone to ground. If he pressed on he could reach them next day.

By the time he made camp his head pounded with a dull ache. He gulped some bitter liquid from the canteen Nattie gave him and shuddered, then swallowed a spoonful of the jam she had packed. He looked up at the stars, remembering Nattie laughing beside him as the wind whipped her hair.

The pain in his head eased. He was tired but restless. He reached into his saddlebag for the shirt she had worn and, feeling foolish, held it to his face. The scent—plain brown soap, she would have told him—brought her to him. He folded the shirt under his head, and slept.

He moved on before first light. A short ride brought him to the base of a ridge where he tethered Bella. Alan scouted along the ridgeline until he saw a ramshackle cabin below. Adits in the hillside marked it as an old mining camp. Smoke rose from the stovepipe.

Got it in one, he thought.

From the concealing shelter of a jumble of boulders, he hallooed the cabin and explained that he wished the occupants to step outside, unarmed. They responded with a flurry of inaccurate gunfire. Alan seized the opportunity to sight in his new rifle. He methodically shot holes in the stovepipe until he was satisfied with his aim. This prompted more gunfire.

Apparently they're well-stocked with ammunition, thought Alan. So was he, but a long siege didn't suit his plans. Using boulders for cover, he made his way to a heap of abandoned mining equipment. With some effort, he maneuvered a section of sluice into position to launch rocks at the cabin. The inhabitants protested but remained inside, so he intensified his assault. He found a rusty wheel and hefted it into the trough, then watched in awe as it flew through a corner of the cabin. Timbers groaned as they twisted and sagged into a precarious balance, prompting renewed cursing and gunfire.

" 'Yet breathing out threatenings and slaughter,' " said Alan.

Inspired now, he loaded the sluice with the largest rock he could lift. It took a bad bounce and missed its target, but the next went through the walls like a cannonball. He was wrestling with a nicely rounded rock when he heard shouts of surrender. Firearms were thrown out through the crooked door, followed by three men. He regretfully left the rock in place and went down to claim his captives.

Chapter 18

Nattie was miserable. Her head ached, her nose ran, her throat tickled, she was hot with covers on and cold with them off. She was desperate for distraction, which arrived in the form of her eldest brother. Tomás described the storm's damage, the repairs that had been completed and those that continued. Nattie asked how the Stocktons came through the storm, but Tomás had little to say. Nattie studied him closely but his manner was disappointingly normal. He was more interested in talking about Alan.

"Ranger McTurk. I've heard of him. Dime-novel nonsense. He's reputed to be a wild man, even for Texas," said Tomás disapprovingly.

"Well, he's settled down to be a rancher now."

"Except when he's skylarking around the territory engaged in espionage."

"It's useful espionage for us," retorted Nattie. "It might bring that rail line you want."

"Settle down, infant. If I can bait you that easily Robby will drive you mad."

Tomás got up from his chair and said, "By the way, two men rode through this morning, looking for a friend of theirs, they said. They didn't seem to be especially friendly, though."

"What did you tell them?"

"I'm afraid we may have pointed them in the wrong direction if they were looking for your ranger." He turned to go.

"He's not my ranger," Nattie called after him.

Robby and Ignacio came in after supper to regale her with stories of Mrs. Beamish. Robby sprawled across the foot of the bed and said, "You have to come down at least once before she goes home—if she ever does," said Ignacio, "to see her tea ceremony."

"Like the Japanese—?"

"No no no. This is much more entertaining. First she explains that she's much too agitated to drink tea, so she wants just a cup of hot water."

Robby was a clever mimic. His tone was that of a querulous martyr.

"Then she graciously accepts Tía's offer of a slice of lemon—" added Ignacio.

"And perhaps a bit of sugar wouldn't be amiss, and then Papí offers a drop of brandy to help calm her nerves—"

"Brilliant man—"

"And the drops have grown larger each day, which might account for her afternoon nap getting longer."

"A truly brilliant man," said Ignacio with deep feeling. "I stand in awe of his perspicacity."

"Indubitably," agreed Robby.

"Tie game, boys," said Nattie, her laugh turning into a cough.

Before they left, Robby told her that Alethia planned to ride over on Saturday, "if you're well enough for company."

"I'm sure I'll be ambulatory before then," Nattie told him.

"Five. You'll have to do better than that to beat us."

With that, Robby and Ignacio were gone. Nattie sat by the window and saw them ride out, wishing she could go too. Instead she went back to bed with Chinche purring beside her.

"Don't get too used to me joining you in your sloth," Nattie told him. "Tomorrow I'm getting up and rejoining the humans."

She tried to begin a letter to Flo but couldn't concentrate. She wondered where Alan was now. Nattie returned to the window, her mind roaming far beyond the limits of her sight.

Tía brought a tray of ginger cookies and *cenizo* tea. She pulled her spectacles and needlework out of her apron and settled in.

"Don't tell me you're hiding from Mrs. Beamish now."

"Not at all," replied Tía calmly. "Your father sent her in the carriage to see how her house is coming along."

"How *is* her house coming along?"

"It will be ready in a day or so, although I'm sure she'd be reluctant to go home without seeing you. Perhaps you could come down soon, even if just for a moment."

"Of course."

Nattie understood perfectly. Mrs. Beamish wouldn't leave before she obtained the latest grist for the gossip mill, so she must oblige with a brief visit.

"Mrs. Beamish will be so pleased. And you can plead illness when you need to make your escape."

"Tía! Are you condoning deceit and bad manners?" asked Nattie delightedly.

"Not at all. You *are* ill, are you not? And I would never condone unmannerly treatment of a guest, but after several days of her company I won't insist that you share it for long."

"Poor Tía. But Mrs. Dresen says having company was a good distraction to keep you from worrying about me."

"Your father was the one who was concerned," said Tía. "I've given up worrying about you. I just get my remedies in order and wait to see what damage you've done to yourself." She tucked the needle into her work and put it aside. "Which reminds me, let me see your arm."

Tía judged the jagged cut to be healing well.

"Another injury to add to your collection," she said as she re-bandaged it.

"It hardly counts as an injury; not like this one." Nattie felt the scar under her chin. "I really thought I'd shake you that time. But you just said, 'We'll wash it off and see how bad it is.' Like always."

"Ah, but after you were clean and bandaged I sat and shook like a leaf."

"Did you really?"

"I really did. After seeing the front of you covered in blood, and the others trailing behind you looking terrified…"

"I thought Robby was going to be sick. And Ignacio kept saying they should have stopped me."

"As though anyone could ever stop you from risking your neck. That palomino was crazy, and you were crazy to ride her."

"I stayed on longer than the boys," said Nattie, then looked stricken.

"Oh, don't worry. You're not revealing any secrets. Your father and I knew you weren't the only one to try that horse. You were just the only one to hit—what *did* you hit?"

"The snubbing post, maybe, or the fence. Robby thought a hoof grazed me."

Tía shook her head. "And how did you injure yourself this time?"

"I'm not sure. A sharp branch in the water, I suppose."

Tía poured more tea. "Do you feel up to telling me about your latest adventure?"

Nattie welcomed the opportunity to relive her stay at East Camp. The end of her story was punctuated with yawns.

"Sleep now. I'll bring up a tray for you later," Tía told her.

Chinche watched Tía from the window ledge as she opened the door.

"Don't look so innocent," she scolded. "I know you'll be on that bed the minute I'm gone."

Downstairs, Tía heard voices from the room that Martin Johnston called the office. His massive desk was always piled high with papers, usually employed to kindle fires. The real ranch office was Tomás's study upstairs.

She knocked on the half-open door and stepped inside. Tomás and Martin sprawled comfortably in armchairs before the stone fireplace that nearly filled one wall. Shelves of books lined the room. Striped blankets were tossed over a well-worn sofa, and a jumble of ropes, tack, and unidentifiable gear was piled in a corner. The air bore traces of horse, dog, leather and tobacco. Both men rose and Tomás pulled a chair forward for her.

Martin gestured to bottles and glasses on a round table. "Will you join us in a drink, Constancia?"

"Yes, please." She sank gratefully into the chair Tomás offered. "I've hardly seen either of you lately."

Martin handed her a glass.

"You'll need this—Mrs. Beamish is coming back tonight, isn't she?"

Tía nodded. "But she plans to go home Saturday."

"To stars in your crown," said Martin, raising his glass. "You've had the worst of it. We've been able to make ourselves scarce, cleaning up after the storm." He drank, then asked, "How's Nat?"

"Much improved. She'll be up and around soon. Alethia is visiting Saturday. I'm glad the girls are spending more time together. They both miss Flo." Tía sipped her drink.

Tomás stood and stretched.

"I need to clean up before supper. Wouldn't want to offend La Beamish."

They heard his boots thudding up the stairs.

"Those long legs," said Tía. "I think he takes the steps three at a time."

She put down her glass and folded her hands in her lap. "I need to talk you about Nattie. I think our girl is in love."

"Lord help us," said Martin. "Alan McTurk, I suppose."

"Yes. What do you know about him?"

"Not enough. He writes a pretty letter so I reckon he's had an education. I've heard tales about him, but I don't know what's fact and what's fiction. I'll ask around. And if his story is true, we'll soon hear what James and Flo think of him."

"Do you believe his story's true?"

"Yes, I do. But that's not enough to make me entrust my girl to him." Martin swirled the whiskey in his glass. "I thought Nat would be the one to stay with me into my dotage."

"*Más tira el amor que una yunta de bueyes.* This may be the first time she has fallen, but she has fallen hard."

The sound of a carriage was followed by Mrs. Beamish abusing the driver for a too-sudden stop.

That voice would drive a coyote to suicide," said Martin. "I'm off to the barn."

Tía sighed and rose to greet her returning guest.

Chapter 19

On Friday Tía judged Nattie too ill to go outside, and Nattie didn't feel well enough to face Mrs. Beamish's interrogation, so she stayed in her room. She picked up and discarded one book after another. She tried to continue her letter to Flo, but drifted into daydreams. She tried and failed to pile her hair atop her head like Alethia's. She even attempted her needlework, but gave up when the thread tangled and broke.

Robby and Ignacio brought the welcome news that Mrs. Beamish's home was nearly ready for her return, "but she won't leave until she has a go at you. Of course no one has mentioned your ranger, but she's awfully suspicious about why she hasn't seen you. I don't think she believes you're sick—thinks you're just hiding for some nefarious reason. Promise you'll let her grill you tomorrow so we can be rid of her."

"We've all been suffering while you were swanning around the countryside and luxuriating up here in peace. It's your turn," said Ignacio. "And if she stays much longer Mrs. Dresen will murder her."

"She'd be acquitted, of course, but who would cook while she was on trial?" added Robby.

"Yes, all right," Nattie sighed. "I'll offer myself as sacrifice tomorrow."

"Early tomorrow," Robby told her sternly.

Saturday Nattie went down to breakfast. Mrs. Beamish wore her usual dark, ornate clothing that always seemed uncomfortably tight for her plump form. Flat curls framed her round face, giving her the appearance of an ill-tempered infant.

"So, the slug-a-bed makes an appearance at last," Mrs. Beamish greeted her. "You don't look as though lying abed all this time did you much good."

"Good morning, Mrs. Beamish," replied Nattie. "I am so sorry that your house was damaged. I hope everything is satisfactory now?"

"As much as can be expected, considering that the workers are a bunch of Mex—" Mrs. Beamish caught herself. "Of course, I'm sure your father's workers are doing their best. I can't expect to find the same craftsmanship out here that we had in Baltimore."

Baltimore was a favorite theme for Mrs. Beamish.

"I hope your parlor is restored to its former elegance," said Nattie.

As children, she and Flo had dreaded visiting Mrs. Beamish. Her parlor was crowded with dark, massive furniture, carved with designs that looked like angry faces. The little girls perched stiffly on overstuffed sofa cushions covered in a scratchy fabric. ("Made of hair from her dead relatives," Nattie told Flo.) The carpet was dreary and the heavy curtains, always closed to keep out the sun, were dark red. ("The color of dried blood," said Nattie.)

Mrs. Beamish eyed Nattie's plate.

"Your appetite is certainly restored," she said. "I myself have been so distressed that I could only manage tea and a nibble of toast."

Her breakfast plate contradicted this statement. Nattie made sympathetic noises and hid a smile behind her coffee cup.

"Mrs. Beamish goes home today," said Tía. "But you'll have time for a little visit first."

"That would be lovely," said Nattie. "I'm so glad I was well enough to come down today." She sneezed vigorously, begged pardon, and sneezed twice more.

"You look a bit flushed," Tía told her. "You may be feverish."

"I'm fine," protested Nattie, continuing to sneeze.

Mrs. Beamish said, "I don't know why you left your room if you're still sick. So unhygienic."

"Perhaps you should breakfast upstairs. We don't wish to expose our guest to your illness," said Tía.

She deposited Nattie in her room and said "There. You're safe. Mind you stay out of sight until she's gone."

Nattie dropped onto her bed, disturbing the sleeping cat.

"That went well," she told Chinche. "Another hour or so and *la vieja chismosa* will be gone. And Alethia and I can go riding."

Tía hadn't given permission to resume all activities, but Tía would be escorting Mrs. Beamish back to her Mausoleum.

Impatient for her freedom, Nattie went to the window to await the departure of Mrs. Beamish. Although she knew they were miles away, she looked again for a man and a horse. Her mind drifted back to the time she spent with Alan, and leapt forward to imagine when she would see him again. Her fantasy was always the same; she would pause at the top of the stairs and see him standing below. Her hair would be done up in swirls and twists, and she would be wearing The Dress.

Flo had brought The Dress back from her wedding trip to Europe. It was an Italian design, simple and elegant, but what set The Dress above all other garments was the fabric; indigo velvet, the color of the night sky, scattered with touches of silver thread that sparkled like stars. They clustered thickest at the hem, as though she waded in a pool of starlight. In Nattie's fantasy she gracefully descended the stairs to greet Alan, and then—what? Her imagination always failed her at this point.

Nattie sighed. "The problem is that I can only imagine *my* part. I can't do the imagining for anyone else."

She heard noises below and leaned out the window to see the carriage being loaded with a mountain of luggage. Soon Mrs. Beamish and Tía emerged from the house and were driven away. Before the carriage passed through the front gates, Nattie was in the barn. Her fingers flew as she saddled Chico.

She thought of riding out to meet Alethia, but the sound of voices led her to a stand of trees. A group of children had salvaged a swing from a tree blown down by the storm and now debated where to hang it. Nattie joined the discussion as various branches were considered and rejected. Finally a candidate was judged to have suitable height, diameter, and accessibility, and the swing was hauled up to be tied. Nattie was tempted to climb up to help, but she was dressed for company so she advised from the ground.

Once the swing was up, Nattie yielded to endless pleas of "Push me, Nattie! Push me!" She was rescued by a shout from a high branch. A young lookout had spotted Alethia, accompanied by Robby and Ignacio. Nattie removed a child from Chico's saddle and trotted out to greet her friend.

Alethia, resplendent in her green riding dress, was happily chattering to her escorts. She waved to Nattie and galloped forward, talking before she was close enough to be heard.

"...met them at the ford. My father rode with me to see how the work is coming along and they brought me the rest of the way. Tomás stayed there; he's supervising. Look how muddy they are! They don't want to take time to come back to the house to eat so we should bring them dinner. Don't you think?"

Nattie, laughing, said "Hello, Alethia. It's good to see you."

"We're off to wallow in the muck again," Robby said cheerfully.

They waved farewell and raced off, Robby tall and lean, Ignacio broad-shouldered and half a head shorter. "Don't forget pie!" he called back to them.

"I can't *wait* to have you tell me everything that happened," said Alethia. "I've only heard bits and pieces, and none of the most important details."

"Like what?"

"Like...was he handsome or hideous? Were you terribly frightened? Did he fall madly in love with you? Did you—?"

Nattie interrupted the stream of questions. "In-between; sometimes; and no, he didn't seem the least bit mad. I promise I'll tell you all about it. Shall we ride or lounge?"

Alethia voted for lounging so, after a detour to the kitchen, the girls settled comfortably in the courtyard with lemonade and oatmeal cookies. Nattie found herself eager to tell her story again and Alethia was a rewarding audience. Eyes wide, hands clasped tightly in her lap, she scarcely moved as Nattie spoke.

Finally Nattie said, "And then he rode away—"

Alethia slumped in disappointment.

"But he came racing back and took my hand and said he'd return as soon as he could. And then he was gone."

Alethia sighed. "I've never heard anything so thrillingly romantic."

"It didn't seem thrillingly romantic while I was scared and cold and wet. But thanks to your mother I was never hungry."

"She'll be *so* pleased to hear it. You must come and tell her all about your adventure and your Mr. McTurk."

"He's not *my* Mr. McTurk," Nattie said reflexively. "I don't even know if I'll ever see him again. Out of sight, out of mind, you know."

"Absence makes the heart grow fonder," retorted Alethia. "Of course you'll see him again. He said he'll come back, so he will."

The girls discussed, analyzed, and speculated until it was time to pack the noon meal to take to the river. Mrs. Dresen, watching piles of food appear on the table, asked "What size multitude are you girls feeding?"

Alethia counted on her fingers. "Well, there's Ignacio, and Tomás, and—oh! We need pies!" She tried to find an open space on the table.

Nattie continued the count. "Robby, and a crew of three, and the two of us, so that's eight."

Mrs. Dresen surveyed the table. "This would feed twice that. I'll help you pare it down a bit and then we'll load up the donkey cart. Do you want to drive the cart or lead it?"

They decided to ride their horses and lead the donkey. They'd leave the cart for the men to bring back, and be free to roam after the meal.

Finally they set out, the cart rattling and clanking along behind them.

"How did your place come through the storm?" asked Nattie.

"Not too badly. The orchards took some damage, mostly limbs down but a few trees blew over. Oh—a tree fell on the goat pen so they were able to climb out. Papa told Pauline, Deborah and me that it's our job to get them back. We still haven't managed to capture the little beasts. Papa thinks it's funny." Alethia scowled. "I *hate* goats."

"Maybe we could have a goat round-up. Robby and Ignacio can rope a stiff breeze; goats should be easy enough."

"You don't know these goats," Alethia said darkly. "I wish they'd just run away but I swear they stay around to mock us. We'd welcome the help, though."

The meal was well-received. Nattie watched for signs of romance; Alethia seemed flustered, but Robby seemed focused on food and Tomás talked of nothing but the job. As soon as the men finished eating he chivvied them back to work. The girls tidied away the lunch remains and rinsed dishes in the river, running clear now.

Nattie turned to a young man who was pulling branches out of the water. "Elías, is your father home yet?" she asked.

He grinned. "No, but Marisela's about to kick him out. She says if he won't stay off his broken foot he might as well be here. When this job's done, Luis and I'll haul supplies to East Camp for when Papí limps back."

"You'll need kerosene," Nattie said absently, remembering Alan appearing out of the darkness with candles.

The girls packed the cart and said good-bye to the men. It was a perfect day for a ride. The only clouds were piled in great heaps over the mountains like soft reflections of the peaks below. The sun was warm and a breeze rippled the grass. Nattie was pleased to see that

Alethia and her horse moved smoothly together.

Alethia caught Nattie's eye and called, "She's wonderful, isn't she? I call her Duchess because she's so regal and serene."

The girls dismounted and sat in the shade of a cottonwood tree. Nattie leaned against Chico's front legs while he snuffled her hair.

"Will he stay like that?" asked Alethia.

"No, it's a game. Watch."

Chico inched backward until Nattie was flat on her back. She covered her face with her hat.

"Now he'll snort at me."

Chico lowered his head until Nattie felt his warm breath. He snorted a great gust by her ear and tossed his head.

"Thank you, that was lovely," she told him. "Run along and graze now."

She rolled over on her stomach and rested her head on her folded arms, looking at Alethia through half-closed eyes.

"Ooh, I'm hot!" Alethia complained. She wriggled out of her jacket and fanned herself with her hat. "Mama said I'd be too warm in this but I wanted to wear it one more time before it gets packed away for summer. And it does flatter me, don't you think?"

"Did Flo tell you the latest fad?" asked Nattie. "She says the ladies wear their best gowns when they visit each other, no matter how hot it is. They arrive red-faced and nearly suffocating, then they strip down and chat or play cards in their underclothes."

"No! Not really? What if someone should see them?" Alethia was gratifyingly shocked.

"Flo says they giggle and fuss about that possibility, which adds some spice and scandal. And of course there's competition to have the most fashionable unmentionables."

Alethia asked, "Does Flo do it, too?"

"No. She's too sensible, and too busy to sit all day gossiping and playing cards, clothed or otherwise."

The conversation meandered lazily, but Alethia's questions always brought it back to Alan. Nattie remembered she had some questions of her own. She casually brought the conversation around to the storm, and its damage, and the work to clear the ford.

Alethia was happy to follow her lead.

"Papa couldn't believe how much they had done already. He says he hopes for such a hard-working son-in-law someday."

"Someday soon?" asked Nattie.

Alethia's cheeks were pink. "No, of course not! I mean, I don't know—he hasn't said anything, but I can't help wondering. He calls me Lettie, and he looks at me so sweet and serious..."

"Robby serious? It must be love."

Alethia's eyes widened. "Oh no, not Robby! Of course I admire your brother, but—no. I meant Ignacio."

"Ignacio? Really?"

Alethia sat up straight. "And why not? What's wrong with Ignacio?"

"Well, nothing, of course. I'm just surprised. Robby's been in and out of love a dozen times, so naturally I thought—"

"That I would be one more? No, thank you. I don't want a man who's been in love with every girl in the territory. I don't want to wonder if he's comparing me to someone else."

Nattie said, "Tell me more about these sweet, serious gazes from my cousin."

The girls analyzed every detail of every encounter until Nattie was satisfied.

"Yep. Sounds like love to me. So I guess you won't be my sister-in-law. But Ignacio's just about my brother anyway so that's the next best thing."

"Swear you won't say a word to anyone," demanded Alethia.

"I swear. C'mon, Lettie," said Nattie. I'll race you to the house."

As soon as the girls stepped inside, Tía called to Nattie.

"*Mija*, a crate came from Li Jun. It's addressed to you."

"For me? Where is it?"

"In the courtyard. You'll need a hammer—"

But Nattie was already gone. She and Alethia pried the lid off the long crate with Nattie's knife and pulled out handfuls of straw. "My rifle! And my hat," exclaimed Nattie. "Or rather, Tomás's hat." She brushed it off and clapped it on her head. Further digging revealed blankets; "He kept the old ones and sent back new." She smiled to see a rectangular box wrapped in shiny paper; it held an assortment of chocolates.

"Ooh, lovely!" said Alethia.

A pair of gloves was next, then a gleam of color amid the straw caught Nattie's eye. She pulled out a tangle of ribbons of every shade.

"He must have bought out the town," said Alethia.

Nattie sat down and spread the ribbons on her lap, straightening and smoothing them.

"Look." Alethia pointed. "There's something in the glove."

Ribbons cascaded from Nattie's lap as she reached for it. The glove held an envelope addressed to Nattie's father. She quickly examined the second glove and was rewarded with another note, this one addressed to her. She sank back on the chair to read it.

My dear Miss Johnston-with-a-t,

I hope this finds you fully recovered from your mission of mercy. You will be pleased to hear that I continue to benefit from your vile potions.

Armed with information provided by the good people of Dos Rios, I now set off to tie up some loose ends.

Please accept these tokens of my gratitude for your kind assistance in saving my hide. I share Gonzalo's distaste for a watery grave.

Trusting you will excuse my brevity, I remain your devoted servant,

Alan McTurk

As Nattie read the note a third time she realized that Alethia was leaning over the back of her chair, squeaking with excitement.

"What does he say? May I see?"

Nattie obliged by holding the note where they could pore over it together. Alethia interjected comments as she read.

"Vile potions; that's not very courteous, is it?…Loose ends; What does he mean by that, I wonder…Who is Gonzalo?…Ooh! He says 'devoted'! But 'servant' makes it much less exciting, I think. Now, if he said devoted *admirer*…"

"He's joking about the vile potions. Loose ends…I wonder if he knows where the survey crew disappeared to. Gonzalo's a character in The Tempest. And devoted servant—that's just a joke, too."

"He seems a very humorous fellow, your Alan McTurk," said Alethia disapprovingly.

"We barely met," objected Nattie. "You can't expect protestations of love when we hardly know each other! I may never see him again."

But as she spoke she remembered his hands on hers, and his hurried words. She smiled.

"There!" exulted Alethia. "You will see him again; you know it perfectly well!"

The girls ate chocolates and analyzed every word with the intensity of archaeologists deciphering tomb carvings, until Nattie remembered the note to her father.

"It's time I should be going anyway," said Alethia. "Let's deliver it to your father and then I'll start home."

They tidied up the packaging straw and took Nattie's gifts to her room. She spread the ribbons over her quilt and surveyed the colors.

"This one matches your shirt," offered Alethia.

"Mmm. No, I think I'll wear this one," said Nattie, and picked up a length of deep blue-grey.

Chapter 20

Chinche appeared and leapt into the confusion of ribbons on the bed. Nattie unwound ribbons from his paws and found a string to distract him. He sprawled on his back and swatted aimlessly as Alethia dangled it above him.

"Oh, you're hopeless!" she said. "Do I have to put it in your mouth for you?"

"That pretty much sums up his hunting technique," Nattie told her. "He's rarely this active, you know. He'll have to sleep a day and a half to recover."

They left Chinche purring on the bed and went in search of Tía. They found her in the kitchen packing an assortment of delicacies for Alethia to take with her. As custom dictated, Alethia courteously protested, then submitted with many expressions of gratitude.

Nattie, impatient to deliver the note and perhaps learn its contents, jumped in as soon as she could.

"Tía, where's Papí, do you know?"

Tía glanced at the kitchen clock.

"He was going to check the progress on clearing the *acequia*, and then the ford if he had time..."

"Perfect! We're off, then," said Nattie, giving her aunt a kiss on the cheek.

"You come right back from the ford," Tía said sternly. "The boys or your father will escort Alethia home."

129

"Ignacio will go for sure. He wants to see the condition of the road," Nattie said innocently, watching for her aunt's reaction. But if Tía knew anything about Ignacio's romantic inclinations, she concealed it.

"Alethia, tell your mother I'll be over as soon as the carriage can make the trip," said Tía.

When the girls arrived at the ford they found Robby and Ignacio wet-haired and scrubbed, ready to go visiting. Nattie and Alethia said their farewells, then Mr. Johnston pulled himself into his saddle.

"Well, daughter, shall we go home?" he asked. "I want to soak my old bones before supper."

He turned to the crew, sitting on the bank finishing off a pie.

"Tomás, you can haul the tools back in the donkey cart."

Elías grinned. "We may have to eat another pie to make room, *señor.*"

The others nodded solemn assent.

Nattie and her father rode a little way in silence before she said, "I have something for you, Papí. It came in a package from Mr. McTurk. He replaced the gear I made him take." She didn't mention the chocolates and ribbons and gloves.

She gave her father Alan's note. He read it without comment and folded it carefully into his shirt pocket. They rode on in silence.

"Don't you want to know what he says?" asked her father with a sideways glance.

"Of course."

"Well, I expect he gave you much the same information as he gave me. He told me he wrote you. Doesn't want me to suspect him of slinking around behind my back, I suppose."

"I suppose," echoed Nattie faintly.

"Anyway, sounds like he's trying to find our missing surveyors so he can deliver them along with those papers. He's hoping to liven up the rail committee meeting."

"Oh," said Nattie.

"He continues to sing your praises. I'm beginning to think he's suffering from more than a knock on the head."

"Oh," said Nattie.

"Last one home puts the horses up," said her father, and urged his mount into a gallop.

The race ended in a tie, but Nattie volunteered to take care of the horses. She lingered over the job, wishing she could have gone with Alethia. The boys would stay for supper; Nattie envied them their places at the lively table. She was surprised to realize that she felt a bit lonely.

She shook off her mood and chided herself. "You'll visit Alethia in a few days, *and* you have a note from Alan, *and* most of a box of chocolates left, *and* La Beamish has gone home to The Mausoleum. That should be more than enough to make you happy."

She turned the horses out to graze and headed to the house. Tía intercepted her at the bottom of the stairs.

"Fah! I hope you're on your way to bathe before supper. You smell like horses, as usual."

"Sí, Tía. I'll go out to the bath house."

"We do have bath tubs and running water in the house, you know."

"Yes, but the hot spring is nicer. No clanking pipes, and you can see the sky..."

Tía sighed. "Run along, then. There are towels and soap out there already, so you don't need anything except clean clothes and your fragrant self."

Nattie ran up to her room and kicked off her boots. She read Alan's note again before tucking it in a drawer with the ribbons and candy. She threw moccasins and clean clothes into a basket and gave Chinche a quick belly-rub. Her bare feet made no sound on the stairs but somehow Tía knew she was there and called, "Put something on your feet."

"I will on the way back," Nattie replied as she went out the door.

Soft dust rose and fell with each footfall as Nattie trotted along the path to the hot spring. She slowed when the bath-house came into view. It was a rough wooden structure with two doors that opened into separate compartments. Past the bath-house were steps leading down into the sandy-bottomed spring.

Nattie entered a compartment and arranged her clean clothes on the wooden bench. She shucked off her dirty clothes and stuffed them into the basket, then grabbed soap and a cloth and lowered herself into the clear water. The bathing compartment was open to the sky. Nattie paddled her feet and watched drops sparkle in a shaft of light.

She untied her braid and carefully put the ribbon aside. The water lifted her hair as she put her head back and luxuriated in the warmth of sun and water. She stretched, yawned, and gave herself up to analyzing Alan's note.

"So. His head continues to bother him, but the tisane helps. And he got information in Dos Rios, perhaps from Edwin's bereaved Lucy. It wouldn't take much sweet-talk to get her to tell what she knows."

Nattie found it unpleasant to think of Alan sweet-talking Lucy.

"He didn't stay the night in Dos Rios, but went haring off after 'loose ends.' Edwin and company can't have gone too far if he thinks he can collect them and still deliver the papers on time. And he concludes by proclaiming himself my devoted servant. Of course, that's just an expression."

Still, Nattie found it pleasant to consider and she considered it for quite a while. The compartment was all in shadow by the time she got out. She dressed quickly and trotted home, basket in hand and the towel over her shoulders. Nattie had adopted Tía's practice of rinsing her hair with rain water, so she stopped at a mossy barrel under one of the roof *canales*, removed its wooden cover and lifted a battered tin ladle from a hook. She bent forward, her hair reaching the ground, and ladled cool water over her head. As a child she had loved seeing her reflection in the stillness of the dark water and searching for tiny frogs in the fringe of tall grass at the base of the barrel.

Nattie watched the water flow away in silver rivulets. The supper bell clanged and she dashed inside, forgetting the basket of clothes, and tossed the towel on a bench before skidding to her seat just as her father stood to say grace. Tomas scowled, Tía sighed, and Bertram Kemp, the ranch foreman, grinned behind his flowing mustache. Soon dishes were passed around the large table.

"Would you care for some enchiladas, Mr. Kemp?" asked Tía.

"You know the answer to that, Doña Constancia. I've been eating chuckwagon chow for the last week. Don't misunderstand me; I haven't been suffering, but I doubt there's a dish anywhere that can compare to your enchiladas."

Tía piled his plate high as he continued.

"This outfit's known for good food. You should see that Gilbreath lad pack it away. He says it's almost as good as his mama's."

Mr. Johnston said, "Can't expect men to do their best work on beans and weevilly biscuits. How's that young'un working out?"

Mr. Kemp carefully wiped his mustache. "Well, he's calm and patient with the animals. Quiet, works hard. Can stay on a horse, but with that bad arm he can't hardly rope a stump, much less a steer. Seems to know quite a bit about dirt and what to grow in it." This was said with the mild disdain of the drover for the farmer. "You might think about moving him from cattle to crops."

"I could put him to use," Mr. Johnston replied. "I've been thinking we need a new strain of grass. Drought-resistant, high nutrition, able to hold soil in place during a hard rain..."

Nattie's attention drifted until she heard 'McTurk.' Her head snapped up and Tomás snorted.

"Pull your ears back in, Nat," he said. "They're swiveling like a jackrabbit's."

She ignored him and focused on Mr. Kemp.

"From what I heard in San Antone, he's a hard man to figure. He didn't kill the scoundrels who shot him and robbed his stage, but he beat a man down for striking a woman. And she was just a—I mean to say, she wasn't the sort of woman that..."

Tía rescued him. "More enchiladas, Mr. Kemp?"

"Yes, please. You've outdone yourself, Doña Constancia. I've never tasted anything so good."

"You always say that," she replied.

"It's always true," said Mr. Kemp.

"Hear, hear," added Mr. Johnston. "But save some praise and room for Mrs. Dresen's dessert. She made"—he paused for dramatic effect—"her chocolate cake."

Mrs. Dresen was true to her word. She had promised to make her renowned cake once Mrs. Beamish was gone. "I'll not waste it on that old harpy," the cook had sniffed. "If she dared criticize it like she does everything else, well, I don't know what I'd do."

"Snatch the hair right off her head?" Nattie had suggested. "Slap the nose off her face? Knock her cross-eyed and bow-legged?"

"Honestly, child, where do you get such awful expressions?"

Nattie laughed. "Heard them somewhere, I guess."

Those were Mrs. Dresen's favorite threats, used on impertinent ranch hands who hung around the kitchen door teasing for treats and dodging her broom and dish towel until she relented and gave them a cookie or wedge of pie.

Mr. Kemp continued. "McTurk was well-regarded all over town. One night he'd be whooping it up at a fiesta and the next he'd be waltzing at the Hilmar place."

"Hilmar, the baker?" asked Mr. Johnston.

Mr. Kemp nodded. "Last I heard he had two flour mills and I don't know how many bakeries. His daughter was considered the town beauty, all pink and white like a cake in one of her pa's shop windows. Folks said she was sweet on McTurk, but eventually she gave up on him and married a lawyer. Later McTurk started ranching. I heard he had some English partners; fellers with more money than sense, I expect. One of 'em is supposed to be royalty or some such."

Nattie was pleased to hear that Alan had resisted the charms of the baker's daughter. She imagined bright blue eyes and yellow ringlets, a tinkling laugh and a dainty milk-white hand resting on Alan's shoulder as they waltzed.

The conversation turned to stories of dude ranchers. Nattie drifted away again, dreamily waltzing with Alan, until a slice of chocolate cake was placed before her.

"Bliss," she said.

Sunday morning, Tía was surprised to find Nattie ready to accompany her to Mass. In fact, she was somewhat surprised to find her at all. Nattie had been known to vanish to avoid "being yammered at for an eternity. My soul may be immortal, but I'm not. I don't want to spend half my life listening to Father Ochoa drone on and on about sin and—well, that's all he talks about, isn't it?"

"And when do you listen?" asked Tía. "You fidget, you squirm, you sigh, but listen? No."

Tía was further surprised that Nattie's behavior was almost irreproachable during Mass, even though Father Ochoa seemed to be more than usually disappointed in his flock, as he explained at more than the usual length. But Nattie stood, sat, knelt, and uttered the responses, her face serene, her heart grateful, her mind elsewhere. She wondered if Alan had arrived at Flo's. Her sister would insist that he stay until he was fully recovered, and then—what? Would he return? She imagined Alan appearing at the door, looking at her with those blue-grey eyes, taking her hand... Tía heard Nattie sigh and saw her smile. Tía shook her head and sighed, too.

Chapter 21

Alan's conversation with the three sham surveyors was less than cordial. He directed Edwin to tie the hands of the others, then he tied Edwin's. Alan rolled a smoke and squatted in front of his three prisoners, one long leg extended, as he studied them in silence. Sullivan scowled and cursed, Langelaar was watchful, and Edwin looked ready to cry.

Alan said nothing until his cigarette burned short, then he flicked it away and stood up.

"Right," he said. "I could take the lot of you with me but that would slow me down. One of you will suffice. I'm running short of time and patience, so…"

He raised his pistol and Edwin broke.

"Take me! I can tell you everything! Just don't kill me—"

"Shut up, you idiot, or I'll kill you myself!" shouted Sullivan. "He's bluffing! He won't—"

Sullivan was silenced by a bullet whining past his ear.

Langelaar spoke to Edwin, not unkindly. "Stop blubbing, boy. I do not think he is going to kill us, but if so, well, there it is, yes?"

Langelaar's fatalism was lost on Edwin, who continued to shout disjointed bits of information. Alan listened until he had all he needed, then told Edwin to calm himself. Edwin subsided into quivering gulps while Alan explained his plan.

"Now Edwin, listen carefully, because you're a key player in the little drama that's about to unfold. I'm going to untie you, do you understand?"

Edwin's head bobbed. Alan continued.

"Sullivan will accompany me to the rail committee meeting. I'll leave you two your horses to get home on," said Alan. "Edwin, in thirty minutes you will untie Langelaar. I'll be watching until we cross the ridge so mind you don't get inventive." He paused and added, "If you're willing to let this end now, so am I."

Langelaar said, "I'd offer you my hand on it, but as you can see…"

"If you tell me you're a little tied up, I *will* shoot you," replied Alan mildly.

While Edwin saddled the horses and gathered Sullivan's gear, Alan emptied their weapons of bullets and tossed them down the slope. He asked Sullivan, "Would you prefer to have your arms tied or your feet hobbled?"

Sullivan, red-faced with anger, responded with threats and curses.

"Right," Alan replied. "Arms it is. A bold choice. I myself would be afraid of landing face-first in cactus."

Alan led Sullivan's horse and followed his prisoner as he stumbled up the gully, still cursing.

"Save your breath to cool your porridge," Alan admonished him, only to hear porridge cursed long and loud.

"Now that doesn't even make sense," said Alan, and embarked upon a lecture extolling the virtues of porridge that lasted until they gained the ridge line. He flourished his hat in a salute to Edwin and Langelaar and they vanished over the ridge.

Sullivan spent the trip complaining, making threats, offering bribes, and explaining that he was the innocent victim of a misunderstanding. As they rode into the outskirts of a small town in a vast valley surrounded by mountains, Sullivan's grumbling escalated into shouts that he had been abducted by a band of outlaws. People stared as Alan led his captive's horse to a large house with a wide covered porch.

Alan slapped his hat against his leg, sending up a cloud of dust. "Mr. Sullivan, I'm flattered, but I don't think that I make up a 'band.' And you may want to quiet down before I gag you. I'm hungry, dirty and thoroughly tired of your company. I can leave you here to discuss your recent activities or I can shoot you. I have no preference, but you might."

Drawn by Sullivan's calls for help, a fair-haired young man stepped out onto the porch. Alan dismounted and went to meet him. The man said, "You must be McTurk. Welcome; I'm glad you made it. I'm James Peller."

"Pleased to meet you. I have papers for you, and this is Sullivan. He was playing at being a surveyor down by Dos Rios. You may find him useful."

Alan pulled Sullivan down from the saddle. "I'd leave his hands tied," he said. "His manners leave much to be desired."

Alan cut the leather cord around his neck and handed the pouch to James. He swung up into the saddle and said, "If you'll excuse me, I'd like to find a stable, a meal and a bath. When I come back you can tell me what you want done with Sullivan."

James said, "My wife would never forgive me if I let you go to the hotel, and we can stable the horses here. Come inside and let Flo feed you. After that you can clean up and get some rest. I'll handle Sullivan."

James led Alan up the steps to the porch. A woman appeared at the door.

"Mr. McTurk, I'm delighted you're here! Come through to the kitchen; it's cozier. Coffee?" Without waiting for an answer, she put a steaming mug in front of him. "Here's cream and sugar. I'll have a plate for you in half a second. Your room is ready, and you can bathe if you wish, and I'll call the barber in if you like, but I think that can wait until tomorrow, don't you? I expect you'd rather rest."

"I'll leave you in my wife's capable hands," James said. Alan remembered Nattie's note. He gave it to Flo, who tucked it in her waistband while she prepared his food.

When she was sure he had everything he wanted, Flo sat down across from Alan and opened the note.

She gave him a stern look and said, "I'll tend to your head when you've finished eating." She paused. "No protest? You're a better patient than Nat describes."

"Your sister told me not to bother arguing with you."

As Flo read the note her forehead creased the same way Nattie's did when deep in thought. She was taller, with light-brown hair and hazel eyes, but there was a marked resemblance to her sister.

Flo glanced up. "Nat wrote this very carefully to leave out as much information as possible. Tomorrow you must tell me all that she omitted."

She piled his plate high again, ignoring his protests. While he ate she heated water and gathered jars, strainers, and cloths.

"It sounds like Nat's treatment was effective so we'll continue it, along with something later to help you sleep," Flo told him.

Alan luxuriated in a hot bath, and obediently drank Flo's not-unpleasant concoction before he went to bed. He was surprised to find the sun well up by the time he woke. He dressed quickly and went downstairs where a plump young woman was sweeping the entryway.

"Good morning," said Alan.

"Good morning," she replied. "Let me get you a cup of coffee—unless you'd prefer tea?—and I'll tell Mrs. Peller you're up. Miss Pardee will have your breakfast ready in a moment."

"Coffee's fine, thank you."

She settled him at the dining room table and brought him a steaming cup. A few minutes later Flo appeared, carrying a broad-brimmed straw hat and a garden basket.

"I see Louise has taken care of you. You look *much* better! How do you feel? How's your head?" she asked.

"I feel quite well, thank you," Alan replied. "I must have slept the clock around."

"You were long overdue for a good rest," Flo told him. "And now you need breakfast."

"Do I have time to check on my horse first?"

"Of course. Jeremy, our stableman, is enchanted with her. Oh, and Sullivan is being escorted north to tell his story to interested parties. James hopes you don't mind."

"Not in the least. I'm delighted to be rid of him."

"James said he blustered and blathered until they threatened to return him to you. Then he became a fount of information."

Alan laughed as he stepped outside, cup in hand.

"Breakfast in ten minutes," Flo called after him.

Alan found a stocky man with an impressive black beard brushing Bella and crooning soft endearments. Her coat shone, her hooves were polished, and her mane and tail were elaborately braided. Alan raised an eyebrow.

"Sorry, sir," Jeremy told Alan in a Yorkshire accent without a trace of repentance. "She takes me back to my old days, this one."

"Well, her sire's from England," Alan said. "Her dam was running wild in New Mexico territory. I'd guess she's a descendant of the Spanish Barb. She's fast, tough, smart—"

Flo called from the back porch. "Mr. McTurk, come and eat before it gets cold."

Flo looked on approvingly while Alan demolished heaps of bacon, eggs, and biscuits. When he assured her he couldn't eat another bite she removed his plate and said, "Now let me see that lump on your head."

She gently pressed and prodded, then nodded in satisfaction. "The cut has healed nicely and there's almost no swelling. Is it still painful?"

"Not really. A bit tender to the touch, that's all."

"Well, I think we should continue the poultice for a day or so, and Nat insisted that you see a doctor so I won't go against her orders. Besides, Doc Knowles always wants to know the local news so it will please him to meet you."

"I'm flattered to be considered newsworthy."

Flo said, "Don't let it go to your head. Last month's big excitement was that the new grocer's dog had a litter of nine puppies."

"I certainly couldn't compete with that," said Alan.

"I'll ask Doc Knowles to call this afternoon. Would you prefer to have the barber in, or go to the shop? "

"I'll go out. I'd like to stretch my legs."

Alan thanked her for breakfast and stepped onto the porch. A small boy waited on the steps.

"I am to take you wherever you wish to go," he said.

"I'd appreciate that," said Alan. "What is your name?"

"Eduardo. Also Lalo. I used to be called Lalito when I was young, but now I allow only Señora Peller to call me so. My sister Catalina and I help the Pellers."

"Indeed. And what do you do?"

"Oh, all kinds of things," the boy shrugged. "I am very busy always. Señora Peller says she doesn't know how she would manage without me."

"Well, Eduardo-also-Lalo, I believe your first job is to find me a barber."

Lalo was an informative tour guide, giving a running commentary on every house and store they passed. When they reached the barbershop Alan asked, "Do you have other duties or will you wait?"

"I will wait. Perhaps you will want to go somewhere else afterwards."

While Alan relaxed with a hot towel on his face, he heard the drumming of heels against chair legs.

"Are those boots attached to a boy?" he asked.

"They are," answered the barber. "Is he yours?"

"No, he's just on loan. Ask him if he'd like a haircut, would you? Or a shave, if he feels the need."

Soon Lalo was installed in the next chair. The barber patiently answered his endless questions as his hair was trimmed, pomaded, and slicked down. Alan studied Lalo's small, serious reflection.

"I think we're both presentable," he said. "Now, I've heard that it's possible to find ice cream in this town. Shall we go see if that's true? Or would your parents not want you to spoil your appetite?"

Lalo said, "No parents, only my sister. She would want me to have ice cream, I think."

"Then it's settled."

They strolled to the drugstore and ordered ice cream; chocolate for Lalo and peach for Alan. Then Lalo led Alan to Peller's Mercantile. They found James and an older woman in earnest discussion over a set of dishes. James called to Alan.

"Ah, Mr. McTurk! Can you settle a question for us? Isn't there a crack in this teacup? Right there, d'you see?"

Alan squinted at the cup. He saw nothing, but thought it best to agree.

James exclaimed, "There, Mrs. Meyerson! The cup is damaged so I must reduce the price of the set. I think half-price would be fair, if you'd care to take it off my hands..."

"You know I would," the woman replied. She gently traced the floral design edging a plate. "I've been admiring these dishes since you got them in. You are far too generous, Mr. Peller."

James arranged to have the dishes delivered. Lalo perched on a tall stool behind the notions counter and sorted buttons while James showed Alan around the store.

"Was there really a crack in that teacup?" Alan asked.

"Perhaps not. But she wouldn't accept the lower price any other way. I'd give that woman anything in the store if she'd take it. She nursed my wife tirelessly last year. I'm convinced she and Flo's aunt saved her life."

"Nattie told me about her Tía Constancia. She sounds like a remarkable woman."

"She is that. Now shall we collect your little shadow and go home for dinner?"

As they strolled along the plank sidewalk, James proudly pointed out new businesses, the school, the firehouse, the newspaper office—"I tell you, Mr. McTurk, this town has grown beyond all recognition. Not long ago it was little more than a scattering of adobe huts, every other one a saloon or worse, but now—why, this could be the state capital someday. It's exciting to see."

Alan asked, "More exciting than managing the family stores in San Francisco?"

"Yes, indeed. There was a comfortable existence all planned out for me, but I'd rather be here."

"My story is much the same. What does your family think of you abandoning civilization?"

James said, "My father is supportive. Sometimes I think he's a bit envious. My mother feels that I have fallen far below my station. And your family?"

"My mother misses me but wants me to be happy. My father wants all his chicks to stay safely in the nest. Bad enough that I left, but my sister Edith and her husband followed me. Fortunately my youngest sister shows no desire to roam."

"My sister Margaret can't bear the wilderness, as she calls it," said James. "But Elizabeth comes to visit; she and Flo were friends at school. That's how my wife and I met."

Flo was shelling peas on the front porch when they arrived at the house. With her was a dark-haired, bespectacled young woman.

Flo said, "Catalina, I don't think you've met Mr. McTurk. Alan, this is Catalina Pérez. She is Lalo's sister and my dear friend." The women admired Lalo's haircut and heard Alan's confession of mid-morning ice cream.

"I'm sure that won't prevent Lalito from eating his dinner, will it, *mijo*?" asked Flo.

The child shook his head vigorously.

"Now go wash up, all of you," said Flo. As she led them inside James slipped an arm around her waist. Alan heard him ask, "How are you feeling? Are you taking it easy?"

She smiled at her husband. "I feel fine, truly. The most strenuous work I've done is gather eggs."

"Promise me you'll lie down this afternoon," said James.

Flo put her hand over his. "I promise."

Chapter 22

Nattie hovered over Tía's shoulder as she sorted the mail. As soon as she saw her sister's handwriting she plucked the thick envelope from Tía's hand and was out the door. Sometimes Flo's letters were deceptively plump, stuffed full of recipes or fabric samples or fashion illustrations, but this envelope crackled with the promise of numerous sheets of paper. She bridled Cisco and galloped out to read undisturbed. She tore open the envelope and skimmed the pages of Flo's tidy script until she saw the name she hoped for.

A Mr. McTurk, with whom you are recently acquainted, arrived with the sham surveyor Sullivan. Of course we insisted that he stay with us. He seemed exhausted and I could see his head pained him although he denied it. He was much better after a meal and a good night's sleep. His head wound is healing well and bothers him very little, or so he says. He spoke highly of your care. In fact, every conversation seemed somehow to turn to you. What do you know of him? I've tried to pump James for information, but he's been busy sending telegrams and having meetings. I wish the railroad would make a decision so I can have my husband back. Of course, then he'll be consumed by another issue—he's determined to civilize the Territory into statehood.

Mr. McTurk made quite an impression. Lalito wanted to accompany him everywhere so sometimes they walked together, and sometimes McT pulled him in his little wagon, and sometimes they rode Bella, who is now braided up like an English steeplechaser. They made a fetching picture. A number of ladies made excuses to visit while he was with us. He flirted outrageously with—"

The page ended. Nattie riffled through the pages searching for the rest of the sentence. Finally she saw *"old Señora Martínez. This was a great disappointment to Annabelle Morgan, who was doing her best to fascinate him. She has adopted the most horrifying tittering laugh—am I awful for wishing her to be unhappy, just until she gives it up?"*

Nattie had no objection to wishing misfortune upon Anabelle Morgan.

McT has left us now. The committee called him north on more of this endless railroad business. He asked me to assure you that most of his journey will be a restful train ride. Lalito was desolate to see him go, but McT promised to come back. He gave Lalo a pocket watch to help manage his busy schedule. Be sure to ask the time when next you see him.

I am charged to tell you that McT plans to see Papa as soon as he can. I am also to relay enough thanks and admiration to fill another letter, so consider it said.

Truly, dear, you were incredibly brave and strong and I'm very proud of you, although horrified at the risks you took. McT is quite correct to think so highly of you.

I hope you're gratified by such a long letter. As for me, I'm quite worn out so will close now. Give my love to everyone. I miss you all, so very much."

Nattie slid off Chico's back and stretched out in the shade of a tree. Alan thought highly of her. What did that mean, exactly?

Conversations turned to her…That was only natural, considering that she was a common acquaintance.

She sat up abruptly. Were her ribbons and chocolates like Lalo's pocket watch, gifts to soothe a child unhappy to be left behind? She closed her eyes and remembered the moment when Alan rode back to her and promised to return. Had she read too much into it? No, she decided. She had looked into his eyes, heard his voice.

She turned Flo's letter back to the beginning. She memorized the passages concerning Alan, then lost herself in a daydream. The Dress swirled around her as she paused at the door of a room filled with people. Alan came swiftly to her, leaving Annabelle Morgan in mid-titter, and took her hand...

The sound of fast hoofbeats jarred her back to reality.

Robby pulled his horse to a halt and said "Telegram—Flo—It's bad."

Chapter 23

Nattie would remember that day and night in flashes, like pictures glimpsed while flipping through a book. There was a blur of activity, and then she was mounted on a tough little mustang.

Tía kissed her and whispered "*Vaya con Dios. And remember you'll be no help to your sister if you break your neck.*"

Papí said, "I'd tell you to go carefully if I thought it'd be any use. We'll follow as close as we can."

Then she and Robby were off. The horses soon settled into an easy gallop that ate up the miles. They rode on as the sun set and the moon rose, giving enough light to set the road apart from the deeper darkness around it. Nattie prayed in rhythm with the hoofbeats; *Dios te salve, Maria. Llena eres de gracia, El Señor es contigo…*An owl swooped low and flew alongside her for a few silent beats of its wings. *Bendita tú eres entre todas las mujeres, y bendito es el fruto de tu vientre…*

They changed horses at West Camp, and again at the Madero ranch. People offered food but Nattie couldn't eat. Then she was on a gangly roan and Robby rode a gray, ghostly in the moonlight. The sky lightened in front of them and a coyote, on its way home from the night's hunt, watched them pass. They made way as the east-bound stage flashed past them, with pale blurs of faces at the windows. They rode on. *Santa María, Madre de Dios, ruega por nosotros pecadores, ahora y en la hora de nuestra muerte…*

Nattie jerked awake from a half-sleep, startled to find the sun was up and buildings were visible in the valley below. Soon they were riding past the lumberyard and Trujillo's freight company and on through the quiet morning streets. Nattie felt limp with relief as the house came in sight. There was no black bunting, no sign of death. Jeremy appeared as they hitched the sweating horses. Nattie slid out of the saddle and held the saddlehorn until her legs stopped trembling. Mrs. Meyerson opened the door and hurried to greet them.

"Good news, good news! Your sister's expected to recover. The doctor says the worst is over. She's asleep now, but you can see her as soon as she wakes."

She looked past them.

"It's just us for now," Nattie told her. "The others are coming by carriage. They'll be here tomorrow."

Mrs. Meyerson said, "You must be exhausted. Sit down and I'll fix you a plate. I think everyone in town has brought food."

"I'd like to wash first. I want to be ready to see Flo." Nattie looked down at her shirt and trousers. "I'll need to borrow clean clothes until mine get here."

"I'll borrow some of James' duds," said Robby. "These picked up a pound of dust on the road."

While Nattie bathed, Mrs. Meyerson laid out some of Flo's clothes for her. The shirt fit well enough once she rolled up the sleeves, but the skirt dragged on the floor. There was no need to pull on her boots, Nattie decided, and padded on bare feet to the kitchen. Mrs. Meyerson put a heaping plate before her.

"My word, it's a pleasure to feed people with healthy appetites. I wish we could find something to tempt Flo. She does try, but she's just too exhausted to eat, poor thing. It'll do her a world of good to see you. Maybe you can persuade her to take some nourishment." She fanned herself with her apron. "This heat isn't helping. But clouds are building so there may be a break in the weather soon."

"How is she? Really?" Nattie's eyes searched the older woman's face.

Mrs. Meyerson reached across the table and patted Nattie's hand. "She's recovering, but she lost a lot of blood and she's very weak and tired. And she's sad, of course, and afraid she'll never have children."

"How is James?"

"Frantic with worry. I don't think he's slept more than five minutes at a stretch. He's hardly left her side."

"And Lalo? How is he?"

Mrs. Meyerson sighed. "Poor little mite. He just sits quiet in the hall, drawing pictures to slip under her door. The Soames family—they're new, I don't think you know them—have offered to keep him for a bit. Their dog had pups and young Lydia promised him the pick of the litter. She is very good with him."

She stretched. "I sent Catalina to have a lie-down. Now that you're here perhaps I could go home for a while."

Robby appeared with wet hair slicked back. Mrs. Meyerson said, "I'll go tell James you're here. He needs rest; try to convince him to lie down. Then come up and see your sister." She hesitated. "I should tell you that she looks poorly. Very poorly."

A few moments later James thudded down the stairs and dropped heavily into a chair. Robby awkwardly patted his shoulder and Nattie hugged him. She fixed him a plate and a glass of buttermilk. "No coffee," she told him. "You're going to get some sleep. We'll stay with Flo, and we promise to wake you if there's any change."

James tried to smile. "You're as bossy as your sister."

Robby said, "She's right, *hermano*. You'd better get the roses back in your cheeks or she'll dose you with potions."

"Perhaps you're right. Flo's resting easy now so I'll try to do the same. But you promise—"

"—to wake you if there's any change. Yes." Nattie put her hand over his. "She'll be all right. She comes from tough stock, you know." She picked up his plate and glass. "Now off to bed with you. And

Robby, you should get some rest now, too. I'll take the first watch."

Nattie crept into Flo's shaded room and settled into a chair by the bed. Despite Mrs. Meyerson's warning, she was shocked to see Flo's face as colorless as marble. Her features were gaunt, and the hand resting on her chest looked frail and lifeless. Nattie watched the slow rise and fall of breath, willing it to continue. When Robby slipped in and whispered, "I'll keep watch. You rest now," Nattie shook her head, but soon her eyes closed and she slept.

Her sister's eyes were on her when she woke. Flo lifted her hand and Nattie rushed to take it. She kissed it and held it to her cheek. The long, pale fingers felt cold against her skin.

"You rode?" Flo's voice was a whisper.

"Robby and I did."

"I knew you would." Flo closed her eyes and Nattie held her hand while people came and went and the room darkened. Catalina lit the lamp on the bureau and opened the window to the cooling air. Lightning flickered across the mountains. The curtains snapped in the wind and thunder rattled the glass. Nattie moved to close the window but Flo's small voice stopped her.

"Leave it open. I want to see the storm."

"All right. Will you try to eat a little?" Nattie slipped her arm around her sister and arranged pillows behind her. "Mrs. Meyerson made a lovely pudding, and Doc Knowles left something for you to take, and I made one of Tía's tisanes…"

Flo smiled. "Will it do any good to protest?"

"Not a bit." Nattie touched her lips to Flo's forehead. "No fever. Are you in pain?"

"Not really. I just feel a bit…floaty."

"From blood loss and the doctor's concoctions, no doubt. He wants you to rest."

"I will. In a little while." She sighed. "How is James? I know I've worried him. And Lalito?"

The storm filled the room with light and sound and a hard rain began to fall.

"Everyone's fine. Lalo has a puppy. Now drink this."

Flo said, "If I eat, and take my medicine, will you tell me about your adventure with Mr. McTurk? Then I'll rest, I promise."

"All right. But you already know what happened."

"I want details. Men don't tell stories properly."

Flo obediently ate and drank until Nattie was satisfied, then patted the bed.

"Come tell me all about it."

Nattie rested her head next to her sister's and spoke softly as the storm subsided. Flo's eyes closed. When the rain stopped and thunder was just a muttering in the distance, Nattie closed her eyes too, and slept until James came in.

Chapter 24

Nattie quietly closed the door behind her and sank down on the top stair. She craved sleep, but was reluctant to leave in case James needed help. Only five minutes, she promised herself. Five minutes, and then she'd go to bed. She leaned against the wall and closed her eyes. When she opened them, Alan stood before her. It seemed right and natural that he should be there.

"How is she?"

"The doctor says she'll pull through. But she's terribly weak, and there's the risk of infection..."

Alan sat on the step below Nattie. He wanted to gather her into his arms and hold her.

"How can I help?" he asked.

Nattie longed to rest her head on his shoulder.

"She needs to eat. Ice cream might tempt her. Perhaps you could get some in the morning?"

Alan stood up. "I'll get it now. What flavor?"

"Vanilla, I suppose. But—the drugstore's closed. You need to wait—"

"Now is better. Anything else?"

"No, but—you understand, the store is *closed*."

Alan grinned. "Right. A minor impediment. I'll be back before you know it."

He ran lightly down the stairs and disappeared. Nattie closed her eyes and wondered if she had dreamt him.

When she opened her eyes again, Alan sat next to her, holding a parcel.

"Here you go. Vanilla for Flo, chocolate for you and Lalo, and some sort of fruit concoction for whoever wants it."

"How did you get this? You didn't break in, did you?"

"No need. I simply persuaded the druggist to open his store. He was happy to help."

Nattie shook her head. "Knowing Mr. Metzen, I doubt it." She stood. "Let's take your ill-gotten loot to the kitchen."

Alan objected, "It isn't loot if you pay for it."

Nattie filled two bowls and took them upstairs. She asked James, "How long has it been since you ate?"

Flo spoke. "He hasn't done anything but watch over me. He needs a caretaker himself."

"Well, tomorrow you'll be smothered in caretakers. But for now I'm in charge and I want you both to eat," said Nattie.

"Ice cream! Where did this come from?" James offered Flo a spoonful.

"From the goodness of Mr. Metzen's heart, according to Mr. McTurk."

Flo's face brightened. "Alan is back? Oh, good! Of course he must stay with us. We can put him in the front bedroom."

"I'll get him settled in. Unless he spends the night in jail for theft."

Nattie took the empty bowls downstairs and found Alan dozing in an armchair. His eyes opened as she settled on the ottoman in front of him.

"Thank you," she said quietly. "Flo ate enough to even satisfy James."

"I'm glad to hear it. What else do you need?"

"Nothing at the moment, besides sleep. And chocolate ice cream."

Alan opted for the fruit concoction. They ate in silence at the kitchen table until Nattie asked, "Where did you come from?"

"Connecticut," said Alan.

"Ha. No, I mean—how did you come to be here? Now?"

"Oh. Well, I was still in Prescott, bogged down in this infernal railroad business. James was supposed to join the fun but word came that Flo was ill, so I came back to see if I could be of use."

"You must have ridden hard."

"Same as you and your brother, I expect."

"Yep. I'll be sore tomorrow." Nattie stretched. "Flo and James insist that you stay here. I'm about to wake Robby so you should get some sleep now."

Alan said, "I won't argue. Promise to wake me if I'm needed."

"I will."

"And what about you? Will you be able to put worry aside and sleep?"

Nattie covered a yawn. "I'm not entirely sure that I'm awake now."

Robby stumbled in, hitching a suspender over his shoulder. He nodded to Alan.

"McTurk, isn't it?"

Alan stood and offered his hand.

"It is. Good to meet you."

Nattie poured coffee for Robby while he perused the food that covered every surface. He cut a great slab of pie and dropped into a chair.

"Alright, I'm up. Go get some rest, Nat. You look terrible."

"I don't doubt it," she replied, smoothing loose strands of hair from her face.

Nattie showed Alan to his room. "Good night, then," she said.

"Good night. And—you don't look terrible. You could never look terrible."

He was rewarded with a quick smile, then she was gone. He intended to spend a little time thinking about that smile, but sleep overcame him as soon as he stretched out atop the bed.

Nattie dropped onto her bed and pulled a quilt over her. She intended to enjoy Alan's parting comment for a while, but she fell asleep as soon as she closed her eyes.

She woke to bright sunlight and a breeze stirring the curtains. She re-braided her hair, splashed water on her face, and judged her reflection to be not quite terrible. That would have to do.

She found Miss Pardee busy in the kitchen. The cook was a lanky woman with gray hair neatly tucked up.

"Sit down, sit down," she said. "I'll fix you a plate. The doctor has come and gone, pleased with our girl's progress. James is resting, under protest. Robby rode out to meet your family and give them the good news, and Mr. McTurk and Catalina have gone to collect Lalo and his new puppy, which is to be kept in the stable but you know that Lalo will smuggle it into the house at every opportunity."

"Or he'll be sneaking out to sleep in the stable," said Nattie.

"Well, the diversion will do him good. He's terrified that he'll lose Flo, same as his parents. They sickened and died within a day of each other, poor souls."

Miss Pardee put another biscuit on Nattie's plate and said, "When you see Lalo, be sure to ask him the time. He's so proud of that pocket watch Mr. McTurk gave him, I think it spends more time out of his pocket than in."

"I hope Mr. McTurk slept well."

"Oh yes, he's fresh as a daisy this morning. Fresher, perhaps. He praised my cooking to the skies—said I was a culinary goddess, and a thing of beauty and a joy forever, among other things. Quoting poetry to me, the cheeky devil." Miss Pardee did her best to sound disapproving.

Nattie laughed. "You know it's all true. That's why we adore you so."

She brought her dishes to the sink, giving Miss Pardee a hug in passing. Through the window she saw Lalo and a morsel of brown fur chasing each other around Alan, Catalina, and a girl she guessed to be Lydia Soames. She looked down at her ill-fitting clothes and sighed.

"I look like an orphan," she said.

"No one expects you to look like you just stepped out of a bandbox," Miss Pardee reassured her.

Nattie smoothed her hair in front of the entryway mirror, sighed again, and stepped out to the back porch. Lalo ran to meet her, the puppy at his heels. She caught him up and kissed him on both cheeks.

"*Miro*, Miss Nat! I have a dog!"

"That little bit of a thing is a dog?" she asked. "I thought it was some fluff you found in your pocket."

She sat on the step with Lalo on her lap and scooped up the dog.

"He's little because he's a puppy. But he'll grow to be very big," Lalo informed her.

"If he grows into those paws he'll be huge. Say, Lalo, do you happen to know the time?" she asked.

He proudly produced his pocket watch and solemnly told her it was 8:32. Then he held the watch to her ear so she could hear it tick. The puppy wriggled up to lick her other ear.

Lydia came and sat next to them. Catalina gave her little brother a kiss on the head as she passed by to go indoors. Nattie caught her hand.

"Cata, you can't have had much sleep. Perhaps you could rest for a bit."

"Perhaps I will. It's so good to have you here." Her eyes filled. "I was so afraid—"

Nattie shifted the boy and dog to Lydia's lap and jumped up to hug Catalina. Her eyes filled, too. She stepped back and gently shook Catalina's shoulders.

"Look at us, getting all weepy when the crisis is past. What would Flo say? And look, we've worried Lalo." The boy's chin was quivering.

"Lalo, I do think you picked the best puppy of the litter. There are nine," Lydia told Nattie. "And this one is the smartest and bravest."

"He is!" agreed Lalo as he raced away, the puppy waddling after him. "And the fastest, too!"

Catalina laughed and went inside.

Nattie turned to Lydia. "I know you've been a great help. Thank you for all you've done."

Lydia smiled. "I'd do anything for your sister. She has always been so thoughtful. She visits my mother and brings books to her…"

"Is your mother ill?" asked Nattie.

"Oh no. She just doesn't go out much. She's more comfortable at home."

"I see," said Nattie, although she didn't.

"Not everyone is as kind to her as Mrs. Peller." Lydia's eyes were fixed on her hands in her lap. "Because of what happened to her, you know."

"I'm afraid I don't understand."

"You must have heard the story. Everyone has. Mother and her sister were captured by a band of renegade Yavapai. Her sister was injured when they were taken, and she died soon after. I'm named for her. Mother escaped by throwing herself down a rocky outcrop covered with cactus. Years later, cactus thorns still worked their way to the surface and Papa would pull them out."

"That was your mother? What an extraordinary woman! Who could find fault with her?"

"People can find fault with just about anything, I think. She and my father were betrothed when she was taken, and they married as soon as she recovered. I was born a year later, but still people said— well, they said a lot of things."

"People are idiots," stated Nattie firmly. Lydia giggled. Nattie added, "Do you know, before Flo and James were married, his mother said my family was a bunch of half-breed savages. I'm not supposed to know that, of course."

"No! Did she really?"

"Oh yes. She objected to James courting Flo because our mother was Mexican, and she was convinced that we lived in an adobe hut in the wilds of the borderlands. When James' family came to visit, the old harridan was sure they'd be attacked by *bandidos*. So of course Robby and Ignacio and I went whooping out to greet their carriage. We raced around it until she told her husband to give us money to make us go away. He winked and tossed us each a dollar piece. When we officially met them later, all prim and proper, Mrs. Peller was still talking about how they'd been set upon by savages and she'd feared for her life. She didn't even recognize us until we gave back the money. James and his father thought it was a fine joke, but Flo wasn't pleased."

A shout and laughter drew their attention. Alan was on the ground with Lalo on his chest and the puppy licking his chin. "Help," he called. "I'm outnumbered!"

The girls ran to his aid. Lydia picked up the dog and Nattie took Lalo's hands and swung him in a circle. James stepped out on the porch and pointed to a window overhead where Flo smiled and waved.

"She's out of bed?" asked Nattie.

"No, she's still too weak. I moved the bed by the window so she could see the fun."

James took Lalo and held him high while Flo blew kisses.

"Is *Señora* Flo well now? Can I take her my puppy?"

"Not quite yet, but soon."

Lydia said, "Look, your puppy is sleepy. Let's make him a nice bed in the stable."

James went inside. Alan dusted himself and sat on the porch swing, legs stretched out. Nattie joined him. They rocked in silence for a few minutes. Nattie's skirt fluttered, revealing her bare feet.

"No shoes?" asked Alan.

"Only my boots." She asked, "Mr. Metzen isn't filing charges?"

"No charges to file. I just explained what I needed and he was most cooperative."

"Were you holding a gun on him? Or did you just threaten?"

Alan said, "Nothing of the sort. Metzen seems to be a somewhat excitable chap, though. He may have heard a threat where none was expressed."

Nattie said, "Maybe he'll get over it if we buy a lot of ice cream."

"A sensible plan," agreed Alan.

Lydia and Lalo appeared, arguing.

"Lalo insists that he needs to take a blanket off his bed for the puppy. I told him perhaps we could find material to make him a bed." Unlike Nattie, Lydia had benefited from her sewing lessons.

Alan jumped up. "We must go shopping. Lalo, can you recommend a store?"

"Peller's. Peller's is best," the boy informed him.

"I wonder if it's open now. Lalo, what time is it?"

It was an hour before the little procession left the house. Lydia, who was close to Nattie's size, ran home to fetch clothes for her to borrow. Lalo padded his little wagon with a blanket ("From his bed," sighed Cata) and climbed in with his puppy. Finally all was ready and they set off with Alan pulling the wagon.

When they passed the drug store, Mr. Metzen was sweeping the walk in front. He quickly went inside when he saw them. There were gashes and nicks in the door and a pile of swept-up splinters.

"Looks like someone was playing mumblety-peg," said Nattie. "We are going to have to buy a *lot* of ice cream."

At Peller's, Lalo decided on a brightly-colored striped ticking. He hopped from one foot to the other as the package was wrapped, and insisted on carrying it himself. After he dropped it several times, Nattie suggested that the puppy would like company and deposited Lalo and the package in the wagon.

Alan asked, "Should we stop in for ice cream? Or is it too soon to start making amends?"

"Definitely too soon," said Nattie. "I think it would be best if you stay away from Mr. Metzen. Lydia and I will take charge of placating him. Perhaps we can organize an ice cream social when Flo is feeling better." And that will show the old biddies in this town who Lydia's friends are, Nattie thought with satisfaction.

"And what can I do to help?" asked Alan.

"You can charm the old bid—ladies who attend."

"That sounds like no fun at all," he protested.

"Consider it penance for your game of mumblety-peg."

Lydia's eyes were wide.

"I'm afraid you have fallen in with bad company," Alan told her. "Which reminds me, this young gent and I look like ruffians. I think we need a shave. What say you, Lalo? We can't get ice cream this time but—" With a flourish, he produced two small paper bags of chocolates. He gave one to Lydia and the other to Lalo. "You ladies can share these, and Lalo will save some of his for his sister."

"None for you?" asked Lydia.

"None for me; I'm doing penance."

Alan handed the parcels to Nattie, bowed, and paced solemnly away, pulling Lalo and puppy in the wagon.

"Mr. McTurk is very good with Lalo," said Lydia.

"He is, isn't he?" agreed Nattie. She was happy to discuss him on the walk home.

After a short visit with Flo, Lydia and Nattie helped Cata with a final check of the bedrooms. Nattie flopped on a bed and rested her chin in her hand. "There, that takes care of everyone. I can't wait for them to be here."

Lydia glanced at the clock. "Look at the time! Mama will be wondering what happened to me, and I need to start work on the dog bed. Lalo won't give me a minute's peace until it's done. Catalina, would you like him to stay with us tonight?"

"That might be best. But don't let him sleep with that dog!"

Lydia laughed. "I'll try, but Mama and Papa love to spoil him. I'll bring him home tomorrow, along with the dog, and the new bed that will go unused if Lalo has his way."

"You're probably right," agreed Cata. "The Pellers love to spoil him, too. I'm sure the puppy will be with him every moment."

The girls said their farewells. Nattie peeked into Flo's room and found her sister talking quietly with Mrs. Meyerson.

The older woman stood. "Well, my dears, since all is calm I'll take myself home. Send word if you need me, and tell your Aunt Constancia I'll stop in soon. It's been too long since I've seen her." She kissed them both and said goodbye.

"You look *much* better," Nattie told her sister.

"I feel better; well enough to want out of this bed. I'm tired of everyone worrying about me." She stared out the window. "Nat, do you think I'll ever have a baby?"

"Of course you will. You were meant to be a mother."

"That's what Mrs. Meyerson says, but this is the second time..."

Nattie took her hand. "Remember Señora Garza? She was sure she'd never be blessed with children, but last year she had her"— Nattie counted on her fingers—"fourth. No, fifth." She smoothed the blankets. "What does James say?"

"He wants me to go to San Francisco so I can be under a specialist's care."

"Ugh. Within range of his mother? Maybe you could go to the other coast. Or Europe."

"I'll suggest that to James," said Flo. Meanwhile, I'm so glad you're here to distract me. Tell me, what have you been doing all morning?"

Nattie recounted the events of the day. Flo laughed when she described the splintered drugstore door.

"James and Alan have already arranged to replace it. Old Metzen told James that Alan hammered on the door until he came down from his rooms over the store. He told Alan he wouldn't open until morning. Alan said he'd wait, and started whistling and chucking his knife into the door, just to pass the time, of course. Mr. Metzen said he couldn't sleep for the noise, and whenever he peeked out the window Alan would just tip his hat and smile. Before long Metzen decided to end the siege and sold him the ice cream he wanted. Alan insisted on paying a great deal more than required, thanked him profusely, and left. James vouched for Alan, but Metzen insists he's a madman."

Nattie said, "I'm sure there are many who would agree."

"And what about you? What do you think of Alan McTurk? James says he had quite the reputation as a dashing, daring ranger. And Cata thinks he's handsome. Do you think he's handsome?"

"Well, I suppose, perhaps…"

"Nat, you're blushing! All right, I won't tease. I'll leave that to Robby and Ignacio. So…what do you think of Lydia Soames?"

"I like her. She seems level-headed. Easy to talk to. What's her mother like?"

"Much the same. Unassuming, intelligent, a voracious reader. Does lovely needlework. She tends to be wary, with good reason; some people treat her like a sideshow exhibit, and quiz her about her ordeal. She deserves better."

"She deserves a statue." Nattie paused. "I want to invite Lydia and her mother to visit the ranch."

"To advance the friendship, or to poke the local harpies in the eye?"

"Mostly the former, but I wouldn't mind giving the old biddies something to cluck about."

"Ah, Nat," said Flo. "Always leaping to the defense of the downtrodden. Remember when we saw old Mr. Smythe whipping his mule up the hill? You cussed him up one side and down the other and said you'd lay him out cold. You weren't much bigger than the whip handle, but he stopped."

"Probably from astonishment."

"Well, his mouth *was* hanging open, but that was usual for him."

There was a soft knock on the door and Cata entered, carrying a tray with three mugs. "I made *champurrado*."

"Ooh, lovely!" Flo exclaimed. "Yours is as good as Tía's, but don't tell her I said so." She sipped the rich chocolate drink. "Has everyone been fed?"

"Miss Pardee put out a spread that would feed an army," Nattie told her. "Trust me, no one's going hungry."

"When do you expect your family to arrive?" asked Cata.

"Within the hour," Nattie told her.

Flo said, "James went to check on the store but he'll be back soon. Where has everyone else gone off to? It's awfully quiet."

"Probably because Lalo went home with Lydia," Cata said. "I think Mr. McTurk is out discussing horses with Jeremy. Oh, he asked me to tell you he took a room at the hotel since we have more family arriving."

"That was very thoughtful, but unnecessary. Nat, go tell him he must join us for supper tonight."

Nattie walked slowly through the house and sat on the porch swing to gather her thoughts, but they scattered like sparrows. What would her family think of Alan? What would he think of them? What would Tía bring her to wear? She briefly indulged in her favorite fantasy of sweeping down the stairs in The Dress, Alan taking her hand… She laughed at herself and jumped off the swing. Tía would bring sensible clothes, but at least they'd fit.

Nattie could hear conversation as she neared the stable. Three voices; James must be back. The interior was cool and dim. Nattie greeted each stall's resident as she passed; the mounts that she and Robby had ridden, a carriage horse, Lalo's gentle old pony, and Dinah, a temperamental buckskin. The men were gathered around Bella at the far end of the passageway.

"Hallo, Jeremy. How are our borrowed horses doing?" asked Nattie.

"Well, you and your brother didn't quite ride them into the

ground, but near enough. They'll be fit to go home in a day or so."

"Good to hear." She pointed to an empty stall. "Where's Sinbad?"

"Your brother has him, and I hope he isn't racing him around the countryside."

"I doubt even Robby could get any speed out of that horse." She turned to Alan. "Mr. McTurk, Flo hopes you'll join us for supper tonight. And by hopes, I mean insists."

"I'll be happy to. It will give your father the chance to horsewhip me."

Nattie said, "We generally save the evening's entertainment until after dessert, so you'll get to eat first."

Alan gave Bella a last pat. "Don't spoil her too much," he told Jeremy. "She'll think she's too good to be a ranch horse."

James, Alan and Nattie walked out together.

"I want to see Flo before everyone arrives," said James. "Alan, supper's at six." The screen door to the kitchen slammed behind him.

Nattie and Alan sat on the porch swing. Alan glanced down.

"Still no shoes," he said.

"Still out of jail," said Nattie.

"Not a bad day, all round."

Nattie said, "I haven't thanked you for the ribbons and chocolates. And gloves."

"You haven't lost them?"

"Not yet." She didn't tell him they were safely tucked in a drawer, along with the candy box that now held her hair ribbons.

"Someday we need to exchange stories of what happened after we parted ways, but there isn't time now," said Alan. "Your family will be here soon so I will leave you to greet them. Goodbye for now."

He stood and kissed her hand, then disappeared around the corner of the house.

"Goodbye," Nattie said faintly. The warmth of his lips lingered on her hand as the swing slowed to a stop.

Chapter 25

The sound of an approaching carriage brought Nattie to her feet. She bolted through the house and threw herself into the confusion of greetings. James helped Tía from the carriage as Tomás stretched his long frame and Robby hitched the horses to the rail. Cata shepherded everyone inside where trays of sandwiches and cold drinks waited. James ran upstairs and reappeared with Flo in his arms.

"Clear the sofa," he said. "She insisted on coming down for a few minutes." Flo soon disappeared beneath an onslaught of affection. The men looked on as Flo, Nattie and Tía embraced.

"All three of them speaking at once in two languages and somehow they understand each other," said James.

"I think they read each others' minds," Tomás told him. "Speech is just a formality."

"Well, I hope they've said all they need to for now." James took his wife's hand. "Time for you to be back in bed, my dear."

Flo sighed. "All right. I promised I wouldn't argue."

As James carried her up the stairs, she looked back over his shoulder to give instructions about meals and linens and rooms.

"Stop fussing," Nattie told her. "You're only going upstairs, not off on an Arctic expedition. I'm sure we can manage."

"All right. But do remember to ask Louise to cut flowers for the table, and set a place for Mr. McTurk..." Her voice trailed away down the hall.

"Where is this McTurk feller, anyway?" asked Mr. Johnston.

Nattie said, "He took a room at the hotel today since the house would be full of family."

"Cleared out, did he? Maybe he cleared right out of town," said her father.

"His horse is in the stable here, so I doubt it," Nattie replied.

James came downstairs carrying his hat.

Mr. Johnston said, "Maybe we'll go check out this McTurk. We can escort him back for supper."

"I want to stop in at the store, but I could meet you at the hotel," said James.

Tomás asked, "Are you sure we can handle him, Nat? I hear this McTurk is a tough customer."

"Four against one? Pretty risky," Nattie answered. "Too bad Ignacio isn't here."

Robby said, "He's probably up the south windmill right now. It seized up and of course the cows would rather stand there and beller for water than go to the next one. Or he might be off chasing the Stocktons' goats. He said he'd give it a try on his own."

"Oh, good," said Nattie. She'd get a full report from Alethia.

After she helped Tía settle in, Nattie unpacked her own clothes. After some deliberation she put on a dark green skirt, a white shirt patterned with tiny violets, and amethyst earrings. As she finished unpacking she spotted soft beaded deerskin.

"My moccasins! Bless you, Tía!" She slipped them on and wiggled her toes. "There. I'm shod." She trotted downstairs and saw the front door close behind her father and brothers as they marched off to interrogate Alan.

Waiting was torture. She needed distraction, but Flo and Tía were resting. She found Louise preparing the dining room and tried to help, but after she knocked over a vase of flowers Louise gently steered her toward the kitchen. Miss Pardee and her niece Sally were preparing supper. They gave her a bib apron and a cake to decorate.

She focused intently on sprinkling colored sugar into swirls and curlicues.

"A little shaky, but not bad," said Miss Pardee.

Nattie heard male voices and her hand twitched, depositing a mound of green sugar on the cake. She ran to a front window and was relieved to see that the men were laughing as they approached. She considered making a dash for the kitchen but there wasn't time, so she licked sugar from her fingers and prepared to meet them.

Robby was the first to enter. "You look uncommonly domestic," he said as he dropped into a chair.

Nattie looked down. She had forgotten the apron. She tried to pull it off over her head but it was still tied in back.

"Robby, help me get this thing off!"

A familiar voice said, "Here, let me." She felt hands at her back, untying the bow. Then the apron was lifted up and off and she was looking into Alan's grey-blue eyes.

Mr. Johnston said, "Mr. McTurk, perhaps you'd show me that mare of yours."

Robby and Tomás left with them. Nattie turned to James as soon as her family was out of earshot.

"Well?" she asked. "How did it go?"

"Oh, fine, fine. You know your father has checked up on Alan already."

"Oh." Nattie let out a long breath. "Well, that's good. No horsewhipping."

"Nope. Possibly horse-thieving, if your father likes Alan's horse as much as I expect."

"I've told Alan to promise him a foal. That might stave him off." She started for the kitchen. "I suppose you'll all be talking horseflesh for a while. I'll bring out some beer."

Bella was the center of attention when Nattie brought a tray of cold bottles to the stable. Alan came forward and took the tray. He put it on a crate and pulled another one forward for her to sit.

Tomás said, "You should have Jeremy braid your hair, Nat. He does fine work."

"Thanks. I'll consider it," she replied. "Papa, I hope you haven't been badgering Mr. McTurk."

"Of course not. We're just discussing how I can get this bloodline into my stock."

"Mmm-hmm. I know how those discussions go. Stand your ground, Mr. McTurk."

Back in the kitchen, she surveyed her unfinished cake. She removed most of the stray sugar and added a flourish to cover the splotch. Miss Pardee judged it to be presentable, so Nattie gratefully left it and went out to the back porch. She sat on the swing, watching bees dart among the flowers. Alan appeared in the stable doorway, carrying the empty tray.

"Thought I'd return this," he said, holding up the tray.

"Thanks. I'll take it in."

He joined her on the swing. Nattie felt as if every cell in her body was aware of Alan's presence.

Alan glanced down at the hem of her skirt swirling around her feet.

"No bare toes today?"

"Nope. I'm embracing civilization." She put the tray on a small table. "Tell me, how was your information received by the rail committee? Was it worth a near-drowning?"

"I'd say so. The letters caused quite a stir. The scoundrels who were exposed by them suddenly remembered urgent business at home and disappeared. And Sullivan quite enjoyed being the center of attention. His story became more dramatic each time he told it."

"What will happen to him?"

"Nothing, I suppose. Play-acting at being a surveyor isn't illegal, or at least not worth prosecuting. Have you heard anything about the other two?" asked Alan.

"Langelaar didn't stay long in Dos Rios, and Edwin didn't get the hero's welcome he hoped for. His beloved Lucy was none too pleased to see him. She preferred the role of bereft lady-love."

"Understandable. Edwin doesn't have much to commend him," said Alan.

"How did you find them? Did Lucy tell you where they were?"

"She didn't know much. The town layabouts were more use. By the time I left I had three places to look. I got lucky and found them at the first one."

He told Nattie about his journey after he left her.

"So a few days after nearly drowning and having your head cracked open, you were hoisting boulders and dodging bullets," Nattie said.

"Rocks, not boulders. And Sullivan and company are terrible shots. I was safe as houses. And what about you? What happened when you went home?" asked Alan.

"You had all the excitement. I just had a cold."

"And did your aunt fuss, and make you take noxious potions?"

Nattie said, "Of course. That's why I'm well now. What about you? Have you recovered?"

"Yep. All the bumps and bruises have pretty much healed. No permanent damage."

Alan turned to look at Nattie. "How's your arm? Did it scar?"

"Only a little." She pushed up her sleeve. "See? It's barely noticeable. You can take credit. Tía said your bandaging was neatly done."

"I'm honored," Alan said. "And what about the lecturing?"

"There was surprisingly little. Between cleaning up after the storm and dealing with a horrid house guest, everyone was distracted."

Alan asked, "Who is this horrid being and why let it in?"

Nattie explained about Mrs. Beamish, "of Baltimore. That's extremely important. She mentions it frequently."

"Too bad all your neighbors can't be like Mrs. Stockton," said Alan. "I'd like to send her something, to thank her for the feast she provided. Perhaps you could advise me?"

"Of course. I want to get gifts for the girls, too. Would tomorrow suit?"

James stuck his head out the door. "May I join you two? Tía is entertaining Flo with all the home news so I'm not needed.' He pulled up a wicker chair. "Flo's eager to be up and around. The doctor says she can start coming downstairs tomorrow. Good thing, too. She's about to climb out the window, like Nat would."

"That room's no good. No vines or branches or pipes to shinny down," said Nattie.

James asked, "Have you reconnoitered every room in this house for escape routes?"

"Of course."

"I thought you're embracing civilization," said Alan.

"That doesn't mean I want to spend every waking moment with it," Nattie told him.

Robby appeared from the stable and sat on the steps. "I've had my fill of horse talk," he said.

Nattie asked him, "If you wanted to get out of your room here, how would you do it?"

"Tree. It's a bit of a reach, though."

"There. You see? I'm not the only one." Nattie primly smoothed her skirt.

James shook his head. "Barbarians, both of you."

Robby objected. "Not at all. We're tacticians. Sometimes it's best if people don't know exactly where you are."

"Or who you are," added Nattie. She turned to Alan. "When Robby and I were children we looked very much alike, so during our escapades we tried to dress the same. Papa had a tracker to keep an eye on us—"

"Of course we weren't supposed to know that," interjected Robby.

"—so we did our best to lead him a merry chase. And we figured if witnesses to our misdeeds weren't able to tell who did what, Papa wouldn't know who to punish."

"Did it work?" asked Alan.

"No. Papa just punished both of us. We always got into trouble together so I really can't fault his logic. He said it didn't matter who was the lookout and who grabbed handfuls of cookie dough from the kitchen, we were both upsetting Li Jun."

"Tell Alan about cutting your hair," said Robby.

"Inaccurate. I *didn't* cut my hair."

Alan said, "Very well. Tell me about not cutting your hair."

Nattie sighed. "I wanted short hair, to look more like Robby, but Papa absolutely forbade me to cut off my braids. Plural. So I found shears in the barn and prepared to cut off *one* braid. I thought he'd have to let me cut off the other one to match and if not, no harm done. But Tía was suspicious—"

"—because Nat gave in too easily—"

"—and she caught me before I'd hacked much off. I was confined to the house for quite a while after that."

"No wonder your father's hair is white," said Alan. "I'm surprised he didn't tear it out."

Tomás joined them. He said, "If anyone's interested, there's a lively discussion of 'horseshoes: past, present and future' in the stable."

No one moved.

He added, "James, Pa is trying to lure Jeremy away to work for him."

"As usual," said James. "Any success?"

"No."

"Also as usual. But it pleases Jeremy to be lured."

Nattie asked Alan, "And is he still trying to lure Bella away?"

"No. I managed to fob him off with an invitation to the Gila River ranch. My partners might be willing to sell him a horse or two."

"That's not your home place, is it?" asked Tomás.

"No. Home is farther east, in the Davis Mountains."

"Will you take Pa there, too?"

"No need," said Alan. "The only exceptional animal there is Bella. Although my sister is quite proud of her chickens."

James said, "The chicken really is a remarkable creature. If you have chickens and a garden you don't need anything else."

"Well, when you figure out how to make boots and saddles out of feathers, you let us know," Robby told him.

Tomás stood up. "If you boys are going to squabble I'm going back to the horseshoe lecture."

"I'll join you," said Robby. "Jeremy's a traditionalist; there'll be sparks when Pa starts in about The Horseshoe of the Future."

"I'll pass. I have letters to write," James said.

Once again Alan and Nattie were alone. The air between them felt charged with energy. Nattie stood and examined a pot of geraniums on the porch rail.

"Tell me about your ranch," she said.

"It's small, as Texas spreads go, but growing. It's beautiful country; good water, good grazing, and the occasional flood or fire or hailstorm to keep things interesting. Gus, my brother-in-law, is becoming a fair cattleman, and my sister tends the house and garden. And the all-important chickens, of course."

"Do they have children?"

"They're expecting their first."

"That's happy news," Nattie said. "Are your parents pleased?"

"Oh yes. But my father wants Edith to have the baby at home, in New Haven. He's convinced she can't get proper medical care out here in the wild. Edith refuses to consider it, and she's angry at Father for worrying Gus."

"Isn't there a doctor where you live?"

"There is, and he's good, but Father will worry anyway. He'd be appalled that our doctor is also the dentist, coroner, mortician and sometimes veterinarian."

"You can't blame him," said Nattie. "He lost his wife and children. An experience like that stays with you forever."

Alan said, "That's true. And there's no denying the risk, even in a city with all the doctors you could ask for."

"James and Flo are struggling with the same issue. James wants to take Flo to specialists in San Francisco, which would be helpful, but his mother is there, which would be awful. James is the only son so Mama Peller is determined that he must carry on the family name. To hear her talk you'd think they were royalty."

"They're pillars of San Francisco society, aren't they?" Alan asked.

"Yes, but she's ashamed of how they achieved their exalted status. Mrs. Peller doesn't mind spending her husband's fortune, but she seems embarrassed that he started out as a small storekeeper. Apparently honest work is uncouth somehow."

"Ah, if only there was enough inherited wealth to go around. None of us would ever have to do a lick of work."

"Says the man with an inheritance."

"Yes, but I've worked like a demon to build on it," Alan said. "And what about you? You could do nothing but sit on a cushion and sew a fine seam if you choose."

"Ugh!" said Nattie. She sat down on the steps. "I'll stick with horses."

Alan said, "Speaking of horses, I'd like to take Bella out to stretch her legs tomorrow. Will you join me?"

"I'd love to. James asked me to school their mare while I'm here. Let's go in the morning, before the heat of the day. And then we can go shopping in the afternoon, if you like."

Miss Pardee stuck her head out the door.

"It's nearly time for supper," she said. "Would you let the others know? I hate to ring the bell in case Mrs. Peller is sleeping."

Alan stood and offered his hand to pull Nattie to her feet. For a moment they stood close, then Alan kissed Nattie's hand and vaulted over the porch railing. He walked backwards to the stable, his eyes on

Nattie until he vanished in the doorway.

Nattie absently picked up the tray from the side table. Miss Pardee watched as she drifted through the kitchen with the forgotten tray in her hand. Nattie went to her room and put the tray on the bureau, where she would be surprised to find it later. She dropped backwards on the bed and wondered what Alan's lips would feel like on hers...She jumped up and studied her reflection in the mirror, half-afraid that it would betray her thoughts. Her cheeks had a bit more color than usual and her eyes were bright, but no one should notice anything out of the ordinary. Still, perhaps she should put it to the test. She tiptoed down the hall to Flo's room and peeked in the open door. Flo looked up from the tray on her lap.

"Shouldn't you be downstairs?" she asked.

Nattie stared blankly at her sister.

"At supper." Flo waved her fork. "Evening meal. People around a table, wondering where you are..."

"Right! Supper! I should go."

Nattie careened to a halt at the dining room door and paused to catch her breath. The men stood as she entered. Miss Pardee's niece, Sally, was clearing the soup bowls. Nattie hugged her aunt as she passed behind her chair.

"*Lo siento, llego tarde*, Tía," she said.

"Miss Pardee will be disappointed that you missed her delicious soup."

Miss Pardee was justifiably proud of her soups.

Tomás pulled out her chair and she took her seat between him and Cata. Alan was directly across the table.

"Naturally," thought Nattie. She decided to keep her gaze fixed safely on a painting above his right shoulder. She relaxed as she listened to James' plans to expand the store; nothing there to make her cheeks flare.

"And of course Lalo advises me daily on what I should carry," said James. "It seems to depend on the book he likes best at the moment. Lately he insists that we should sell Wellington boots and huge umbrellas to use as boats."

"Ah, the story of the duck family!" said Cata.

"Exactly. I've ordered him some rain boots, but he'll probably outgrow them by the rainy season. We'll have to make a puddle for him to splash in."

Nattie asked, "Is he still fascinated by trains?"

"Oh yes. I don't think that will ever change," replied Cata.

"Too bad the train won't be going through here," said Tomás. "Lalo and his watch would make sure it ran on time."

This led to a discussion of the railroad skullduggery, and Alan's part in uncovering it. His account of the capture of the fraudulent survey team had Mr. Johnston whooping with laughter.

"Well, that's one for the books," said Mr. Johnston, wiping his eyes. "Robby, just think if he'd had your trebuchet."

"Too hard to transport."

"Fortunately. That limited you to destroying things at home," said Tomás.

"We didn't destroy anything," said Robby.

"You wrecked the carriage shed."

"We only put a hole in the roof. The shed was fine."

"Wait," said Alan. "You have a trebuchet? An actual, working trebuchet?"

"Well, it might need a bit of an overhaul," said Robby. "We haven't used it in years."

"Not since they destroyed the carriage shed," said Tomás.

Alan asked, "Where did you get a trebuchet?"

"Nat and Ignacio and I built it," said Robby. "We had no idea it would work so well."

"The aim could have been better," Tomás said.

"Can't blame the machine for that," said Nattie. "We were inexperienced."

"What was that thing that caught fire, some kind of engine…" said Tía.

Tomás said, "You'll have to be more specific. The trebuchet was one of the few things that *didn't* burn."

"Stirling engine, Tía. Tomás, don't exaggerate," said Nattie.

"All right, I withdraw the accusation. Some of your projects didn't burn. They exploded."

"Trebuchet, Stirling engine…did you perhaps have the Modern Boy's Encyclopedia?" asked Alan.

"Yes!" said Robby. "Did you?"

"Yes indeed. I mostly built boats, which quickly went to the bottom of Long Island Sound. My encyclopedia disappeared after one of my creations burned to the waterline and left me swimming for shore."

"Ours vanished, too. A pity. We had a lot of fun with that book. Did you make the bow and arrows?" Robby asked.

"Of course. I got pretty good at knapping chert to make arrowheads. Still have a little sliver of rock in my hand. Did you make the slingshot?"

"Of course. You could put a rock through a plank with that thing."

Mr. Johnston shook his head. "I swear I don't know how any of you survived."

Louise served coffee and brought in the cake. Nattie's decoration was much admired. After dessert, the men adjourned to the porch to smoke and talk while the ladies went to the sitting room. Nattie curled up at her aunt's side.

"My wild little deer," said Tía, putting her arm around Nattie. "I remember when you first let me hug you. I could only hold you loosely. You always needed to know you could escape if you wished."

Nattie wriggled closer. "I've hardly seen you since you arrived," she said.

"I know. It seems that everyone is going a dozen different

directions. Tomorrow Robby will return the Madero horses, and as soon as Flo can come downstairs she wants Doc Knowles and the Soames family and Mrs. Meyerson to come to dinner, which will be—" Tía counted on her fingers—"about all the table can accommodate, I think. Mrs. Meyerson is coming to visit me tomorrow morning, and Lydia will bring Lalo back."

"I like Lydia. Could we invite her family to visit us?"

"I don't see why not. Your father is like Flo; happiest when the house is full of people."

"James wants me to work Dinah, so I'll ride out with Robby tomorrow if he makes an early start. And I told Mr. McTurk I'd help him look for a gift for Mrs. Stockton in the afternoon. Maybe Lydia would like to come, too."

"I may have you do a bit of shopping for me, as well. And now you should go apologize to Miss Pardee for your tardiness, and I'll try to remember all the supper conversation for Flo. Tomorrow she can start spending some time downstairs, thank goodness."

Nattie found Miss Pardee scrubbing the kitchen table. She found a cloth and wiped the sink. When everything was clean and ready for breakfast preparation they sat at the table.

"I'm sorry I was late for supper," said Nattie.

"I was about to send Sally to look for you. It's not like you to miss a meal. Are you ill?"

"No. No, I'm fine. I don't know what happened. I was thinking, and time just—went."

"You seemed a bit distracted when you came in earlier."

"I suppose I was." Nattie stood, walked around the table, and sat again. "Miss Pardee, were you ever in love?"

"Oh yes. Long ago. He was a brown-eyed butcher's assistant and I was cooking for a hotel. I was so shy I couldn't even speak; I'd just shove my list at him. We got past that, though."

"What happened?"

"He went off to war, and didn't come back."

Nattie's eyes glistened. Miss Pardee reached across the table and took her hands.

"There now, child. It was a long time ago." She went to the stove and spooned some liquid into a bowl. "Here, I kept some soup warm for you."

Nattie tasted the silky broth. "You are a marvel, Miss P."

"I tell you, when I was in love with my butcher's boy, everything I cooked was either the best I'd ever made, or the worst. I don't miss that. There's something to be said for calm." She ladled more soup into Nattie's bowl. "And what about you? You're in love, are you? With that Mr. McTurk?"

"I don't know. Maybe."

Miss Pardee said, "According to the novels Sally reads, there should be lots of swooning and sighing and silly misunderstandings."

Nattie laughed. "No, nothing like that. Just—confusion."

"Well, he seems a decent fellow and your family likes him. You'll work it out."

Miss Pardee took Nattie's empty bowl. "Time for me to be off home. Goodnight, my dear."

"Goodnight."

Nattie looked out the door to the porch where the men were gathered. "No, don't get up. I'm just saying goodnight. Robby, when are you going to the Madero place tomorrow?"

They agreed on a time and she slipped back inside. Perhaps she and Alan would find themselves alone. "And what will happen then?" she wondered. "Swooning, sighing, and misunderstandings, I suppose." She sat by the window and thought about Alan.

Chapter 26

Nattie woke early, eager to start the day. She dressed quickly and started downstairs, then went back to retrieve the errant tray from her room. Miss Pardee and Sally were busy in the kitchen.

"May I help?" Nattie asked.

"Have your coffee first. Then you can make tortillas."

"As long as you don't mind if they aren't perfectly round." Nattie poured coffee and asked, "Sally, how is your mother? It's been ages since I've seen her."

"She's well, thank you. Her hats are very popular at Mr. Peller's store. She says she can't work fast enough to keep up."

"A hat! That would be just the thing!" said Nattie.

Miss Pardee and Sally turned to look at her.

"Mr. McTurk wants a gift for our neighbor, Mrs. Stockton. The food she sent kept us fed while we were stranded by the storm. I bet she'd love a new hat."

"Mama could make one special for her," said Sally. She launched into a lengthy description of styles and trim. "What type of hat does she usually wear?"

"A sort of sun hat, I suppose, for gardening."

Sally's face fell.

"But that doesn't mean she wouldn't like something special," added Nattie hastily.

Tomas and Robby came in, boots clumping on the wood floor.

"Feed me, Miss P." said Robby. "I'm starving."

"Breakfast will be ready soon. Here; roll up some egg and bacon in a tortilla and leave me be."

"I adore you, I worship you—" Robby's words were cut short by a huge mouthful of food.

Miss Pardee said, "Tomás, be sure to go up and lend an arm to Flo. She's coming down to breakfast today."

"Oh good," said Nattie. "She'll be so happy to take charge of us at last."

"Your sister is very sensible," said Miss Pardee. "You'd do well to take a page from her book."

"I could try, but Tomás and Flo got all the sense. Robby and I are the family flibbertigibbets."

"Five," said Robby. "Quite inconsequential."

"Also five. Tie game."

"Six. In-con-see-quen-she-al."

"Don't make me get the dictionary," warned Nattie.

"All right. I'll magnanimously give you the tie."

"Still five."

"Flibbertigibbets, indeed," said Miss Pardee. She slapped Robby's hand as he grabbed a handful of bacon. "Out of my kitchen, the lot of you."

They retreated to the back porch.

"If we saddle the horses now we could leave right after we eat," said Nattie.

"Eager for a ride with your ranger?" asked Tomás.

"Maybe I am. Or maybe I'm thinking that Robby has a long ride out to the Madero place and back."

"Maybe I'll stay the night there," said Robby. "I'd like to catch up with Antonio and Javi."

"And Josefina? I hear she's home from school now, and very pretty," said Tomás. "You may not be the only one hanging around the Madero place, *hermancito*."

"Ah, but do the others have my charm?"

"He says as he licks bacon grease off his fingers," Nattie said.

"Well of course I'm not being charming *now*," said Robby. "What would be the point?"

"The point of what, *mijo*?" Tía joined them on the porch.

"Wasting my charm on these two."

"Well then, come waste some charm on me." Tía turned her cheek to Robby for a kiss.

Robby struck a dramatic pose. "Your loveliness rivals the breaking dawn."

"Which broke some time ago," said Tía. "But thank you just the same."

"Coffee or tea this morning?" Nattie asked her aunt.

"Tea, I think. *Gracias, querida.*"

Nattie nearly collided with Alan in the kitchen doorway.

"Oh, hullo! I'm getting my aunt a cup of tea."

"May I help?" asked Alan.

They seemed drawn to each other like magnets. Cups and saucers clattered as they reached for them at the same time. Nattie knocked over the tea canister. Alan spilled the milk. Miss Pardee shook her head.

"Perhaps you should leave that to me."

She shooed them into the dining room where Louise was setting the table.

"Morning, Louise," said Nattie. She took a stack of napkins to fold.

Alan said, "Good morning, Miss Louise. Tell me—do you have any sisters who might be willing to work at a ranch in the middle of nowhere? My sister's going to have a baby to tend to, so I'd like to get her more help with the house and the chickens and such."

"No sisters, but I have two little brothers who are determined to be drovers."

"Really? I'm always looking for good hands. How old are they?"

"Eight and ten."

"Oh. Perhaps in a few years, then."

Nattie said, "You'd do better to hire a married couple. If you bring in a single woman you'll have every man within fifty miles come a-courting." She turned to Louise. "What about the Mulcahys? Are they still in town?"

"Oh yes. And Mr. Mulcahy's none too happy about it. He says he hates city life."

"Sounds like a man who'd be happy in the middle of nowhere," said Alan.

Louise told him, "He's a prospector, or was. Mrs. Mulcahy finally put her foot down and told him he's too old to go traipsing around the mountains. Now he does odd jobs around town."

"And what does Mrs. Mulcahy do?" asked Alan.

"She works at the hotel. I'm sure you've seen her."

"Is she a little dumpling of a woman, always smiling?"

"That's her. She might be willing to try ranch life. Especially if it gets Mr. Mulcahy to stop moaning about how a man can't even walk what with people in the way."

"They may be just the thing," said Alan. "I'll look into it."

The door opened to reveal a smiling Flo, supported by James and Tomás. Alan pulled out a chair for her.

"It's so good to rejoin the world!" said Flo. "Louise, please ask Miss Pardee to ring the bell for breakfast whenever she's ready."

Soon there was a clanging from the back porch, followed by a clamor of footsteps and voices. Mr. Johnston stooped to kiss his elder daughter on the top of her head.

"You smell like horses, Papa," said Flo.

"I was up early so I went out to talk to Jeremy. I can't adopt these city hours like the rest of you wastrels."

Robby said, "Why not enjoy it while I have the chance? I've seen plenty of rosy-fingered dawns. It won't hurt me to miss a few."

Louise and Miss Pardee brought in platter after platter of food.

Buttermilk pancakes, scrambled eggs, lamb chops, fried potatoes, *chorizo*, tortillas, fruit compote; there was barely room on the table for it all.

"James, I must thank you for inviting me to breakfast," said Alan. "This is remarkable."

Flo said, "Miss Pardee loves to feed a full table. Or, almost full— when is Lalo coming home?"

"Lydia will bring him back at noon. Along with the puppy, of course," answered Cata.

"Hasn't he named that dog yet?" asked James.

"Oh, he's named it. Many times. He keeps changing his mind, though."

"Maybe we can help," said Robby. "What about Argos? Or Sirius?"

"Let's ask Flo," said Tomás.

"Don't tease," she replied.

Tía said to Alan, "Flo named her white cat Snowball and her black pony Midnight. Perfectly serviceable names, if you ask me."

"What about Gyp?" asked Nattie.

"That nasty little mutt in David Copperfield?" Robby shook his head.

"No, Adam Bede's dog. He's the only sensible character in the entire book."

Flo said, "We should let Lalo decide. It's his dog, after all."

The conversation turned to plans for the day.

"Good luck with Dinah," James told Nattie. "I can't decide if that horse is just stupid or too smart for her own good."

"The latter, I think," said Nattie.

"That's what Jeremy says. Do you know she unlatched the pony's stall and let him out, but stayed in her own, all innocent? She has a devious mind, that one. And once she takes a dislike to someone there's no getting past it. The farrier can't bring his assistant anymore or she throws a fit."

"I don't blame her," Nattie said. "The young fool could have killed her with that knot he tied. And that's more evidence that she's smart. A normal horse would have panicked and strangled itself. But when she felt the rope get tight she moved forward."

"Well, I like her," said Flo. "I don't care to ride a horse that just plods along. I might as well sit on the sofa."

"Speaking of equine sofas, may I borrow Sinbad for a day or so?" asked Robby.

"Oh yes, I heard you plan to visit the Maderos. I take it you saw Josefina on your way here?" asked Flo.

"Why does everyone assume that's the reason? I've been friends with her brothers since we were tadpoles."

"Good. They can warn her about you," Flo replied. "By the way, I want to send a few things with you."

"I know what that means. Fortunately I'll have two extra horses for pack animals." Robby looked at the clock. "Time to be off. Are you two ready?"

"I just need to saddle Dinah," said Nattie. "Does she still suck air when she's cinched?"

"Every time," said James.

Alan helped Nattie saddle her horse. "See? Blown up like a balloon," said Nattie. She led Dinah around until she visibly deflated, then tightened the cinch again. They sat on the porch waiting for Robby, who finally appeared with his arms full of bags and bundles.

"I knew Flo would send half the house," he said. "And Miss Pardee packed some vittles so you won't starve before midday."

"After that breakfast I doubt I'll ever need to eat again," said Alan.

At last they set off, Robby leading the two borrowed horses, with Alan and Nattie following behind.

"Dinah always wants to take the lead, so this is good practice," said Nattie. "Watch she doesn't grab your reins—that's one of her pranks when she gets bored. She really needs to be a working horse. I tried her in a pen of calves and she thought cutting cattle was the best game ever."

"I'm surprised your father hasn't taken her for the ranch."

"He might. We have a pinto gelding that would be perfect for Flo. And then this girl would be too busy to act up." She patted Dinah's neck. "I'm going to take her in and out of the lead position. We'll be back in a bit."

Nattie felt Alan's eyes on her as she moved Dinah in front of Robby's horse. Dinah snorted and tossed her head when they fell back to rejoin Alan and Bella, but she didn't try to pull forward.

Soon they reached their destination, a level field edged with trees and a creek.

Nattie told Robby, "Give the Maderas my best. When will you be back?"

"That depends on how quickly the lovely Josefina tosses me out on my ear."

"Oh. In that case, see you soon."

Robby said, "I promised Dinah an apple if she throws you."

He urged Sinbad into a trot and rode away. Alan hooked one leg around his saddle horn and settled in to watch the lesson.

Nattie said, "All right, Dinah. No pretend stumbles, no twisting your head around to look at me, and none of that bone-jarring trot. Show Bella what a good horse you are."

She and Dinah worked on changing leads. Nattie glanced at Alan and saw he was grinning broadly. She pulled Dinah to a halt and asked, "What's so funny?"

Alan said, "I swear the two of you have the very same look of concentration."

"She's doing well, isn't she?" Nattie said, "That's enough school for now. It's time for recess."

She set Dinah at a gap in the trees and they soared over the creek. Bella's ears pricked forward.

"What do you say, my girl? Shall we join in?" asked Alan.

Soon both horses were turning and jumping as though they were yoked together. Nattie pulled Dinah to a halt.

"Time for a rest. You'd do this all day, I know."

The riders dismounted. The horses drank from the creek and Alan offered Nattie his canteen. As she handed it back, she looked past him and pointed to the sky.

Alan turned to see two hawks soaring and wheeling, riding invisible currents. He reached for Nattie's outstretched hand and turned her to face him. Their eyes met and held, and he put his arms around her and pulled her close. She tensed for a heartbeat and he loosened his grasp, then her arms were around his neck and she was soft and yielding against his body as he kissed her forehead, her cheeks, her lips. Tentative kisses became fierce and deep. Nattie lost herself in the need to be closer to him, part of him—they pulled apart and stared at each other, breathing heavily.

"I…hmm. I can't think," said Alan.

"Me neither."

He removed Nattie's glove and kissed her palm.

"That's not helping," she told him.

"I don't know if I should dunk my head in the creek or kiss you again," said Alan.

"I think…you should kiss me."

He did. Nattie said, "My knees are wobbling."

Alan picked her up and carried to a shady spot under a tree. He stretched out with his back against the trunk and Nattie at his side.

"Take down your hair," said Alan. It fanned out in dark waves across his chest as she rested her head on his shoulder.

"Ah, you're lovely," he said. "When I first saw you I knew you were the most beautiful woman I'd ever seen."

"When you first saw me I had a towel over my head."

"A mere towel can not contain your beauty." He brushed a strand of hair away from her cheek. "What did you think when you first saw me?"

"I thought you might be dead."

"Not the most auspicious beginning. Still, here we are."

Nattie nestled against him.

"I want to stay here forever," she said.

"Like the holy men who meditate and people bring them food?"

"I doubt they get to kiss anyone, though," said Nattie. "How terrible for them."

"Indeed. To live without this..." He kissed her again.

Nattie sighed. "I suppose we have to leave, but we can come back tomorrow."

"What about the day after that?" asked Alan.

"Oh, yes. I will clear my calendar of everything except 'kiss Alan.'"

"In that case, dear heart, I'll agree to take you home. We'd better get started if we're to be on time for dinner."

Nattie braided her hair and brushed off her clothes.

"I lost a glove," she told Alan. "Unless you kept it as a souvenir."

"No. I don't need a glove to remind me of those eyes"—he kissed them—"and that throat"—another kiss—"and those lips—." His inventory took some time, and the ride home was slowed by frequent pauses. Nattie said it was good training for Dinah, who stood patiently while her rider was distracted.

They were still some distance from the house when they heard the dinner bell. They turned the horses over to Jeremy, shared a brief kiss outside the dining room door, and entered just as Mr. Johnston stood for the blessing. They were studiously casual, careful to give no clues about what had passed between them, and deceived no one. Nattie was grateful when Lydia spoke.

"Lalo has named his puppy," she said.

"Indeed? What is it?" asked Tomás.

"Hamilton," Lalo announced proudly.

"Hamilton? Where did that come from?" asked Flo.

"It's on my watch. See? It says Hamilton."

The watch made its way around the table so everyone could see the name on its face.

"Where is Hamilton now?" asked Cata.

No one answered.

She said, "In the house, I suppose."

Lydia said, "I think he's in the kitchen. Miss Pardee made him a bed by the stove."

Cata shook her head. "Next he'll be begging under the table."

"I doubt it," said Lydia. "Miss Pardee fed him so much he can barely stand."

"Give up, Cata," said Tía. "You must pick your battles. Just be grateful no one's trying to bring goats or lambs or ponies indoors."

"We weren't bringing them in permanently," Nattie protested. "Just for a visit."

"Poor Tía," said Tomás.

"Oh, no. You don't get to be all high and mighty," said Flo. "Remember your chicken?"

"What's this about a chicken?" James was all ears.

"Tomás had a pet hen that followed him around like a dog. He was always trying to sneak her indoors. And what did you name her?"

"I was very young," said Tomás with great dignity.

"Yes, and what did you name her?" repeated Flo.

"Mrs. Cluck," said Tomás.

"Indeed. So let's have no more mocking of Snowball and Midnight."

James said, "Chickens are much more intelligent than people think. Did you know—"

Nattie knew that James' chicken dissertation would go on until Flo gently changed the subject, so she let her mind drift to Alan's arms around her, Alan's mouth on hers... She suddenly realized someone had asked her a question.

"Oh yes," she said. "Very intelligent."

"What are you talking about?" asked Flo.

"I'm not sure. Are we talking about chickens?"

"No. I asked you what you're shopping for this afternoon."

"Oh. That's a very intelligent question. I meant."

Flo rolled her eyes.

Nattie hurried on. "I'd like to find some little gifts for the Stockton girls. And for Mrs. Dresen. I can't decide if I should get her something for the kitchen or something wildly impractical for herself. So perhaps both."

Alan said, "And I want to find something for Mrs. Stockton. Perhaps her husband, as well. Does he smoke?"

Mr. Johnston answered, "He enjoys the occasional cigar."

"That might do, then."

Flo said, "I have some fashion periodicals to send Alethia. And cuttings from my garden for Mrs. Stockton. I do miss them both."

"They miss you, too," said Nattie. "Perhaps you could stay at the ranch for a while when you get your full strength. You could escape the summer heat."

"Would I go too?" asked Lalo.

Flo replied, "Of course! And Cata. Perhaps Lydia, as well."

Nattie told Lydia, "I hope you can visit sooner than that. Maybe you could go home with us."

"You're not leaving soon, are you?" asked Flo.

"I'll head home in a day or so," said Tomás. "Can't leave things unattended for too long."

Nattie looked at Alan. When would he leave? Her throat tightened at the thought. How could she watch him ride away now that she had felt his body against hers, felt his kiss?

Alan's eyes met hers. He gave her a trace of a smile and a slight shake of his head. *No, I won't leave you.* Nattie relaxed. The future would take care of itself.

Alan asked, "Will Lalo be available to guide us around town this afternoon?"

"If you can wait until he has a nap," replied Cata. "His eyelids are drooping."

Lalo sat upright. "I'm not tired! I was thinking!"

Lydia said, "I'm sure Hamilton will need a nap after his big meal. The two of you can rest together."

After much negotiation it was agreed that both would rest in Lalo's room, on their separate beds. A yawning Lalo said his goodbyes and Cata took him to collect Hamilton from the kitchen.

"Do you think they'll both end up in the boy's bed or the dog's?" asked Mr. Johnston.

"I predict that Lalo will put the dog's bed on his, thus fulfilling the letter of the law if not the intent," said Alan.

Nattie hoped for a moment alone with Alan before the shopping expedition, but he said, "If you'll excuse me, I'll attempt to find the Post Office without Lalo's guidance. I have letters to mail. My family must be wondering about me."

Nattie hoped she could walk him to the door alone, but "It's time I got back to the store," said James. "I'll go with you."

Nattie said, "I need to change before we go shopping." She hoped for a private moment to review the morning's events but Lydia said, "May I go up with you? I need to borrow a hat. Mine doesn't have much of a brim and I'll be squinting against the sun."

When they entered Nattie's room Lydia dropped into a chair. As Nattie offered her a hat she said "Never mind that. What happened?"

"What do you mean?"

"What happened between you and Mr. McTurk?"

Nattie sat on the bed. "You can tell?"

"*Everyone* can tell. The way you look at each other, and how you try not to look at each other—"

"Oh."

"So tell. Has he kissed you?"

"Oh yes. Yes indeed. This morning."

"I knew it! Was it wonderful?"

"*So* wonderful."

Lydia sighed. "Have you told Flo?" she asked.

"I don't suppose I need to since everybody knows already."

"What will your family think?"

"I don't know. But I'm sure they'll tell me."

"Forgive me for badgering you with questions. You don't have to tell me anything if you don't want to. It's just so exciting and romantic…" Lydia sighed again.

"I don't mind. It's nice to have someone to talk to."

"Did he ask you to marry him?"

Nattie hesitated. "We haven't talked about that yet."

"Oh. Well, it's plain that he loves you. And of course you love him."

"I don't think I could live without him," Nattie said. "I always thought that kind of thing sounded ridiculous, but now I feel like I'm missing part of myself when I'm not with him." She moved to the window and looked out. "I wonder if he feels the same."

Lydia said, "I don't know if men feel things the way we do. I mean, they go haring off to the gold fields or wars or expeditions and leave their loved ones behind without a thought, seems like."

"But what about your father? He kept searching for your mother when everyone else had given up. I think your parents' story is the best kind of romantic."

"I suppose it is, isn't it?"

"Of course it is, and don't let the old biddies tell you any different." Nattie opened the wardrobe. "Now help me decide what to wear. Then I'll have to go down and face my nosy family."

They found Flo and Tía in the sitting room. To Nattie's great relief, the conversation was about shopping lists and embroidery floss.

Tía told Lydia, "I hope your mother will bring some of her work when she comes to supper tomorrow night."

"She always carries her embroidery bag. And she wants to see how you do…dish something?"

"*Deshilado*," said Tía.

Cata stuck her head in.

"Mr. McTurk was right. Lalo put the dog's bed on his and they both slept in it."

Flo asked, "Are they up now?"

"Yes, they're outside. Lalo has his wagon so padded you'd think that dog was made of spun sugar."

Nattie glanced at the mantel clock. "Do I have all the lists? Oh! I need to ask Miss Pardee to recommend some kitchen gadget for Mrs. Dresen."

Miss Pardee had her hands in a mixing bowl. She dusted them off and took a metal object from a shelf.

"I'm quite pleased with this chopper," she told Nattie. "It clamps on to the table, like this, and you just turn the handle. It saves a great deal of time. Mr. Peller brought it home from his store. I'm sure you could find one there."

"That's perfect! I knew you'd know just the thing."

Nattie heard Alan's voice outside.

Miss Pardee said, "There's your young man now. Run along, and be home on time for supper."

Chapter 27

Finally the little group was ready to set off. Their first stop was Peller's Mercantile. James and his employees took charge of the many lists and soon the counter was laden with purchases.

Nattie said, "Now I need something pretty for Mrs. Dresen. Something that has nothing to do with cooking."

James said, "Let me show you the shawls we just got in."

Soon the counter was draped in bright colors. Nattie selected a black shawl embroidered with flowers in turquoise and coral.

"Do you think Li Jun's wife would like one?" asked Alan.

"I'm sure she would," answered Nattie, turning over the soft fabrics.

"Good. And if there's another food grinder I'll send that to Li Jun. He was most helpful. Help me pick out some toys for their children."

Their hands met frequently as they looked at marbles, tops, dolls, and puzzles.

"You're very good at estimating their ages," Nattie said. "Most men haven't a clue."

"I'm a man of many talents," replied Alan, juggling rubber balls. "We should get one of these for Hamilton. Lalo, come pick out a ball for your dog."

Nattie chose a cloth doll for Deborah Stockton, art supplies for Pauline, a bonnet for the baby, and a paisley shawl in blues and greens to complement Alethia's red hair. She unfolded an ivory shawl embroidered with birds and flowers in soft colors.

"This is perfect for Cata," said Nattie. Lydia agreed, so it was added to the pile. Alan found a box of cigars for Mr. Stockton and said, "Now on to the difficult task; hats. Ladies, you must advise me."

"Sally said her mother could make whatever you want," Nattie told him.

"That would be splendid if I had any idea what I want."

Lydia and Nattie modeled the hats. Alan judged one to be too severe, another too plain, and another "just silly. Why would a woman want a bird nesting on her head?" Finally one met with his approval. "It has enough of a brim to be serviceable, with just the right note of frivolity."

They left their purchases to be wrapped and delivered. "Now where?" asked Alan.

"I need to buy a novel for Molly Stockton," said Nattie.

"Very well. And after that I'll leave you all to have ice cream while I run an errand."

"I don't think Mr. Metzen allows dogs in," said Lydia.

"Then I'll take Hamilton with me," Alan replied. "He'll be useful, actually."

Nattie persuaded Alan to leave them at the corner. "It's probably best if Mr. Metzen doesn't see you," she said.

"Still holding a grudge, is he? Very well. I'll be back in half an hour."

Nattie watched him stroll away, remembering his arms lifting her off the ground, her fingers in his hair...

"So, shall we go?" asked Lydia.

"Oh! Yes. Of course," said Nattie. "C'mon, Lalo."

They had finished their ice cream when they heard a rap on the window. Alan was outside, holding Hamilton and gesturing for Lalo to come outside. The girls followed to find the boy examining a leather collar on his puppy's neck.

"Lalo, look," said Nattie. "There's a metal plate on it. Look what it says."

Lalo traced the engraved letters.

"Hamilton. It says Hamilton!"

He pulled out his pocket watch.

"See, it's the same! Thank you very much, Mr. Alan," he said.

"My pleasure. Perhaps we should move along now."

Alan gestured to the store. Mr. Metzen was wiping the counter and glaring at them.

"Is all our shopping done? Shall we head for home?" asked Nattie.

She and Lydia paused in front of the tailor's to allow Alan, pulling Lalo and Hamilton in the wagon, to catch up. Behind them, a woman burst out of the stationer's.

"Mr. McTurk? Is that you? I knew it was you! We met in Abilene, remember? You and my husband were buying cattle. I'm here visiting my sister, Mrs. Manning; perhaps you know her. How nice to see you and your son again! But this can't be your son; I remember he was quite fair."

"How do you do? No, this is Lalo. He lives with the Pellers. We were just on our way—"

"And how is your wife? Is she here with you?"

Nattie felt like the she was collapsing in upon herself. Her face was numb, and her vision narrowed to a sign on the window in front of her. "Repairing Neatly Done." She read it over and over without comprehension. From a great distance she heard Lydia's voice.

"Mr. McTurk, do stay and talk with your friend. Come on, Lalo. Bring your wagon."

Nattie was grateful for the support of Lydia's arm linked in hers as they walked away.

"Thank you," she whispered. Her voice caught in her throat. "Thank you. I—"

"Don't try to talk. You're white as a sheet. Can you walk? Should we sit down somewhere?"

"No. No. I just want to go home."

"Miss Nat, are you ill? You can ride in my wagon," said Lalo.

"No, I can walk. Perhaps you could hold my hand, though."

Lalo's warm hand slipped into hers. Alan had a son. And a wife. A wife. It wasn't possible. But Alan hadn't denied it. Had he? Perhaps she misunderstood. Perhaps this was just a silly misunderstanding. Swoons and sighs and silly misunderstandings, Miss Pardee had said. Nattie looked behind her. If it was a misunderstanding, shouldn't Alan be hurrying to explain?

Lalo raced ahead as they neared the house. Nattie turned to Lydia.

"You must promise me that you'll tell no one. No one, you understand? Not a word."

"But your family will know something's wrong," Lydia protested.

"I'll tell them later. I can't face questions right now. Just let me have some time to sort it out."

"All right. Do you want me to stay with you or leave you alone?"

"Stay, please. I keep going over and over it, thinking I must have misunderstood him. Did I?"

Lydia slowly shook her head. "I wish I could say yes."

"Oh God." Nattie closed her eyes.

"Let's get you inside so you can lie down."

Lydia closed the curtains and said, "I'll get you something to drink."

Nattie collapsed on her bed and stared at the ceiling. Her mind raced. How could she have been so blind? Were there clues? There must have been clues. A tear trickled from the corner of her eye; she angrily wiped it away.

There was a soft knock on the door and Lydia entered with a tray.

"I made you a cup of tea with lots of sugar, and here's a cold cloth for your head. I told your aunt you had a bit of a headache and were going to nap, so you'll be undisturbed for a while."

"There's no word from Alan?"

"No. I'm sorry."

"It must be true, then. He has no explanation so it's true. That's right, isn't it?"

Lydia smoothed the cloth on Nattie's forehead. "I don't know what to think. It was so plain that he loved you..."

"Papa asked about him. How could he miss that he's married? How could I be so stupid?"

"Not stupid. You had no reason to doubt him. He's the one to blame. Be angry at him."

"I wish I could feel angry. It would be better than this. I just want to run and run until I can't think any more."

Lydia took Nattie's hand. "Try to rest. I have to go home now but I'll come back if I can."

"Thank you, but there's no need. I think I will try to sleep."

"Good. I'll see you tomorrow morning, then."

As soon as the door closed behind Lydia, Nattie jumped up and changed into riding clothes. She scribbled a note so her family wouldn't worry if they found her room empty. When she was sure everyone was at supper, she slipped into Robby's room and opened the window. She could barely reach the nearest tree branch, but she grasped it and scrambled to the ground. The garden shielded her from sight as she hurried to the dark stable. She saddled Dinah and led her to the alley behind the stable, remembering to re-cinch the saddle. Then they were off, galloping on the road that led out of town.

Nattie slowed Dinah to a walk as they neared the field where she and Alan had embraced—when? Was it just this morning? She felt old, as if years had passed. There was the tree where she and Alan had talked of tomorrow, and the day after that...

She remembered her lost glove. Suddenly it seemed very important that she find it. She dismounted by the creek where Alan had removed her glove and kissed her palm; her fingers closed over the memory. The rising moon gave light to see but there was no trace of her former happiness, not even footprints to mark where they embraced. She sank to her knees and sobbed, her head bowed to the ground. When she could cry no more, she plunged her face in the cold creek water. Then she dried her face on her sleeve and started back to town.

Nattie saw the glow of her father's cigar on the porch as she tied Dinah to the hitching post by the stable. As she put the saddle away she was surprised to see Bella's sleek head emerge over a stall door.

"Still here, are you? I thought he'd be high-tailing it back to his wife by now."

When Nattie came out, her father was rubbing Dinah's head.

"Feel better?" he asked.

"Not really." She began to brush the horse.

"Do you want a lantern?"

"No. There's enough light."

"Do you have another brush?"

She handed it across Dinah's back.

"Do you want to talk about it?" her father asked.

"No. There's nothing to talk about."

198

"All right. I won't press you." He came around to her and wrapped his arms around her. "Ah, *mi pobrecita*. I wish I could make it all better."

"Papí, I just want to go home. Could Tomás and I go tomorrow? Early?"

"I'll talk to him. You go in and get some rest. I'll finish up here."

Nattie reached her room unseen, but as she opened the door Tía looked out from Flo's room.

"There you are at last! Will you come to us? Or would you rather we come to your room?"

I'd rather be miles away, thought Nattie, but she turned and went to her aunt.

"Are you hungry?" asked Tía. "Shall I fix you a plate?"

"No, I'm fine. Just tired."

Flo patted the bed next to her. "Come and lie down. Tía made a poultice for your eyes."

The cloth was soothing, with a familiar scent. Flo patted her hand.

"Poor Nat. Do you want to talk?"

"If I talk I'll cry, and I'm sick of crying. I'll tell you everything later." She lifted the cloth from her eyes and looked at her sister. "Flo, would you mind if I went home tomorrow? With Tomás?"

"Of course I don't mind, if it will help you feel better. You can take Dinah. But you must write to me *soon*."

Tía asked, "What about Lydia's visit?"

"I'll leave a note asking her to come home with you."

Tía stood. "Well, if you're riding home tomorrow you'd better go to bed. Keep that on your eyes; it will take down the puffiness." She brushed Nattie's hair from her face and said, "*Siempre que llovió, paró.* You won't feel like this forever, I promise."

Nattie expected to lie awake all night, but she slept until there was a knock on her door. It was still dark, with only a hint of light on the horizon.

"Nat, are you up? I want to make an early start."

She hurried into her clothes and met Tomás in the kitchen. Miss Pardee gave her a hug but asked no questions. Breakfast was ready and there were packages of food on the table. Tía came in, followed by Flo on her father's arm.

"You didn't have to get up," Nattie told her.

"I know. But I wanted to see you off."

"Will you come home soon?" asked Nattie.

"I will, I promise."

James shuffled in. "You country folk keep ungodly hours," he said.

"Up with the chickens," replied Tomás.

After hugs and farewells, they were finally off. Tomás rode a sturdy horse from the livery stable. Nattie looked away when they passed the field where she had been so happy, so sure of a future with Alan.

They were urged to stay and rest at the Madero ranch, but Nattie was eager to go on. She sat quietly while Tomás gave them news of Flo. Robby pulled her aside.

"What's wrong?" he asked. "Why are you going home? What happened?"

"He's married. Alan is married. With a child."

"I don't believe it! That can't be right." Robby paced a few steps. "What makes you think so?"

Nattie explained.

"So some dotty old woman babbles a load of nonsense and you take it as gospel." Robby snorted. "Honestly, Nat, I thought you had more sense."

"But Rob, he didn't deny it. He hasn't said anything, hasn't explained—"

"That is odd, I'll grant you that. But I won't believe anything until I hear it from him. I'll go back today and have it out with him. Is he still in town?"

"I think so. Bella was in the stable when we left."

"That's another thing. If he's a scoundrel, why would he stick around?"

"Robby, I was there. I heard it. Please don't try to explain it away." Please don't give me hope, she thought. Just let me accept the truth and start surviving it.

Robby slung an arm around her and she rested her head against him.

"I'm so tired, Rob. I don't think I've ever been so tired."

"You'll feel better once you're home," he said. "Now let's go talk to Tomás about what to do with all these horses we've collected."

The livery horse and Sinbad went back to town with Robby. Tomás and Nattie rode the West Camp horses and led Dinah. Nattie let her mind empty of everything except the sound of hooves, the smell of dust, the movement of the horse beneath her. Dusk brought a cool following breeze that dried the sweat on her back. She half-dozed until she was roused by Tomás' voice.

"Nat. Nat, we're here."

They turned the horses loose in the corral and trudged wearily to the house. Tomás turned to the stairs. "G'night, infant," he said. He awkwardly patted her shoulder. "Get some rest."

Nattie paused in the courtyard. The air was sweet and the fountain splashed in the corner. She pushed aside the memory of opening the crate from Alan.

Chinche mewed from the shadows. She scooped him up and buried her face in his fur. "Let's go to bed," she told him.

Chapter 28

Nattie slept until mid-morning. She considered getting up, but Chinche was sprawled across her neck and purring in her ear so she went back to sleep. It was after noon before she went downstairs. Mrs. Dresen was having her afternoon nap, but there was a pot of chicken and dumplings on the stove and chocolate cake on the table. Nattie stood a spoon in a cup of coffee, put a fork in her mouth, stacked a cake plate on top of a bowl of soup and carefully carried it to her room. She'd have to face people eventually, but now she wanted to hide away.

She ate by the window, looking out at the familiar view. Chinche accepted bits of chicken as his due and licked the bowl, then bumped Nattie's nose with his forehead. She scratched his ears as she planned her day. First a ride, then a long soak in the spring. Then she should start a letter to Flo. The thought of explaining left her weary. Robby would tell them. Let them all talk and speculate and question. She was done with it. She never wanted to think of Alan again.

The day dragged by. At supper, Tomás, Ignacio and Mr. Cole talked about livestock and grazing. The memory of a supper conversation about Alan invaded her thoughts and she shook her head. What an infatuated little fool she had been.

After supper she braced herself and ventured into the kitchen. Mrs. Dresen gave her a hug but asked no questions. She just said, "My poor girl. If you ever want to talk, I'm here." Nattie's throat tightened. She shook her head and retreated to her room.

The next day she sought solace in the courtyard garden. She pruned and weeded as the sun moved across the tile floor, followed by Chinche and her father's old dog. As her hands restored order to the garden her mind sifted through what Alan had said, and left unsaid. He never said 'I love you,' but neither had she. He had told her about his life, but admitted it wasn't a complete history. His son must be near Lalo's age; that explained why he was so good with the boy. She hadn't given it a thought. She hadn't thought about anything, really. She had just followed her feelings. She wouldn't make that mistake again.

When it was too dark to tell weed from flower she sat on the wide Talavera tile border of the fountain and looked up at the sky. Clouds blocked the stars. She felt the dog's wet nose push into her hand.

"Ah, Moose. You miss Papí, don't you? He'll be home soon." And then she'd have to face a house full of people. But for now it was quiet, and no one questioned her. Alan had said she didn't ask many questions. She should have asked more. Her father had asked about him, though. Maybe there were clues to be found there.

After supper she knocked on Tomás' office door.

"Hallo, infant. Clear the papers off a chair and sit down. It's amazing how things piled up while I was away. What can I do for you?"

"Well, you know how Papí checked into Alan McTurk when he first showed up?"

"Yes. I was the one who did the checking. We wanted to be sure he was an upright citizen. Why?"

"You didn't find out anything about his family?"

"He lives with his sister and her husband. But you knew that."

"But—what about a wife? And child?"

"Oh. So that's the way of it. No, there was no mention of him being married. But secrets are easy to keep out here. I'm sorry, Nat. I thought he was a good 'un." He paused. "Does Pa know? Do you want me to telegraph him?"

"No. I just want to forget I ever met him."

"Give it time." Tomás stood beside her and put his hand on her shoulder. "You'll find someone."

"Nope. I'm going to stay here forever with Papí and Tía and you."

"But I'm not going to stay here forever, you know."

"Really? You want to leave? And do what?"

"I want to study law, then come back here to practice. I realized I enjoy sorting out legal matters more than anything else."

"Have you told Papí?"

"We've talked about it."

"When will you go?"

"Soon, I hope."

"First Flo, now you... And Ignacio will leave when he marries Alethia."

"And Robby seemed quite comfortable at the Madero place. Maybe he managed to charm Josefina," said Tomás.

"I didn't notice. Too wrapped up in my own misery." Nattie stood. "Well, I guess I'll be the only one to stay home. I never really thought about doing anything else until now."

"No, you never were one for affairs of the heart."

"What about you? Have you ever been smitten?"

"Oh, I suppose so, now and again." He turned back to his papers.

"Goodnight, Tomás."

"Goodnight, infant."

Nattie tried to start a letter to Flo, but gave up and leaned out the window into the night air. A breeze fluttered the curtains and blew the blank pages from her desk. She tossed them in a drawer and climbed the stairs to the roof. She undid her braid and felt the breeze lift her hair, remembering a night at East Camp when the wind blew out the candles.

The clouds had moved on and the stars were bright. She saw The Pleiades but didn't try to count the sisters. "No one stays at home anymore," she told the night sky. "Except me." She watched the stars until clouds returned to hide them.

Chapter 29

The next morning Nattie saddled Chico and rode out with no destination in mind. Ignacio saw her and galloped over.

"*¡Hola! ¿Cómo estás?* You look better today. Lettie wondered if you'd like company. She has missed you."

"I've missed her, too. Tell her I'd love to see her in a few days, perhaps."

"I will. Where are you going?"

"Nowhere particular."

"Go see the ford. It's all cleared now. And there's a new bridge at Alamosa Station. Everything's back to normal."

Nattie thought, "Repairing Neatly Done." She said, "Good. That's good. *Adiós*, Ignacio."

"*Adiós*. Enjoy your ride."

The ford was as good a destination as any. The shaded road was cool and dim. Sunlight filtered through leaves to make wavering bright disks on the soft dirt. Birds swooped in and out of trees where their companions called.

The river murmured softly as it flowed over the ford. Nattie sat on the bank and tossed pebbles into the clear water. If she hadn't found Alan in the flood her heart would still be intact. Did she wish that? No, she decided. She could wish she'd never met him, but she couldn't regret saving his life.

Nattie took off her boots, rolled up her trousers and waded in. The shallow water pushed against her with surprising force. She scooped up cold handfuls and splashed her face and neck, then pulled on her boots and turned Chico toward home.

Tomás met her in the courtyard, waving a handful of papers.

"This is odd. A Dos Rios lad just brought you a stack of telegrams. A letter from Flo, too."

"Telegrams?" Nattie felt a flicker of hope and sternly squashed it. She took the papers and sat down by the fountain.

"Oh. This is from James." "THINGS NOT AS THEY SEEM—SOMEWHAT BUT NOT ENTIRELY"

"What on earth?" She looked at Tomás, who shrugged.

The next was from Robby. She smoothed the flimsy paper on her knee. "DESPAIR NOT—AWAIT EXPLANATION—APPLY PERSPICACITY"

She shook her head. "He's babbling."

She opened another. "This one's from Papí. Maybe it will make sense." "ALL CLEAR IN FULLNESS OF TIME—YOUR DECISION BUT PLEASE LISTEN—HOME SOON"

Tomás said, "I think that's the longest telegram Pa ever sent."

The last was from Jeremy. "WILL BRAY HIM IF YOU WISH BUT NO NEED MAYBE"

She handed the telegrams to Tomás. "I don't even know what that means. I don't know what any of it means. Have they all gone mad?"

"I suspect drink," said Tomás.

"But—all of them? All drunk and sending cryptic telegrams? What is going on?"

She tore into Flo's letter.

Dearest,

I am hurrying to send this with the stage driver who will send it on from Dos Rios. I must tell you what has happened since you left, as much as I understand it.

First of all, McT sent to have Bella moved to the livery stable. Miss Pardee told Jeremy that McT caused you pain so he decided to " 'ave it owt wi' the cur." Apparently Jeremy found McT miserable in his cups, took pity on him and joined him in a drink. Or several.

When Miss P told us Jeremy hadn't returned, Papa and James went to see what had happened to him and to perhaps offer McT some gentle correction of their own. They didn't come back, so when Robby got here he went after them, and ages later they all came rolling home drunk as lords. No one will tell me what McT said—they say it's his place to tell you.

Perhaps you already know all this—there was a mention of telegrams. All James will say is that he'll never again try to match a Yorkshireman in drink.

Must close. Write!

Your loving sister, Flo

Nattie was stunned. "What in the *hell*," she said. "They're all carousing with that—that—*cur*. And they keep his secrets for him? And intervene for him? Drink only excuses so much. I will *never* forgive them."

She looked at the telegrams again. "Await explanation…listen…your decision." What had Flo said? "They say it's his place to tell you." Did that mean Alan was coming to her?

"Oh no. No no no." She paced the courtyard. "He can't come here. I can't see him." She stopped. What if he was already on his way? She raced upstairs and looked out her window. No horseman approached. What should she do? Go stay with the Stocktons or Li Jun? No. No more running. She would receive him with quiet dignity, hear him out, and firmly dismiss him.

Tomás looked in. "Just wanted to make sure you aren't aiming a rifle out that window."

"No. I'm fine. Mr. McTurk may come here. Briefly. And I'll listen, as Papí requests. But I'll be stone sober, so whatever he said to buffalo a pack of intoxicated sympathizers won't work on *me*. What did James say—things are somewhat as they seem, but not entirely?

Well, you can't be somewhat married."

"But Nat, have you considered that maybe McTurk does have some valid explanation?"

"Then why didn't he come and tell it to me? No. I'm not that stupid trusting girl he hornswoggled. Not anymore."

"Perhaps you're right. Anyway, I'd rather see you outraged than miserable."

Nattie preferred being outraged, too. But by the next morning her temper had cooled to resignation. She would have to see Alan one last time. It would be painful, but then it would be over and she could start forgetting him.

She dressed in dark blue, hoping to look severe and uncompromising, but she was pleased to see that the gown showed her figure to full advantage. She sat primly in the parlor until boredom drove her out to the courtyard, but the garden failed to soothe her. She was sitting by the fountain, passing her hand through the water and watching ripples collide, when Ignacio hurried in. He soaked his neckerchief in the water and ran it over his face, then flicked it at her.

"Hey Nat, put on some work clothes and come help with Mama-cow."

"What's she done now?"

"Got her head stuck in a tree. I think you're light enough to climb up and rig a rope."

Nattie splashed him and stood up.

"All right. Give me a minute to change."

"I'll saddle Chico and meet you outside."

Nattie ran upstairs and put on battered trousers and an old shirt. Ignacio filled her in on the cow's latest misadventure as they rode.

"She must have pulled herself up to eat leaves, although there's no shortage of grass, and when she dropped back down her neck got stuck in the fork of the tree. Fortunately she's too stupid to be upset about it or she'd have broken her neck trying to get loose. It's just one thing after another with her. I swear, I'd butcher her where she stands if she wasn't such a good wet nurse."

"Probably because she's too stupid to realize the calves aren't hers," said Nattie. She asked, "Why not just cut off one side of the fork?"

"We will if we have to, but the tree's on a bank so it's awkward to get at, and it might take too long. If she tires and starts to sag she'll strangle herself. I'm hoping we can just get her head high enough to push it back through."

They arrived to find several hands smoking and swapping stories of livestock predicaments.

"What do you think, Nat?" asked Ignacio.

She kicked off her boots. "It looks like the branches will support my weight, but I don't know if they'll pulley her."

Ignacio handed her a rope. "Guess we'll find out."

Nattie patted Mama-cow and said a few soothing words, then scrambled up into the tree. She wrapped her legs around a branch and hung upside down to take hold of the horns. The cow's tongue slurped across her cheek and left a smear of green.

"We may not need a rope," she said. "She doesn't need to come up much at all. If you could raise her just a little I can turn her head and she'll pop right out."

"Worth a try," said Ignacio. "On the count of three, heave!"

The men grunted as they lifted the cow's front end while she tried to eat Nattie's braid. Nattie wrestled the cow's head into place and shoved it back through the fork. Mama-cow's front hooves dropped to the ground and she was free. Nattie pulled herself right-side-up and wiped away sweat as the cow calmly wandered off to graze. As Nattie turned to climb down, her eyes met Alan's.

Chapter 30

Nattie expected to feel angry, or sad, but she just felt empty. Alan sat quiet on his horse as she dropped to the ground and pulled on her boots.

"Hello, Mr. McTurk." Her voice was steady. Ignacio moved beside her and raised his eyebrows in a question.

"It's all right. Mr. McTurk and I have some matters to discuss before he rides on."

Nattie swung up into her saddle. They rode in silence as she led the way to a hilltop scattered with boulders. She settled cross-legged on a rock and looked out over the broad valley below.

Alan stood in front of her and cleared his throat. "I've been rehearsing what to say all the way here, but I'm just going to jump in. I'm not married. Never was. I do have a son."

Nattie sat like stone. Alan went on.

"His mother was a whore. She died when he was born. That's the bare bones of it. I'd like to tell you everything, if you'll allow me."

Nattie didn't look at him, but she inclined her head. Alan turned to face the distant mountains, and began.

"When I first saw Sophie, she was curled at the feet of a man who had knocked her down. I intervened. Her face was bruised and bleeding, and she was so weak she could barely stand, so I took her to my rooms and brought in a doctor. He said she was under-nourished and anemic. By the time she recovered we had settled in pretty comfortably together, so we just went on like that.

"Her father died when she was thirteen, and her mother a year later. Sophie and her older sister Helen were sent to live with an aunt who had a brute of a husband. Sophie never said much about that. Eventually they ran."

Alan picked up a rock and sent it soaring out into empty air.

"They scraped along for a few years, until her sister found a fancy man who said he'd set her up in Shreveport. He wouldn't take Sophie; said she looked consumptive and no man would want her. Helen promised to send for her as soon as she got settled. But her man took everything she had and disappeared. And then Marie-Elise took her in."

Nattie's head lifted.

"The most improper Marie-Elise?"

"Right. She runs a popular establishment in Shreveport." Alan sat on a rock and looked at Nattie, but her gaze stayed fixed on the valley. "So. The man who beat Sophie was an exalted member of San Antonio society. He pitched a fit because I'd rearranged his face a little, so I was transferred to a small town where I was less likely to cause trouble. When Helen wrote and asked Sophie to join her, we were playing house like a couple of children. I told Sophie she could stay if she wanted, and she did. Then one day I came home and found a note. She had gone to join Helen in Shreveport.

"I should have gone after her but, truth be told, I was relieved that I didn't have to make the decision to stay together or not. So I just let her go and didn't think much about it, until Helen wrote me, months later. She said Sophie had left because she was expecting my child and didn't want to obligate me."

Alan paused. "The birth was difficult. Marie-Elise brought in the best doctors, but Sophie died a few days later. She named the child Samuel, after her father, and Alan, after me.

"I went to see the baby. He had a houseful of women caring for him, so I left him in Shreveport until I could figure out what to do.

Then I got the inheritance from Great-Aunt Alice. I resigned from the Rangers, bought my land, and offered my sister and her husband a place there. As soon as we were settled, I brought Sam home."

There was a long silence. Nattie asked, "What is he like?"

"He's tall for his age. Looks like me, but with Sophie's smile and coloring. He's quick to learn, and soft-hearted, and asks endless questions."

"Did Helen come with him?"

"No. She saved her money and bought a little shop in Shreveport, selling sweets and tobacco and the like. I'm trying to persuade her to move nearer to us but she's doing well where she is. She's a clever businesswoman."

"Was Sophie clever?"

"Not in the usual sense, I suppose. She liked cooking, and could read well enough to follow a recipe. She loved needlework. The house was covered in doilies."

Nattie turned to look at Alan. "Would you have married her?"

"I don't know. Perhaps. I enjoyed making her happy, and she was grateful, but we didn't love each other."

"Did she hope that you would go after her?"

"I don't think so. Helen said Sophie was delighted to be the pet of the establishment, with all the women coddling her. She'd love the gravestone they chose; an angel holding a cherub."

Alan pushed his hat up and rubbed his forehead. "Sophia Adelaide Muller. I didn't even know her full name until I saw it carved there."

"S.A.M. Your son's name. He has the same initials, too."

"Yes. Helen said Sophie was very pleased about that."

"Have you told your family about Sam?"

"No. Not yet."

"Why not? Are you ashamed of him?"

"No! No, not at all."

"Ashamed of his mother, then?"

"No. I suppose…I'm ashamed of how careless I was with her. I gave no thought to the future, her future. She deserved better."

"Did she ever ask you for a future?"

"No. We were both happy enough just rattling along together. But I wasn't there when she gave birth. I wasn't there when she died." He looked away. "That's part of the reason I didn't tell you about Sam."

"And the other?"

"That's obvious, isn't it? I have a son whose mother was a whore. I couldn't ask you to overlook that."

Nattie sat quiet for a moment, then stood and pointed south. "There's a house down there, right on the border. Half on this side and half in Mexico. It was built by a man with two wives. He says he only ever intended to have one, but it got away from him somehow. They weren't welcome in civilized society so they came out here. The wives live on opposite sides of the border. I'm not sure how that solves anything but from what I hear, everyone's happy and no one troubles them about it."

She turned and pointed again. "See that ridge? On the other side is the Swoboda place. One day Emil pushed back from the supper table, said he'd had enough, and walked out. Olga thought he meant he'd had enough to eat, but he rode off and never came back. Left her with a houseful of children to feed. A year or so later there was another baby on the way, so Olga and her farm hand announced they were married. Maybe they are; most likely they aren't. But the farm's prospering and the children are thriving and people around here are happy to see it.

"My father hired a young man named Marcus Gilbreath. He does pretty well despite having a crippled arm. Years ago his father ran off to find gold. The family would have starved without help from folks around. Mrs. Gilbreath wrote begging him to come home, but he always said he was too close to a big strike to leave. Finally Marcus set out to find him. Turned out his father was spending everything he earned, which wasn't much, on drink and gambling. Marcus refused to leave without him, so his own father grabbed him by the arm and threw him out into the street. The boy's arm snapped like a sapling. By the time he got home it had mended crooked.

Nattie turned and gazed steadily at Alan. "You know how things are out here, how we live. Did you really think I'd take issue with a man being a good father to his child, however that child came to be? Maybe your New Haven people would look down their long blue noses, but I'm not some prissy thin-lipped holier-than-thou Elsie Dinsmore embroidering Bible verses while I judge and condemn everyone around me. You're a damn fool, Alan McTurk."

Alan's mouth opened, and closed again. He said, "I can't argue with that. I know I should have told you straight away. At first I convinced myself that it didn't matter because I wouldn't allow myself to care for you. But then I did care, very much, and the thought of losing you was unbearable. So I just bumbled along, hoping it would all work out somehow. And I hurt you."

Nattie looked away. "You did hurt me," she said quietly. "You hurt me terribly."

"I know. I'm so sorry. And I have no right to ask, but—is there the slightest chance you can forgive me?"

Nattie was silent.

"If you tell me to go, I will. I won't promise to give up all hope and never darken your door again, but I'll go." Alan stepped forward to stand beside her.

"Look," said Nattie. She pointed to two hawks soaring and falling together, so close that they could see the feathers move.

Alan took Nattie's hand. After a long moment, she rested her head against his shoulder. They stood like that, without speaking, until the hawks flew away.

"Does this mean you forgive me?" asked Alan.

Nattie's eyes narrowed. "It means—I'm considering it."

Alan faced her and took both her hands in his.

"I ask you to consider this, too," he said. "You must know that I love you. I'm fool enough to hope that you love me, and that you will be my wife. I've never wanted anything more."

Nattie's eyes searched his.

"Convince me," she said.

Chapter 31

The sun was low by the time Nattie agreed she was convinced.

"All right, yes! Yes, I forgive you. Yes, I love you. Yes, I'll marry you. Now let me catch my breath."

"Only for a moment. I don't want you to change your mind."

"I won't, I promise. But we should go let Tomás know that I didn't shoot you and all is well. He'll be pleased to hear that your defenders were right."

"All is well, indeed. All is perfect," Alan replied. "But—what defenders?"

"Your drinking partners. They sent telegrams urging me to give you a chance. Although Jeremy offered to thrash you if I preferred. At least, I think that's what he meant."

"He was the most sober of all of us when we called it a night, so he probably had the best judgment. I staggered over to see you next morning—I was half-dead already and figured I might as well let you finish me off—and Jeremy was inhumanly bright-eyed and bushy-tailed. He told me you had gone, so I followed. I would have been here sooner but Bella threw a shoe and we had to go back."

"A tiresome journey. Still, you seem remarkably energetic," said Nattie.

"I rested at the blacksmith's. He said no one ever fell asleep by his anvil before."

Nattie put her hands on his chest and stepped back.

"We really must go," she said. "Mama-cow slobbered all over me and I think she ate my hair ribbon. And you're covered in dust. If we leave now we'll have time to make ourselves presentable before supper."

"I do want to make a good impression. But I have a question before we go; what do you think of short engagements?"

"I think they're eminently sensible," said Nattie.

"Good. And what is your ideal honeymoon destination?"

"The ocean."

"Do you mean a trip to Europe or some such?"

"No." Nattie shook her head. "No people. Just us, and the sea."

"Perfect," said Alan. "I'll teach you how to sail. We could take a small boat up the California coast..."

As they rode, they finalized their wedding plans.

"So we're agreed," said Nattie. "It will be small, as soon as possible, and the rest doesn't matter."

"No fussing over all the wedding bits and bobs?"

"I'll leave the details to Flo and Tía. If it starts to get out of hand I'll threaten to elope."

"A tempting idea. No frills, no waiting..."

"They'd never forgive me. Besides, we won't have to wait too long. We have to marry while your sister can still travel."

"Good point."

"Do you think the rest of your family will come?" Nattie asked.

"I expect so."

"Good. They can meet Sam. Speaking of which, when will I meet Sam?"

"Soon, I hope. Perhaps you could go home with me before the wedding—chaperoned, of course—to see the place and meet everyone. Do you think we can leave Flo and Tía unsupervised?"

"I'll risk it."

They rode on under a sky set ablaze by the setting sun, and never noticed it at all.

Chapter 32

Chinche poked his nose out from under the bed.

"It's safe. They've gone," Nattie told him. "You can come out, but stay away from my dress."

Her room had been full of chatter and rustling skirts as hands flew around her, buttoning and tying and arranging. Now it was blessedly quiet, a moment to think before she went downstairs to the waiting crowd. She took a slow breath and studied her reflection. The clusters of silver thread sparked like stars against the deep blue of The Dress.

"But that's not a wedding gown!" Tía had protested.

"It is if I get married in it," said Nattie.

"But what will people think?" asked Flo.

"Whatever they like," said Nattie.

Her dress was blue, the pearls that gleamed at her throat were borrowed from Flo, and Miss Pardee had given her an old sixpence for her shoe. Her ring was old, too, but newly hers. She stretched out her hand to admire it once again. Alan had given it to her on that first night of reclaimed happiness...

~ ~ ~

They had found Tomás in his office and given him a somewhat

incoherent account of events. After a barely-touched supper, Nattie and Alan escaped to the flower-scented courtyard. They sat close together by the fountain, Alan's arm around Nattie and her head on his shoulder. Alan suddenly jumped up and patted his pockets, then knelt with a flourish.

"Natividad Irazema Johnston-with-a-t, will you do me the honor of being my wife?"

"Didn't we settle this a few hours ago?" asked Nattie.

"Yes, but I enjoy asking you to marry me. I especially enjoy hearing you say yes. Besides, I forgot the ring before."

He took a velvet box from his pocket and removed a small object that gleamed in the faint light. "This belonged to Great-Aunt Alice. She'd be delighted to know that it's yours now."

"Do you always carry it with you, just in case you feel like proposing marriage?"

"I asked my sister to send it. Just in case I found the courage to ask you."

He slipped the ring on Nattie's finger and she leaned forward to kiss him.

"It's lovely," she said.

"You can't even see it," Alan chided. He produced a box of matches. In the sudden flare of light Nattie could see a pearl surrounded by seven garnets.

"Like the Seven Sisters," she said, remembering the night sky over East Camp and a wild wind moving her hair…

~ ~ ~

Now her hair was piled atop her head in dark shining coils. Nattie cautiously tilted her head one way, then the other. Nothing budged. Alethia had promised it would stay up through the dancing.

And after the dancing, she and Alan would ride to a hunting cabin high in the hills.

Tía and Flo had objected in unison. "That old place! For a honeymoon?"

"Yep. We'll take a pack mule and have everything we need. It's perfect. Far from everyone…"

Nattie smoothed the soft fabric of The Dress and closed her eyes, imagining being alone with Alan, lips to lips, skin to skin… She caught her breath.

"No more of that," she told herself. "You have a wedding to get through first." She stood and turned before the mirror, watching her skirt swirl around her feet.

Chinche jumped onto the windowsill and licked a paw.

"You'll like our new house," Nattie told him. "It has a porch all the way round so you'll always be able to find a sunny patch."

She looked around her room. It already felt like a memory. She had a new home waiting for her, in Texas…

~ ~ ~

Alan had lifted her over a wobbly step onto the porch of the little tin-roofed house. He tested a creaking floorboard and said, "I don't remember it being so…so…"

"Charmingly rustic," Nattie said firmly. "And it has beautiful views." She stretched across the sagging porch railing. "Look, you can see the main house if you lean way out. Edith and I can wave to each other as we hang out the wash."

Alan asked, "Will it do, just until we build a new one? It's sturdy, and it has a good well, and a room for Sam—"

Nattie took his hand. "You don't have to convince me. It's perfect. It just needs a little spit and polish."

She rubbed dirt from a window and peered into the kitchen where Mrs. Mulcahy was tut-tutting about the dust and Mr. Mulcahy was muttering about repairs. They had chaperoned the trip to Alan's ranch. Edith and Gus and Sam would provide respectability on the way back.

Mrs. Mulcahy stepped briskly out onto the porch.

"Don't you worry," she said. "I'll keep my man out of those mountains until everything is ship-shape, as you might say. When you come back it will be a tidy little home for you and the little boy."

~ ~ ~

Nattie opened her bedroom door and listened to the buzz of conversation downstairs. As expected, Tía and Flo had added dozens of people to the guest list. Fortunately Flo's mother-in-law had declared her health was too delicate for the long journey. Even better, Mrs. Beamish had sent her regrets.

"How odd," Tía had said. "Mrs. Beamish lives for occasions like this. I wonder why she isn't coming."

Nattie and Lydia exchanged a glance.

"Nat, you didn't do anything to discourage her attending, did you?" asked Flo.

"No, not a thing," said Nattie. Alan, on the other hand…

~ ~ ~

Flo had insisted on an engagement party. Nattie grumbled, but gave in.

"The house is already full of people. I suppose it makes no difference to squeeze in some more for an evening."

"It won't be that many. Just a few friends and neighbors," Flo assured her.

"Which means the whole territory, I suppose. All right. Do your worst."

On the night, it did seem as though the entire territory had crowded in somehow. After several circuits, Nattie dropped on a sofa next to Lydia.

"Whew! I think I've done my duty and spoken to everyone."

"Where's Alan?" asked Lydia.

"He and his father and sister are talking chickens with James. I need punch; shall I bring you some?"

As Nattie maneuvered through the throng she saw Mrs. Beamish scanning the room for victims. Nattie hurried back to Lydia, punch sloshing in the cups she carried, but Mrs. Beamish arrived first. She settled herself next to Lydia, eyes bright with malice, her black skirt rustling like dead leaves.

"You're the Soames girl, aren't you?" she asked.

"Yes, I am. How do you do?"

Mrs. Beamish said, "I don't suppose your mother is here. I've heard she's something of a recluse."

Lydia's smile faded. She said, "My parents will be here for the wedding. Are you acquainted with them?"

"I've shopped at Mr. Soames' store, but we haven't met socially. And I haven't met your mother but of course I've heard of her. She's quite notorious."

Spots of color appeared on Lydia's cheeks.

"How fortunate that you are fair-complected," Mrs. Beamish continued. "You must take after your mother."

"Actually, people say I resemble my father."

"Your father? Mr. Soames, you mean? He must be an extraordinary man, to take your mother back after her time among the savages."

Nattie stood. Courtesy to guests only extended so far. She put a hand on Lydia's shoulder and took a breath but before she could speak, Alan stepped in front of her.

"There you are, Mrs. Beamish! Do you know, I've finally remembered why your name seems so familiar; I've seen a similar one on many a box and barrel on my father's ships; Barrish Brothers Shipping and Storage, of Baltimore. You must have heard of them;

the story of their family scandal traveled up and down the seaboard."

Alan turned to Nattie and Lydia.

"One of the brothers helped himself to the company funds. There were rumors of a gambling habit, or a wife with expensive tastes."

He turned back to Mrs. Beamish.

"You're from Baltimore, aren't you? Perhaps you know more about it. I always wondered what happened to the thieving brother. People said that he and his wife fled out west somewhere…"

Nattie asked, "Did he return the money?"

"Never a penny. Nearly bankrupted the company."

"And his brothers didn't try to find him?"

"Not that I know of. Perhaps they thought it was good riddance to bad rubbish."

Mrs. Beamish looked pale. Alan asked her, "What do you think, Mrs. Beamish?"

"I'm sure I don't know," she said faintly. "I don't believe I was in Baltimore at that time."

"That's fortunate. You wouldn't want to be associated with a scandal like that, even by mistake."

"No. No, of course not."

Mrs. Beamish stood. "I must be going. Yes. Good night."

She rustled away. Alan said, "I wouldn't have thought she could move that fast."

Nattie shook his arm. "How long have you known?"

"Oh, for a while. I'd have kept it to myself if she'd kept a civil tongue in her head."

Lydia said, "Perhaps she won't dare to be hateful anymore."

"That would go against her very nature," said Nattie. "But I expect any mention of Baltimore will shut her down in a hurry."

~ ~ ~

Now Nattie heard music begin downstairs. She picked up the

bouquet of her mother's roses and was surprised to see the petals tremble.

"I'm as nervous as Sam," she thought. He had solemnly accepted his duties as ring-bearer and practiced incessantly with harness rings.

"What if I forget to swap these for the real ones?" he had asked her.

"Then your Daddy and I will be married with harness rings. They'll work just as well."

"What if I drop them?"

"Well, I expect they'll roll across the floor and out the door and we'll have to chase them."

"How will we catch them?"

"We'll rope them with a thread lasso."

"What if—"

Nattie scooped him up in her arms. "What if I spin you until you're dizzy?" she asked.

She twirled him until they collapsed in a heap, laughing.

~ ~ ~

There was a knock on the door. Nattie opened it to her father.

"Are you ready, *mija?*"

"Sí, Papí. Is it time?"

"Yep. Your man's waiting at the foot of the stairs, nervous as a cat. Come down and put him out of his misery."

"Are you sure you don't want to escort me?"

"Naw, my hip's too stiff to handle stairs with any dignity. I'll go down first and wait with Alan. His jaw's going to drop when he sees you."

"That's the plan."

Nattie kissed her father and watched his broad back disappear down the hall. She kissed Chinche on the top of his head, glanced in the mirror one last time, and closed her door behind her. She had planned a stately descent, but when she saw Alan she moved faster and faster, her skirt flowing around her like dark water shimmering with stars. Alan reached for her and she leapt into his open arms.

About the Author

Katy McKay is a retired science teacher who left her native Southwest for a cabin in the woods of the Pacific Northwest.

She volunteers at an animal rescue farm where she tends to a variety of animals including, best of all, horses.

The author (on horseback) and her sister Pauline. California, 1966.

98545588R00131

Made in the USA
Lexington, KY
08 September 2018